Acclaim for Joshua Ferris's

THE
UNNAMED

"*The Unnamed* is a book that draws the reader along as compulsively as its main character is propelled on his endless walks. And the book ends with a singular achievement.... Ferris manages to pull off the rare literary feat of portraying a convincing, unembellished portrait of true love."
—Michael Astor, Associated Press

"You can't break away from the grip of these opening chapters."
—Ron Charles, *Washington Post*

"Ferris's literary magic transforms his bleak story not only into an intriguing novel of ideas but an existential mystery, an eerie road novel, and, in spite of everything, an abiding love story."
—Dan Cryer, *Newsday*

"What's most engrossing is Ferris's portrait of a couple locked in an extreme version of a familiar conflict—the desire to stay together versus an inexplicable yearning to walk away."
—Karen Holt, *O: The Oprah Magazine*

"Riveting."   —Gabriella Stern, *Wall Street Journal*

"You don't often find a marriage as affectingly or affirmingly drawn as this one.... Throughout the book, there is beauty in Ferris's writing, even when charged with despair.... In boldly investigating what it takes 'not to forget what it means to be human,' Ferris makes those secrets sing."
—Lloyd Sachs, *Chicago Sun-Times*

"Spellbinding.... *The Unnamed* unfolds in a hushed, shadowed dimension located somewhere between myth and a David Mamet play."   —Laura Miller, *Salon*

"A compelling and haunting novel....Ferris's prose somehow manages a distinctly lyrical quality even as it socks the reader in the gut." —*New York Press*

"Rich and profound." —Lev Grossman, *Time*

"You may find yourself compelled, in an inexorable, Tim-like way, to keep turning the pages—to see what happens next to this character trapped 'in the present, above time,' with only the most tenuous grasp of his own future." —*Slate*

"Bracingly original....Surprisingly, almost tenderly, and despite his unrelenting refusal to churn out a predictable happy ending, Ferris turns *The Unnamed* into a most unorthodox love story about commitment and sacrifice."
—Connie Ogle, *Miami Herald*

"A bold and moving novel....Josh Ferris's second novel may well outshine his first." —Kevin Grauke, *Philadelphia Inquirer*

"Tim's compulsion to walk is as threatening as the monster in a Stephen King novel. Readers will look for metaphors, but Ferris is a good enough writer and portraitist that it's not necessary. Tim's crucible is real and compelling enough without having to figure out what it 'means.'" —Peter Sagal, NPR.org

"An accomplished and daring work by a writer just now realizing what he is capable of creating."
—Tod Goldberg, *Los Angeles Times*

"At once riveting, horrifying, and deeply sad, *The Unnamed*, like Tim's feet, moves with a propulsion all its own. This is fiction with the force of an avalanche, snowballing unstoppable until it finally comes to rest—when we come to the end, so to speak."
—Heller McAlpin, *San Francisco Chronicle*

THE
UNNAMED

A Novel

JOSHUA FERRIS

A Reagan Arthur Book
BACK BAY BOOKS
Little, Brown and Company
New York   Boston   London

ALSO BY JOSHUA FERRIS

Then We Came to the End

Reagan Arthur / Back Bay Books
Little, Brown and Company
Hachette Book Group
237 Park Avenue, New York, NY 10017
www.hachettebookgroup.com

Originally published in hardcover by Reagan Arthur/Little, Brown and Company, January 2010
First Reagan Arthur/Back Bay paperback edition, September 2010

Reagan Arthur Books is an imprint of Little, Brown and Company. The Reagan Arthur Books name and logo are trademarks of Hachette Book Group, Inc.

Lyrics from "Five Years" by David Bowie appear on page 206.

Library of Congress Cataloging-in-Publication Data
Ferris, Joshua.
The unnamed / Joshua Ferris. — 1st ed.
p. cm.
978-0-316-03401-2 (hc) / 978-0-316-07274-8 (int'l pb) /
978-0-316-03400-5 (pb)
1. Lawyers—Fiction.   2. Compulsive behavior—Fiction.
3. Identity (Psychology)—Fiction.   4. Domestic fiction.
5. Psychological fiction.   I. Title.
PS3606.E774U56 2010
813'.6—dc22   2009010264

10 9 8 7 6 5 4 3 2 1
RRD-IN
Printed in the United States of America

For Chuck Ferris and Patty Haley

THE FEET, MECHANICAL

1

It was the cruelest winter. The winds were rabid off the rivers. Ice came down like poisoned darts. Four blizzards in January alone, and the snowbanks froze into gray barricades as grim and impenetrable as anything in war. Tombstones were buried across the cemetery fields and cars parked curbside were swallowed undigested. The long-term debate about changing weather was put aside for immediate concern for the elderly and the shut-ins, while the children went weeks without school. Deliveries came to a halt and the warehouses clogged up on days the planes were approved to land. There were lines at the grocery store, short tempers, a grudging toward the burden of adjustment. Some clever public services addressed the civic concerns — heat shelters, volunteer home checks. The cold was mother of invention, a vengeful mother whose lessons were delivered at the end of a lash.

The ride home was slow going because of the snow and the traffic. He usually worked by eyelet light but this evening he brought no work home and sat in one quadrant of the car without file opened or pen in hand. They were waiting for him. They didn't know they were waiting for him. The driver had on 1010 WINS, traffic and transit on the ones. Somewhere, out to sea or in the South, it might not be snowing. Here it slanted into the windshield like white ash from a starburst. The frostbite had returned to his fingers and toes. He unbuckled the seat belt and leaned over, stretching his long torso across the backseat, and what the driver thought he didn't care. The sound of the radio faded as one ear was sealed up by the distressed leather and he put a hand on the floor mat and ran his tingling fingertips over the fiber-trapped pebbles. He hadn't called to tell them. He had lost his phone. They were waiting for him, but they didn't know it.

The driver woke him when they reached the house.

He was going to lose the house and everything in it. The rare pleasure of a bath, the copper pots hanging above the kitchen island, his family—again he would lose his family. He stood just inside the door and took stock. Everything in it had been taken for granted. How had that happened again? He had promised himself not to take anything for granted and now he couldn't recall the moment that promise had given way to the everyday. It was not likely one single moment. He set his keys on the table below the mirror and uncharacteristically took his shoes off on the long Persian runner, which he and Jane had bought in Turkey. They had spent a week in Turkey and a week in Egypt. They always had a trip in the works. Their next trip was a Kenyan safari but it would have to be postponed now. He walked through the house in his socks. Inside the kitchen he ran his hand along the dimly lit countertop. He loved his kitchen, the antique cupboard doors, the Moroccan tile backsplash. He walked through the dining room, where they hosted dinner parties for his firm. The long table sat twelve. He reached the stairs and put his hand on the oak newel and took one step after another. Family photographs made the ascent with him. The sound of the grandfather clock ticking away in the living room gave way to the television laughter issuing softly from the bedroom down the hall.

Jane was still beautiful. She was wearing a pair of reading glasses that had a Pop Art zaniness of character, teardrop frames polka-dotted with drops of primary color. Spaghetti straps revealed her slender arms and the nightgown held her firm breasts in place just below a freckled slate and an articulated clavicle. She was doing the crossword. Whenever she got stuck, she glanced up at the late show on the flat screen mounted to the wall and drummed the pen between upper and lower teeth, as if to waken her brain. She looked at him as he entered, surprised to see him home so early. "Hello, banana," she said. He took off his suit coat as if it were a T-shirt, thrusting the back over his head and turning his sleeves inside out. Then he found himself grabbing the hem, a hand on each half of the parted tail, and ripping the thing in two. Hard to break the seam at first, but once the first thread snapped, it went. Jane opened her mouth but nothing came out. He dropped the tattered coat and climbed onto the bed and hunkered down on his hands and knees like a man waiting for an explosion. "What is it?" she said. "Tim, what is it?" His head was lost inside his sheltering arms. "Tim?" She moved over to him and put her arms around him, hugging him from above as if they were about to engage in a wrestling match. "Tim?"

He told her that he had been forced out of the building and into the street. At 43rd and Broadway he hailed a cab, which he hoped would take him back to the office. After getting the cab to pull over, he reached out and opened the back door. But then he walked on. The driver, a Sikh in a pink turban, honked the horn, staring at him through the rearview mirror. Why would someone hail a cab and open the door only to keep walking?

Near Union Square he had tried to call an ambulance, a recourse they had envisioned during his last recurrence. He was on the line with a dispatcher trying to explain the situation when he slipped on a patch of ice coming off a curb and lost his grip. "My phone!" he cried out as he regained his balance. "Somebody! My phone!" He walked on with a tweaked back. "Please get my phone!" Everyone ignored him. His BlackBerry had landed in the middle of the street where it lay defenseless against oncoming cars. He kept moving forward. He told her of all the city scaffolding he walked under, the manic traffic he managed to avoid, the parade of oblivious people he passed. He told her that he had turned tired in the old way by the time he reached a bench, somewhere near the East River, where his body gave out. How he had crumpled up his suit coat for a pillow and taken off his tie, sweating despite the cold. How he woke up in horror an hour later.

"It's back," he said.

2

First thing, she had to dress him. She knew he didn't want to dress. He wanted to shower, crawl into bed, fall asleep—whatever action preserved the routine. Brush his teeth, reach for the light. He was still on top of the bed, frozen in the soldier's huddled field position, his rear up and his arms encircling his head as if to shield it from flying shrapnel. His hair—he still had a full head of dark hair, one of his most distinguished features, he was a handsome, healthy man, ridiculously horse-healthy and aging with the grace of a matinee idol—was disheveled. "Tim," she said, looking over his arm into his one visible and glazed-over eye, "you have to get dressed."

He didn't move. She got off the bed, walked into the bathroom and threw a black waffle-weave robe over her silk nightgown. She was startled by the complacency of the lotions, soaps, creams and deodorants arrayed on their bathroom sink, suddenly insulted by the rosy promises of common beauty products. She took an inventory in her head of all the things she needed and began collecting them from the places in the house where they could be found: his base layer of thermal long underwear and form-fitting insulator pants from the dresser; a sweatshirt and fleece from the walk-in; his heavy down coat; his hat, gloves and scarf. She placed his ski mask in one of the coat pockets along with several disposable heat packs she hoped hadn't reached some unmarked expiration date. She reminded herself to buy more. She almost broke into tears by the washer-dryer. She brought up the GPS and the alpine pack from the basement. She filled the pack quickly: a rain poncho, eyedrops, dryskin lotion, an inflatable pillow, a first-aid kit. And then from the cupboard, trail mix and energy bars and a Nalgene bottle of electrolyte water. She included matches for no specific reason. Then she zipped the pack and walked upstairs.

She went to the bed and began to move him physically as if he were a child. She turned him over and undid his belt and removed his pants and boxers and unbuttoned his shirt, all with little help from him. He was soon lying on the bed naked. She applied a coat of Vaseline to his face and neck and then to his genitals because Vaseline helped with both the chafing and the cold. Then she began to dress him in what she had collected, finishing with the wicking socks and his waterproof boots. She placed the alpine pack in the doorway where it could be grabbed easily on his way out and then she crawled onto the bed beside him.

"No Bagdasarian this time," he said. "No doctors of any kind."

"Okay," she said.

"I mean it," he said. "I got off that gerbil wheel and I'm not getting back on."

"Okay, Tim."

She reached out for the remote and turned off the late show.

"Have I taken you for granted again, Jane?"

A powerful silence settled over them. He lay on his back as overdressed as a child ready for the winter snow. She watched him from her pillow. His eyes were not as wide and his breathing had calmed.

"Let's not do this," she said.

"Do what?"

"Start in with the guilt and the regrets."

He turned to her. "Have I taken you for granted?"

"Everyone takes everyone for granted," she said. "It's a clause in the contract."

"How do you take me for granted?"

"How? In so many ways, Tim."

"Name one."

"I can't even begin," she said. "Okay, for one. The best vacation we ever took and for the life of me I can't remember the name of the island."

He began to smile. "Scrub Island," he said.

"I depend on you for that."

"That's different than taking me for granted."

"Scrub Island," she said. "It was such a clean place, the name makes perfect sense. But I can never remember."

"Wouldn't you like to go back?" he asked.

"I thought Africa was next."

They both knew there was no next, not now, not any time soon, and the silence returned.

"We should buy a place on Scrub Island," he said. "There was such delicious food there. And do you remember the little girl walking the streets in a wedding dress?"

"She'd be grown by now."

"And the ostriches. That man herding them with a bull-whip. Don't you want to go back?"

"Yes," she said. "When you're well again, we'll go back."

"I'm hot," he said.

She got off the bed and opened both windows. The winter's crisp, shocking reality blew in. She turned back toward the bed. Then she remembered the handcuffs.

She walked over to his nightstand and removed them from the drawer. "What about these?" she asked, standing over him at bedside.

He pulled his stare from the unfocused void into which he had lost himself. He looked at the cuffs mournfully, as if they belonged to someone whose death had come on suddenly, and now he was taking stock, with great reluctance, of what to keep and what to throw away. He pursed his lips and shook his head and resumed looking at the ceiling. She put the cuffs back in the drawer.

3

Her sleep was fitful, responsive to every turn he took, the slightest shift. She woke up when she heard Becka come home, and later when Tim began to whistle—he never snored, but when he lay on his back his heavy breathing turned to a tuneless whistle. Their room was insanely cold, she could see her breath in the moonlight between episodes of some surreal dream, but Tim had not even bothered to get under the covers. He lay on the bed dressed for the subzero weather in coat and gloves. She woke every hour that never-ending night, sometimes more than once, and every time she reached out for him to make sure he was there.

It has been a good, long run, she thought.

When the dimmest fraction of darkness gave way to daylight, she opened her eyes and found him gone. She was furious with herself. Yet what could she have done but let him go?

She dressed quickly and left the house, walked down the long drive to the gate, and stood at the entrance looking in both directions. Their neighborhood had been developed to preserve the natural landscape, so that certain houses were set back on hills, some had small ponds out front, and all were safely buffered by trees. Late at night within the limited view of the headlights you could almost believe you were in the country. At the crack of dawn, with everything caught in the interminable cold snap, she found the street empty and quiet. Too early for the brave morning walkers, even for those neighbors who worked in the financial sectors. The black trees all around her stood with their sharp naked branches like burnt-out dendrites. She scanned for footprints in the snow, then returned up the drive.

She got inside the car and rounded the cul-de-sac. Braking at the gate's edge to look both ways, she was gripped by a familiar fear. She did not know which way to turn. He had forgotten to turn on the GPS. She pounded the steering wheel with her open palms.

Anger with God was a tired and useless emotion, anger with God was so terrestrial and neutering. She thought she had arrived at a peaceful negotiation but in fact it was only a dormancy and when her anger at God met her at the end of the drive she was exhausted. She was caught unprepared again, and nothing could have prevented that, no promise made or lesson learned. Enjoy the BBQ, she thought, for no apparent reason. Enjoy the BBQ before God turns it to shit with His rain. She turned left and glided soundlessly down the street, fully aware of the comfort of a slowly heating car and how he would have been deprived of even that for how long now.

Minor mountain banks of greasy snow sat in front of the residential gates, in their valleys a paste of dead leaves or a patch of frozen earth. Cracked snow thin as flint covered the yards. More snow capped the red-brick gateposts. The NBA star's house was gaudy even at dawn, lit up with faux gas lamps like some Frank Lloyd Wright spacecraft. She swung around and down the swooping curve leading to the frontage road and drove in both directions before heading back the way she came. She found him miles away in the opposite direction.

He was lying in a small wood separating two houses, sleeping on an incline behind some linden trees that prevented him from rolling down to the street. She pulled into the opposite lane and threw the car in park, leaving the door hanging open as she climbed up the culvert into the woods. She was relieved to see he had taken the pack, which he had placed under his head for a pillow. The black ski mask gave his prone figure an air of menace. Someone walking past with a dog might have rushed home to call the police. She knelt down beside him, feeling the cold through her jeans. "Tim?" she said, peeling back the mask. "Tim." He opened his eyes with the innocence of a child and looked around him.

"I fell asleep," he said.

"Yes."

"I tried to make it back. I was too tired."

"You did good, you took the pack. Can you stand up?"

"The sleep is even better than last time," he said.

4

He enjoyed against his will those narcoleptic episodes that set him down wherever the walks concluded, the pinched-eye, clenched-fist sleep of a newborn. He had watched Becka as a baby with her smooth pink brow and he couldn't recall ever sleeping with such enviable unburdened purity. Horses ran through his brain the minute his head hit the pillow. He drifted into bad sleep drafting motions. He carried on pointless exchanges with opposing counsel. But this sleep, these black-dot swoons—coming after such punishing miles, after the caloric drain and metabolic change—were invigorating. And he came out of them with perfect clarity. Everything was bright. Even in the landscape of that dead season, even among the black snow, the world was crisp and lucid. He could make out every nub-ended tree branch, he heard the crawl of a crow across a black wire, he smelled the carbon in the decomposing earth. It offered him a brief respite before he was forced to wonder again just where on earth he was.

He limped out from the trees. She brushed his backside of ice and crumbled leaves. He looked down the road. "Here comes Barb Miller," he said.

The car was angled into the street on the wrong side of the road, as if it had swerved to avoid an accident. They stood still as deer and watched their neighbor approach. Barb slowed the SUV and powered down the window.

"Everything okay?" she asked. Her words formed white plumes of smoke in the cold air. Butch Miller sat beside her.

"Oh, everything's fine," said Jane. "Everything's fine. Just something with the car."

Butch leaned over and waved. "Hello," he said through the window.

"Hello, Butch," said Tim.

"Do you need us to call someone?"

"No, no. Triple A is on its way, thank you."

"Thanks, Barb," said Tim.

"Do you want a ride back to the house? You can't stay out here, can you?"

"They promised to be here any minute," said Jane.

Barb smiled and said okay. They waved good-bye and she

started the car rolling again. Butch turned his head and they could see him continue to stare through the tinted windows. They watched the SUV dip and disappear out of sight. Then they exchanged a look that conveyed their shared exhaustion. Triple A? Could they really be at it again? The futility of communicating their predicament to the Millers had turned their kind gesture of help into something onerous and unwanted. To approach the world with evasion and thanklessness — that was no way to live. Jane walked around to the driver's side and she and Tim got in and closed their doors at the same time.

They drove home. Soon after Jane killed the engine, the car began to crackle in the silent garage. "I have to go in," he said.

She was surprised. He had shown such resolve the night before: no gerbil wheel. She wondered whom he intended to see. Bagdasarian? Copter at Mayo? Did he mean Switzerland again?

Then she realized her mistake. He meant in to work.

"I don't think that's a good idea," she said.

"Janey, I'm all rested up. I have to go in."

The night before, she had pushed aside how they would deal with the long-term things like his work, in order to make him safe for that one night. Now she had to deal with the reality of the light of day, and she should not have been surprised that he would want to go in.

"You should take the day off," she said.

"No, that would just be..."

"We need to—"

"...capitulation."

"—to deal with this, Tim. Capitulation? It's called reality."

"But the case," he said.

"Oh, fuck the case!" she said. "It's back, Tim! You said it yourself last night. It's back."

The car was losing heat. He sat unmoving in his fleecy chrysalis of Patagonia and down, staring straight through the windshield at the spare gas tank and paint cans and the coils of extension cords and rubber hoses on the garage shelves. A row of old Vermont license plates had been nailed into the wall. Jane turned away from him in the still car and they sat in silence. Within the minute their breath became visible. She waited for him to say something, preparing the counterargument. After waking he always felt this false rejuvenation, but that strength was fleeting and within hours he could be walking again. And then what would he do, out in the cold with his frostbite and dressed in nothing but suit and tie, walking around Manhattan and ending up God knows where? She was about to remind him of this when he started pounding the glove box with his gloved fist. He rained blow after blow down on the glove box and she let out an involuntary cry and jerked back against the cold window. He stopped hitting the glove box and began to kick it until the latch snapped and the door fell. He continued to kick as if to drive his foot clear through to the engine block. One of the door's lower hinges snapped, and thereafter the glove box had the cockeyed lean of a tired sun visor. It would never be fixed.

When it was over, he withdrew his foot and out spilled a handful of napkins. His heel had compacted the owner's manual and ripped the maintenance records and insurance papers. He returned his feet to the mat and things were calm again, but he would not look at her.

"I have to go in," he said finally.

Her gaze had a fire's intensity.

"Okay," she said. "You should go in."

"I'm trying to tell you that I feel good."

"I will pack your backpack," she said, "with your winter gear, in case you need it, and you can take the pack in with you."

"I have to go in," he repeated.

"I understand."

Then he turned to her. "Do you?"

"Yes," she said.

5

Becka was up for school, showered and sitting at the kitchen table eating a bowl of cereal. At seventeen, she wore a silver loop in her left nostril and never properly washed her hair. She was surprised when the door to the garage opened. She had figured her parents were upstairs. They came into the kitchen brooding and silent. Her father was overburdened with winter clothes and her mother looked pale and terrified.

"What's going on?" she asked.

Nobody said anything. She just knew.

She stood up and hugged her dad, a rare hug. She approached him sideways, resting her head on his shoulder. He took hold of her forearm and squeezed.

"It's not a hundred percent yet," he said.

"It's a hundred percent," said her mom.

Becka had been nine the first time. She remembered driving with her mother into the city. She was scared by her mother's silent, impatient driving. She wondered why she had been picked up at the school bus stop, and where they were going, and what had happened. Her mother turned and smoothed her hair in the stop-and-go traffic over the bridge but said nothing. Becka expected him to be waiting on a street corner with his briefcase and a rumpled newspaper under his arm, dressed in his beige overcoat. Instead they came upon a small triangle of park with a lone tree in a grate and a pair of trash bins, a phone booth and four or five wooden benches. Her mother pulled up to the curb and threw the hazards on. She told Becka to stay put. Taxis raced past as she stepped out. Becka watched as her mother approached a bench and bent down. She touched the man laid out there and he sat up. Becka recognized him only when he stood and began walking toward the car.

They began picking him up more frequently, never in the same place, three times a week, sometimes four. Becka accompanied them to the doctor when she was not in school and sat in the waiting room with her mother. She went with her mother into the room where her father sat on the metal table with the tissue paper and she listened to the doctor and to the questions her mom and dad asked, but she couldn't understand what they were saying. They were saying everything it wasn't. There was confusion and frustration and much talking over one another. She stood behind a glass window holding her mom's hand as her dad moved inside the scary tunnel of an MRI machine. On the ride home they were silent and her father was distant.

Sometimes she came home from school and the car was gone and nobody was in the house. She watched TV until it got dark and ate after-school snacks instead of dinner. Her dad woke her on the sofa and carried her to her room and tucked her into bed. She asked him if he was sick and he said yes. She asked him if he was going to be all right and he said yes.

He started staying home from work, which he'd never done before. One afternoon after school she heard them in the bedroom. The door was ajar. She put her head in and saw her mother standing over him. He was dressed differently, not in a suit and tie but in sweatpants and T-shirt, and he was handcuffed to the headboard. His arms were stretched tight as if they were hanging from iron rings in the wall. He might have been doing calisthenics like at school, the one called bicycle-in-the-air, except his legs moved lower and kind of jerky. The fitted sheet had popped off and all the bedding was bunched up around him. His face was hurting and his T-shirt was stained with sweat. She fled from the doorway.

Soon after her mother came downstairs surprised, almost panicked, to find her there, as if she were a stranger. She told her to be quiet because her father was sleeping.

"Is Daddy addicted to drugs?"

Jane had moved to the sink to fill a pot with water. "What?"

"Because at school they told us about drugs. They showed us a video."

"Daddy is sick," said Jane, and turned the water off.

"Because of drugs?"

"No, sweetie, of course not because of drugs."

"Then how come?"

Jane placed the water on the stove without answering. She went into the pantry for the rice and when she returned she took the meat out of the fridge and bent down for a cutting board. Becka waited for an answer, but her mother continued to squat in front of the cupboard, one hand on the open door, motionless and refusing to look at her. No one looked at her very much lately. Her mother was usually tired. She often told her to clean her room or asked her to go out and play. The house had never been so quiet, a hush timed by strikes from the grandfather clock and broken only when her father was kicking.

"How come he's in handcuffs?" she asked.

Now finally her mother stood with the cutting board and looked at her. "Did you see Daddy in handcuffs?"

Becka nodded from the kitchen table.

"Daddy doesn't want to leave the house," said Jane, setting the cutting board down and the meat on top of it. "We're just trying to keep Daddy inside the house."

Becka didn't want him inside the house. She heard him at night making noises like he was straining to lift something heavy. She heard the rattle of the handcuffs. His curses filled the house and his mumbling carried through the walls. Sometimes she heard nothing at all. Once she tiptoed to the door and put her head in the room and found him bound to the bed, staring into space. He saw her in the doorway and called to her but she ran away. "Becka, come back!" he cried. "Come talk to me." She raced down the stairs. "Becka!" he cried out. "Please!" But she kept going.

It left as quickly as it came and he went back to work. After a few months her memory of him bound to the bed faded. They didn't talk about it. They talked about other things. He came to her recitals again. Once again he woke her in the mornings and made her breakfast and got her ready for school. He never let a day pass without calling her before bedtime. Jane slept in and took care of her at night. That was the routine, the blissful family groove, and it had returned.

6

Was she up for this? She lay in bed under the covers, her breath visible in the slant moonlight. Really up for it? The long matrimonial haul was accomplished in cycles. One cycle of bad breath, one cycle of renewed desire, a third cycle of breakdown and small avoidances, still another of plays and dinners that spurred a conversation between them late at night that reminded her of their like minds and the pleasure they took in each other's talk. And then back to hating him for not taking out the garbage on Wednesday. That was the struggle. Sickness and death, caretaking, the martyrdom of matrimony — that was fluff stuff. When the vows kick in, you don't even blink. You just do. She had to be up for it.

She had nursed him once, and then a second time. About a year and a half of their lives, all told, and by the end of his first recurrence it was a full-time job. He was exonerated of all trifling matters when it returned. They were up against a specter that dwarfed the daily vexings. He could die out there. And so she set to the task of picking him up immediately, of learning how to properly rewarm the skin, of what food to bring with her in the car. She read survivalist manuals and prepared the pack. And when she wasn't picking him up or preparing the pack, she was making the appointments and taking him to the doctor. She was his support staff and counsel. And when she was driving him home from the doctor she was the sounding board for all the confusion, doubt, anger and frustration. And when not the sounding board she was the cheerleader, dragging him out of the morass of self-pity. And when not the cheerleader, the quiet, supportive presence that said simply, I'm here, said without a word, you are not alone. But it was all-consuming, two intense periods of uncertainty and fear to which she gave herself entirely, often at the expense of Becka—after which, once it was over, in a mad dash to catch up with his life, he went back to work. He treated his first day back like any other day, while she was left wondering *just what day is it?* What cycle of their marriage had they left off on? How did she resume ordinary life after so many arguments with doctors and late-night car rides to random street corners? He was fine again, as if nothing had ever happened, but she wasn't unchanged. She was suddenly bereft of purpose. And he wasn't there to say, I'm here, you are not alone. She didn't fault him for that. If anything, she envied him. He had an admirable passion for the work he did, and partnership at Troyer, Barr meant he did important work. But she did no favors to anyone by ignoring her own needs. She wanted what he had, something that would not abandon her to her own devices upon his recovery. She needed a purpose not entirely predicated upon other people, loved ones, the taking care of loved ones. She earned her license and started selling real estate.

Was she really up for a third time? To do it right, she would have to quit. She could not keep showing houses with him lost in the world. But what would happen when it was over? When it was over, if she quit and took care of him for however long, what life would she have to return to?

Jane stepped out of bed into the freezing room and walked down the hall to Becka's. Becka was playing a late-night set of coffeehouse ballads cryptic with yearning, which came to a halt when Jane opened the door.

"What happened to knocking first?"

Gone were the days of her good-faith efforts to fit in with the TV-commercial vision of life. No more running shoes, no more hair gels. She let her heartbreaking weight be what it was, hiding behind the acoustic guitar. Senior year in high school and she refused to so much as order a yearbook. She wore her flannel shirt, Roxy Music tee, black sweatpants. Big surprise.

Jane peered unrepentantly around the room, at the mounds of clothes just waiting for the torch, the slag heap of dirty dishes on desk and nightstand. The room smelled heavily of itself. "Any good developments in here lately, Madame Curie?" she asked.

"I'm making music right now, Mom."

"And a vaccine or two?"

"Do you even realize how old that joke is?"

"What are you doing up? It's one in the morning."

"What are *you* doing up?"

"Can't sleep."

Becka had eight or ten thick dreadlocked strands. They moved about her head the way mitter curtains dance lazily over the car at an automatic car wash, heavy and grayish. Their weight exposed the pale faultlines of her scalp. They cushioned her head as she leaned back on the headboard. "Do you think he fakes it, Mom?" she asked.

"Fakes it?"

"Have you ever Googled it? Google it and see what comes up."

"Google what?"

"Exactly."

"What comes up?"

"Some disease horses get when they eat poisonous plants."

"That doesn't mean he fakes it."

"Not faking, then," she said. "Just…I don't know… mental."

"There's a lot of debate about if it's psychological or not," said Jane. "He doesn't think it is. He thinks—"

"Yeah, I know, I know," she said. "I know he thinks it's the legs. I just have a hard time buying it. I think he's mental."

"You're talking like a real jerk, kiddo."

"He could control it if he really wanted to."

"Like you can control your weight?" said Jane.

It was as if she had slapped the girl in the face, and for a moment, before the recriminations and tears, they stared at each other unmoving and silent, stunned into recognizing, after so long an indifference, the wicked force they could work on each other. Becka threw a guitar pick at her. "Get out."

"I'm sorry, I shouldn't have said that."

"Get out!"

"I was just trying to make you see things from his—"

"Get! Out!"

The room was cold. She was relieved to find him still there, asleep in the down coat on top of the covers, as if he could expect only a brief nap. He was breathing heavily, perspiring through troubled dreams.

She got under the covers. She didn't mind the cold. She preferred it, actually. One day she had been a young woman, and the next a panting complex of symptoms. The hot flashes and night sweats, the mood swings and sleep disruptions. And there was no way, no possible human biological way, of explaining to him, a man, what her body was putting her through. She could talk to her gynecologist, who understood. She could talk to her friends. But the words *hot flash* hit his ears and bounced right off. She imagined how maddening it would be for a doctor to insist that her discomfort was "all in her head," or the burden of explaining symptoms no one had ever heard of. Thankfully she didn't need to. Her problems were widely shared. Pharmaceutical companies spent millions developing medicines to ease her suffering. She was alone with specific hot flashes, but she was not alone in the world with them.

After menopause set in she stopped speculating that he might be crazy. She stopped speculating altogether. She didn't know what had its hold on him. She didn't care. He couldn't know about hot flashes and she couldn't know about walking. They were like two inviolable spheres touching at a fine point in their curves, touching but failing to penetrate, failing to breathe the other's air. She chose to believe him when he told her that his condition was not a disorder of the mind but a malfunction of the body.

The health professionals suggested clinical delusion, hallucinations, even multiple personality disorder. But he said, "I know myself." He said, "I'm not in control, Jane." His mind was intact, his mind was unimpeachable. If he could not gain dominion over his body, that was not "his" doing. Not an occult possession but a hijacking of some obscure order of the body, the frightened soul inside the runaway train of mindless matter, peering out from the conductor's car in horror. That was him. That was her husband. She reached out in the darkness and touched his breathing body.

7

The next day she brokered negotiations in a half daze. She accepted offers and arranged showings for later in the week. She tried calling him at work. When he picked up, he picked up on the first ring; the secretary waited until the third ring. That gave Jane the second ring to hang up and try him again later. She came to the second ring again and again, and then she quickly put the phone down. She didn't want to push through to the secretary. She didn't want to know if he'd left the office. If she didn't know, she could still picture him in a climate-controlled conference room with his associates arrayed around him in their decorous business attire, drinking civilized lattes and assessing the other side's evidence. It was what he wanted, this corporate pastoral. What the glove box had given its life for: the perpetuation, inherently a kind of celebration, of uneventful everyday life. Long live the mundane.

In early evening she tried him again but again he didn't pick up. He didn't pick up because he was walking through the front door of the realty office. She looked up from the telephone and there he was, with flowers.

"I'm sorry about the other morning," he said. "The boxing match with the car." He handed her the flowers, and they went to dinner.

It wasn't the Italian you could get in the city but the food was better than most. The private lighting of the place lent itself to both proposals of marriage and requests for divorce. They sat in back in a dimly lit booth, dipping bread into an olive tapenade, a wine-red rococo carpet underfoot. Outside a new snow had started to fall over the old, adding a pristine frost to the winter's blackening palimpsest.

They had agreed that the alpine pack could remain in the car.

"Five o'clock," she said. "And with flowers. I didn't think that would happen until I announced I had cancer."

He stared at her intensely, as if this were a visit monitored by guards who would soon break them apart and return him to captivity, while she would walk through the parking lot to weep in the car. His expression was earnest enough to appear before God and she expected an apology for something: the late nights, the missed opportunities, the lacunae born of married days. But instead he smiled and picked up his wine and said, "It's not coming back."

"What's not coming back?"

"I've gone two entire days," he said. "It's not coming back."

The waiter appeared. Tim sat back to allow him to move in with the plate. Ordinarily after the food arrived she tucked her hair behind her ears and picked up her silverware. Now she pushed the plate away and leaned into the table on her elbows and looked at him.

"It's happened twice already, Tim."

"You should have seen me today."

"I found you in the woods just yesterday morning, remember?"

"Sitting at my desk. I wasn't going anywhere."

"You know and I know that two times—"

"Are you going to eat?"

She looked down at her plate. "No," she said.

"Why did we come here if you're not going to eat?"

She didn't want to fight. She picked up her fork. He took his first bite.

"Can we just assume?" She didn't know how to continue. "What if it is back? What if?"

He took another bite. "Then I will buy a gun," he said, swallowing, picking up his wineglass again, "and blow my head off."

He drank. She removed her elbows from the table and sat back. Did she just hear him right? He continued to eat his penne. Was he that far gone? She entered a blinded moment. Kill himself? He was the only one in the body. Everyone else was locked out. But this misfortune was not his and his alone! She left the booth.

In the movies they throw cash down on the table but he didn't have any cash so he stood quickly, instantly aware that he had provoked the response he'd wanted and just as quickly regretful of it. He removed a credit card from his wallet and followed her out. She was walking very quickly across a parking lot shared by suburban retailers and a grocery store, car-packed and big as a football field. "Jane!" he cried before he was out the door, and people seated near the window turned their heads and watched them go.

The sidewinding gusts were snow-flecked and bitter and filled his ears with a violent howl. "Janey!" He chased her down. She'd left without her coat and now she hurried away with her arms crossed, hands holding the opposite shoulders and her head lowered into the cold. She turned between two cars to lose him just as he reached for her. She shook him off but he grabbed her again and said, "Please, Jane." She swiveled and hit him with the back of her fist. The blow landed just below his collarbone and made him flinch. "You stupid bastard!" she cried between clenched teeth. Angry tears came from her eyes like stubborn nails jerked out of brickwork. "You don't fucking tell me that?" For some reason it came out as a question, which he couldn't answer. Both confused, both at a loss for words. The little space between them, between cars, was filled with their furious white breath. She put her splayed hands on his chest and pushed him and he stumbled back a few steps while taking hold of her wrists. She yanked loose again.

"It was un-thought-out," he said.

"After everything we've done, you would say that."

"I would never do it," he said.

"How do I know?"

A shopper rattled past them with a cart. He put his arms around her, but she kept her arms hugged to her chest.

"I never would," he said.

8

The next day she drove into the city, the lower Bronx, to a storefront with a red plastic awning advertising African Hair Weaving. She parked at the curb and stepped out as a snowplow sparked past her down the neglected street. Eroded brick surfaces, dull and defaced, ghettoed the neighborhood. Wind picked up the trash. The chain-link fence to a barren lot was curled up at one corner like a pried-open sardine can.

She checked the name and address against what she'd written down. The front window was plastered over with yellowed clippings from hairstyle magazines and framed by a string of red Christmas lights. The same collage covered the door, obscuring what awaited her inside: two black stylists, one albino with pink pigmentation spots, both in heavy blue aprons and tending to matrons in chairs. Their hands paused in their labor as they turned to look at her. There were cords everywhere, cords and spray bottles and dusty fake plants reflected in the mirror-paneled walls. She saw him against the far wall, sleeping on a row of folding chairs.

A gust blew the door open again.

"Slam it now," said the albino.

Jane did as she was told. When she turned around to face them a second time she forced a smile, feeling the interloper again, the tension of her unexpected presence in another random subculture. "That's my husband," she said, pointing to the man in back.

They were mostly quiet on the ride home. When they were out of the city, he said, "They were nice in there. I offered them forty dollars but they wouldn't accept it."

"Why did they agree to take you in?"

"I said I was having chest pains. I said I'd give them money if they let me sit down on one of their chairs, but they wouldn't take it."

"But they gave you the chair."

"You expect the world to greet you with hostility," he said, "and instead they give you a chair and call your wife."

"You can't count on that forever," she said.

They pulled into the garage and she killed the engine but neither of them moved. She figured now, after African Hair Weaving, he would come to his senses. But he remained silent, and she realized that he was determined to persevere. The light clicked off. They sat in the oily darkness as if they were high school lovers at odds, too inarticulate to put their feelings into words, and with nowhere to go to resolve their differences but the car.

"What do you feel when you see a black albino?" he asked.

"Sorrow," she said.

He stared through the windshield. "Me too."

9

Becka was thirteen when he got sick the second time.

Puberty was hell. Everyone said that she'd lose her baby fat but it never happened. There was no sudden onset, no flash gain. She just never slimmed down.

She first asked her mother the difference between a protein and a carb when she was ten years old. For Christmases and birthdays she drew up lists of fitness books and weight-loss how-tos. "Why am I fat?" she asked them. "Nobody else in this family is fat."

They did everything they could—consulted dietitians, endocrinologists, acupuncturists; bought her running gear and memberships to women-only health clubs; ordered elaborate machines and highly engineered plastic devices advertised on TV. Nothing worked.

Tim offered her every one of a father's honest lies about her being the most beautiful girl in the world. At night he secretly wondered why she could not shake the weight. He and Jane talked about it just as often as they did the girl's good grades and dark moods. They were afraid she was headed toward the tabloid destruction of an eating disorder, but she wasn't one for easy answers. She packed a lunch with cold tofu. She asked for an alarm clock and woke early to jog. She was twelve years old in black spandex and fleece vest doing three miles a day in the seventh grade. She wore tailored Glad bags under her running gear and imagined the sweat making its way out of her, surface-bound molecules of dairy-white fat. The greasy squish between the plastic bag and her skin was unpleasant but she liked it almost better than anything else, this hard-earned sensation of loss. This was before the nose ring and the dreadlocks and the midnight trips to the Reddi-wip canister.

Her longer run took her around the elementary school. The pink stucco building was painted with murals. A glassed-in sign outside the front entrance offered a daily message from the principal's office. The message was the same every day now: Enjoy Your Summer, Tigers! See You Next Year.

It was the summer before her freshman year. She cut across the empty blacktop poled for tetherball and sketched with four-square courts and hopscotch and entered the grassy field where the children ran relays and played kickball. Just past the rear fence of the baseball diamond, a well-marked trail led into the woods. The trail opened into clearings in which an outdoor sculpture was coupled with a nearby bench. There were half a dozen such sculptures along the trail—a steel Pink Pearl eraser tall as a tree, another called *Abstract Cactus*—which the village planning commission had installed as a part of a cultural outreach program. She ran across a footbridge into the last of the clearings and there she stopped. The heat materialized instantly. All the stimulated biology of a hard run hummed in her ears along with the summer crickets. She recognized the robe, white cotton with orange pinstripes. He was curled up at the base of *Smiling Bronze Sun* with his cheek on the dirt. His bare feet were bloody. She turned back. She ran home. She woke her mom and told her that Dad was asleep on the sculpture trail.

He woke up after Becka had gone. Utter terror woke him—or utter terror was the condition into which he awoke, hard to tell which. He bolted upright and sprang to his feet in one manic motion, as if expecting to be surrounded by physical threat. The quick rise made him stagger. Slowly he recalled where he was and how he got there. The night before, he had been wheeling the trash down the drive to the curb, one in the morning. It was the second of three bins. He knew halfway down that he would not be back for the third. He knew the sensation as an epileptic knows an aura. As an epileptic feels the dread of an oncoming seizure, he was crestfallen, brokenhearted, instantly depressed by what was now foretold. *It's back.* The first time, that four-month nightmare four years earlier, he had erased from his mind. Something finite, and, so, forgettable. But now, no denying it: a recurrence. Not finite. Chronic. Mother*fucker* his first thought. Don't take me away from my home. There's more garbage. Jane expects it to be taken out. His body's response: too bad. He read into it, because he had to find meaning, a morality tale: you fool, you blithe, oblivious fool. You should have thought about this possibility *last night*. You should have made it home at a decent hour to enjoy being in bed with Jane. He released the bin at the end of the drive and continued walking. He walked past neighbors' houses, he walked barefoot down Route 22. He walked past the supermarket: empty parking lot and an eerie glow. He walked past the Korean Baptist church and the Saks-anchored mall into the dreams of late-night drivers who took home the image of some addled derelict in a cotton robe menacing the soft shoulder. He looked down at his legs. It was like watching footage of legs walking from the point of view of the walker. That was the helplessness, this was the terror: the brakes are gone, the steering wheel has locked, I am at the mercy of this wayward machine. It circled him around to the south entrance of the forest preserve. Five, six miles on foot after a fourteen-hour day, he came to a clearing and crashed. The sleep went as quickly as a cut in a film. Now he was standing again, in the cricket racket, forehead moist with sweat, knees rickety, feet cramped, legs aching with lactic acid. And how do you walk home in a robe with any dignity?

The doctor appointments started up again. He wasn't well that time for thirteen months.

On the night Jane picked him up at African Hair Weaving, he knocked on Becka's door. "Can I come in?" he asked. No response usually meant her begrudging acquiescence, so he turned the knob and eyed her for permission to enter. She sat up against the headboard.

"What do you want?"

"To apologize."

"For what?"

He sat down on the bed. "For ignoring you."

She drew her legs up to her chest and hugged her knees. Her thighs expanded in their black sweatpants.

"Let me try to explain," he said. "I've always felt a strong sense of duty to provide for you and your mom. I've worked hard so that you would never have to want for anything."

She looked at him skeptically. "I don't really think that's why you worked hard."

"And that meant," he said, "that I had to put certain opportunities aside."

"Like what?" she asked. "Like did you want to become a painter on the Left Bank?"

"I mean opportunities with you."

"Or an astronaut? Did I keep you from becoming an astronaut?"

"I would have liked to spend more time with you," he said. "And your mother would have liked me around more."

"So she could have somebody else to bitch at besides me?"

"Becka," he said. He put a hand up. "Give me a second here, okay?"

She frowned and grew quiet.

"But the last couple of years," he said, "the last couple of years have been different."

He stared into the dead aquarium in front of him, a quarter full of rock-and-roll buttons and Mardi Gras beads and CDs and cigarette papers.

"Different how?" she asked.

"The last couple of years," he said, "I haven't really wanted to be around you."

He turned on the bed to look at her, making a small vortex

of the sheets below him. She didn't move. They were never still anymore in each other's presence. There was always some context for movement, some unspoken vectoring away. Now they stared as if startled by each other, years after having forgotten what the other looked like.

"I love you more than anyone in the world," he said, "but I didn't give a damn if I saw you or not. I didn't understand the phase you're in. The duct-taped sneakers, the dreadlocks. The music."

"Right. It's so hard. The Beatles."

"You don't just listen to the Beatles," he said.

"Ew," she said, "the Ramones."

"Point is," he said, "I hid behind my duty. I used work as my excuse to avoid you."

He said he was sorry. He didn't anticipate her saying anything in response and didn't expect it or need to be absolved or even understood. He needed only to come clean. She said nothing as he left the room.

She found him sitting at the kitchen counter slouched over an uneaten orange, looking morose and inward. It had been only a few minutes, five at the most, since he'd left her, but in that time the kitchen had filled entirely with the weight of his self-pity. When he got like this, bundled up in his coat and carrying around his backpack, she wanted nothing more than to beat a retreat the hell away from him. It was like he was dying or something, when he wasn't dying. He was just worried that he couldn't go in to work anymore. It made him grumpy. He wasn't even sick really.

"You think I care?" she asked.

He turned on the stool. She stood on the runner in her torn flannel and concert tee, barefoot, hands on her hips.

"You think I've been waiting around this whole time for an apology? That I give a shit what you think or what you do?"

He put his hands in the pockets of his down jacket. It was a defeated gesture, as if he were the child his daughter was scolding.

"The only reason you're apologizing is because you're sick again. If you weren't, you wouldn't have even thought about it. You could have been stoned on crack since I started high school, nothing would be different. You think too much of yourself, Dad."

And with that she turned and went back upstairs.

10

Coffee and a powdered doughnut sat on his desk. He might have thought to get something more substantial but he didn't care to interrupt the flow of work. Night after night, he sat at his desk just as a sphere of oil sits suspended in dark vinegar—everything blotted out but his own source of light. To save on energy costs, Troyer, Barr and Atkins, LLP, had installed motion sensors on the overhead lights. From six in the morning until ten at night, the lights burned continuously; after ten, the sensors took over. He worked past ten most nights, and most nights found him sufficiently absorbed in something that required only the turn of a page or the click of a mouse—too little activity for the sensors to register. The lights frequently switched off on him. He'd look up, surprised again—not just by the darkened office. By his reentry into the physical world. Self-awareness. Himself as something more than mind thinking. He'd have to stand, a little amused by the crude technology, and wave his arms around, jump up and down, walk over and fan the door, sometimes all three, before the lights would return.

That was happiness.

Twenty-five years ago he had decided to go to law school. It offered interesting study and good career prospects. He made it to Harvard and quickly learned how to chew up and spit out the huge green tomes on civil litigation and constitutional law. He summered at Troyer, Barr and they asked him to return after graduation. But first there was a clerkship with a judge on the Second Circuit. A year later he was married to Jane. He worked hard at Troyer. Document production for the first couple of years, boring as hell, but then junior status gave way to opportunity. He started taking depositions. He showed a gift for strategy in both civil and criminal cases, and a rare composure in the courtroom. He impressed the right people and when his seventh year came around they voted to make him partner. He sat in the best restaurants and ordered the best wines.

But that was never the point. The point was Houston, Seattle, Pittsburgh, Orlando, Charleston, Manhattan—wherever the trial was. The trial, that was the point. The clients. The casework. The war room. He took on a few pro bono causes. And he worked in midtown amid the electricity and the movement. And his view of Central Park was breathtaking. And he liked the people. And the money was great. And the success was addictive. And the pursuit was all-consuming. And the rightness of his place was never in doubt.

Now it was morning, and he was preparing for trial. The case involved a client named R. H. Hobbs who had been accused of stabbing his wife in a methodical way and dumping her body in a decommissioned landfill on Staten Island. The evidence against

R.H. was entirely circumstantial. There was a blood-soaked bedsheet with no trace of a third party's DNA, his thin alibi of being stuck in traffic at the time of the murder, and a sizable life-insurance policy. The district attorney had managed to bring charges against him only by the skin of his teeth. Grand jury testimony revealed a case fraught with uncertainty, and the consensus among Tim and his team was that R.H., despite a loveless marriage, had not committed the crime he had been accused of. R.H.'s private equity firm generated an enormous amount of business for Troyer, Barr, and no one wanted a guilty verdict to interfere with that relationship.

He ate the doughnut over a napkin to catch the powdered sugar and recalled a time when he had watched what he ate. Not as a dieter, not with his daughter's sad South Beach struggle, but with a fanatic's vigilance for good health—for Bagdasarian had suggested that it might be dietary. Cut out the caffeine, Bagdasarian told him, the sugar and the nicotine, and consult a naturopath. And so he did. Because nothing had shown up, repeatedly, on the MRIs, because he was on his third psychiatrist, because the specialist in Switzerland had thrown up his hands, he saw a Trinidadian in Chelsea with golden tubes and magic roots for seven days of colonics and grass-and-carrot smoothies. Jane drove and waited in the naturopath's living room among primitive wood carvings and bright tropical art. They took the highway home, and for the first couple of days there was this breathless, anxious hopefulness. Then he walked right out of the house. Jane picked him up six hours later behind a Starbucks in New Canaan. Nothing came of the marmalade fast or the orange juice cleansings except another possibility to cross off the list, though he could move his bowels like a ten-year-old.

His office was calm and pleasant. The early winter sun brightened the window behind him. Yet as every minute he remained in place moved effortlessly into the next, that new minute came with the increased anxiety that it might be his last. The wonderful warmth, his comfortable chair, the lovely rigor and stasis of practicing law were growing, with time, increasingly impossible to enjoy. He almost believed Naterwaul could be right, that worry alone could cause the attacks. Of course Naterwaul was also the moron who suggested that SoCal yahoo who had him reenact his birth. Those were some dim, desperate days. He'd be goddamned if he was returning to that giant foam womb and working to cry during reentry.

DeWiess, the environmental psychologist with the desert retreat, blamed urban air, cell phone radiation, and a contaminated water table, and gave him a sheet of paper with the names of everyday toxins listed front and back.

At ten he rose to walk down to Peter's office. Standing was hard. His legs were eighty years old again. His first steps were stiff and careful, an easing back into fluid motion that stunned the cantankerous joints. He limped down the hallway.

"Knock knock," he said at Peter's door.

"Hey hey," said Peter.

He entered the office and sat down. Peter was the senior associate on the R. H. Hobbs case. Tim didn't think much of him.

"Maybe I'm in and out these next couple of days, Peter. Maybe, maybe not."

Peter demonstrated the lack of curiosity required of associates when something personal appeared to be driving a partner's decision. His blank expression conveyed the theater of total understanding. He didn't even lean back in his chair. "Sure, Tim."

"We're under the gun, yeah. This thing is pressing down on us. But you don't make a move without me. Understand?"

"Tim, who—"

"Not one move."

"Who am I?"

"You call me, understand? I don't care what it is. I'm always on my cell."

"Of course. Of course."

"From this point forward I'm on my cell. No Kronish. No Wodica."

"No, no way. What for?"

"They don't know the case. You know the case better."

"I'll call you, not a problem."

"And you, I mean this with all due respect."

"Yeah."

"You're just not ready yet."

"No," said Peter. "No. I'm happy to call you, Tim."

Tim nodded and stood. Halfway down the hall, he heard his name being called. He looked back at Peter, who stood in the doorway, but his body kept moving forward.

"Hobbs is due in today, right?"

"Today?"

"Just wondered if you'd be here for that."

"He's due in today?" He was getting farther and farther down the hall.

"I thought you said he was coming in."

"I said that?"

They had to talk louder.

"Tim?"

"You call me, Peter! Understand? You don't make a move without me!"

He turned the corner and disappeared.

"There is no laboratory examination to confirm the presence or absence of the condition," he was told by a doctor named Regis, "so there is no reason to believe the disease has a defined physical cause or, I suppose, even exists at all."

Janowitz of Johns Hopkins had concluded that some compulsion was driving him to walk and suggested group therapy.

Klum dubbed it "benign idiopathic perambulation." He'd had to look up *idiopathic* in the dictionary. "Adj. — of unknown causes, as a disease." He thought the word, divorced of meaning, would have nicely suited Klum and her associates. *Idiopaths.* He also took exception to the word *benign.* Strictly medically speaking perhaps, but if his perambulation kept up, his life was ruined. How benign was that?

The internists made referrals. The specialists ordered scans. The clinics assembled teams.

He saw his first psychiatrist reluctantly, convinced as he was that his problem was not a mental one. Dr. Ruefle began their session by asking about his family history. He offered what little he had. His grandparents were dead; he knew their occupations, but nothing more. His father had died of cancer when he was a boy. On the twentieth anniversary of his death, his mother had been struck by a mirror, beneath which she had been sitting in a restaurant, when it came loose from the wall, and she died of blunt trauma to the head. Dr. Ruefle was never able to make sense of these facts or anything else. Tim lost the last of his patience with her when she suggested he see a genealogical healer, on the chance that something tragic had taken place in his past — an ancestor lost in a death march or some other forced evacuation. He had no idea what "genealogical healing" might entail and dismissed the idea as quackery.

He walked past the reception desk and through the glass doors, beyond the elevators and into the echo chamber of the emergency stairwell, where fire drills were conducted. He took the stairs with a determination he never displayed during drill time, as if now there were something to flee. He kept one hand on the railing. The orange stenciled floor numbers, the fire extinguishers. The toes of his dress shoes hit one note twelve times, reached the switchback, started the note again. He avoided the vertiginous glimpse down the rabbit hole of diminishing floors.

For some people the depressing setback was a return to the hospital, it was some migraine holocaust, lower-back blowout, inconsolable weeping, arthritic flare, new shadow on the CT scan, sudden chest pain.

Hobbs was coming in today?

Twenty floors down he encountered a black man. The man sat on the landing beside the painted piping that emerged from the wall. A thick coiled fire hose was encased in glass above him. He wore a winter coat, black but for the places where the white synthetic fiber cottoned out from tears in the shell. A collection of wrinkled shopping bags was arrayed around him. He had removed his shoes, a pair of high-tops gone brandless with grime. He was inspecting the brick-red bottoms of his feet.

"What are you doing here?"

The man looked up with a foot in hand. "Huh? Oh. Yeah, just…"

"What?"

"Looking for cans."

Tim walked past him and continued to descend. He was forced to turn his head in order to stay in the conversation. "How'd you get past security?"

"It's my brother," said the man.

"What?"

"My brother."

"Who's your brother?" He reached the next landing and within a few stairs lost sight of the man. "You shouldn't be here," he cried up.

"What?"

"I said I don't think you should be sitting in our stairwell!"

His voice echoed through the upper stairs. The man no longer responded. The clop of dress shoes filled the silence. In no time he descended past the twenties and the teens and entered the lobby.

Once he ran with the goal to exhaust himself. Maybe there was no slowing down, but he could speed up. He could move his head, his limbs — hell, he could *dance* so long as he kept moving forward. Like a stutterer in song. He juked and huffed around casual city walkers until he was in New Jersey and his lungs hit a wall and he stopped. But his legs, he realized at once, had every intention of continuing, and continue they would until they were through. He couldn't believe what he had inflicted on himself, his muscles quivering with fatigue, every step like lifting out of quicksand.

He had Jane lock him inside the bedroom. The tidy circles he was forced to walk made him dizzy and half-mad.

He had Horowitz pump him full of a powerful muscle relaxant. Which worked for the time he was out. But after the medication wore off he was out walking again, this time drowsy and nauseous, his longest and most miserable walk, and he swore never to do that again.

They bolted an O-ring into a stud in the wall and tethered him with a chain and a belt made of leather. After a couple of days, that sort of containment was just too barbaric.

When the illness returned a second time, he thought of the treadmill. He'd beat his body at its own game, outwit dumb matter with his mind. But every time chance permitted him to have his body on the treadmill during an episode, he found himself stepping right off the revolving belt, into freedom. His body wouldn't be contained or corralled. It had, it seemed to him, a mind of its own.

The lobby of his office building was set on a mezzanine. To access the street, one still had to ride down the escalator.

Frank Novovian looked up from his post, his eyes burdened with ripe bags, his cold-clock gaze greeting the world without humor. Yet he was deferential to the right people. "Good morning, Mr. Farnsworth," he said.

"Frank, can I have a word?"

"Of course."

Tim stepped onto the escalator. His feet continued to walk. He was forced to turn his head in order to further address the security guard. "Will you walk with me?"

Frank got off his stool and caught up with Tim long after he had stepped off the escalator. He was halfway across the lower lobby by then. "What can I do for you, Mr. Farnsworth?"

"There's a man in our stairwell."

"What man?"

"A homeless man."

"In our stairwell?"

"Know what he's doing there?"

He entered the revolving doors. He gestured for Frank to follow as he fought the wind pushing against the glass.

The uprush of city life, always unexpected. A far cry from his time behind the desk. Taxis heading past, cars, supply trucks, bundled men on bicycles delivering bagged lunches. Faces were as varied as the flags of the earth. A Hasidic Jew pushing a dolly in front of him weaved quickly between blustered walkers. The sidewalks were salt-stained; the cold swallowed him up. He walked into the wind, north, toward Central Park, a wind shaped materially by pole-whipped newspapers and fluttering scarf tails. The fabric of his suit snapped behind him angrily. His teeth were rattling. Poor Frank, forced out in nothing but his standard-issue security man's blazer. Yet Frank followed him dutifully into the crystal heart of the season.

Could he send Frank for the pack? Frank would have to reenter the building, wait for the elevator, walk the hallway, head back down again. By then he'd be searching for one man among eight million.

"Frank," he said, "R. H. Hobbs is expected later today."

"Do you remember the floor the man's on, Mr. Farnsworth?"

"Midthirties?"

Frank unclipped the walkie-talkie from his belt. "Two minutes and he'll no longer be a problem."

"Thank you, Frank."

Frank cocked the walkie-talkie sideways at his mouth and radioed inside. A voice crackled back. He was in midsentence when Tim reached out. "Wait," he said. Frank cut himself short and lowered the walkie-talkie in anticipation of further instruction, continuing to walk alongside him. "Wait a second, Frank."

They approached an intersection clustered by pedestrians waiting for the light to change. He turned down the side street, walking opposite the one-way traffic he was inexplicably, almost mystically spared from throwing himself in front of, and Frank followed. Some failsafe mechanism moved him around red lights and speeding cars, moved his legs with a cat's intuition around any immediate peril. Dr. Urgess had once pointed to that reprieve as proof he was in control at some conscious or at least subconscious level, although Dr. Cox later claimed that the body's involuntary systems, especially its sense of self-preservation, were powerful enough to override and even determine specific brain mechanisms. One located the disease in his mind, the other in his body. First he had believed the one doctor and followed his instructions, and then he had believed the other and followed his instructions. Now he was crossing the street with Frank after the last car in line had made it through the light, and neither Urgess nor Cox had managed for all their curiosity and wisdom to bring a single thing to bear on the problem itself. Thank you for your beautiful theories, you expert professionals, thank you for your empty remedies. Frank kept peering over.

"I'd like you to leave the man alone," said Tim. "Let him stay where he is."

"I thought you wanted him gone."

"Not anymore," he said.

He was thinking of the way he'd been treated at African Hair Weaving the day before. White man walks in and asks for shelter, black women point to the folding chairs. Same white man walks past a homeless man seeking the very same shelter, has black man thrown out into the cold. Dharma guru Bindu Talati's long-ago suggestion that some karmic imbalance might have caused a material rift that provoked his walking had claimed his imagination again, but partly he was just trying to be decent. "As a personal favor," he said.

He looked over to drive the point home and saw that by some miracle a black wool cap had materialized on Frank's once-steaming, egg-bald head. "There are perfectly good heat shelters in the city, Mr. Farnsworth."

"There are, that's true," he said. "But by a strange coincidence I know the man, Frank. We went to high school together. He's fallen on hard times. Will you do me the favor of seeing he stays put as long as he wants? And also make sure no one else harasses him?"

"I didn't know he was a friend of yours."

"A friend of sorts. From a long time ago."

"Consider it taken care of then, Mr. Farnsworth," said Frank, cocking the walkie-talkie at his mouth again.

"And Frank, I have to ask another favor of you," he said. "Would you let me borrow your cap?"

With no hesitation Frank handed him the hat. Handed it off as if that had been the point of bringing it outside with him, its brief respite on top of his head merely a convenient place to store it until the request was made. Tim put the hat on and tucked in his singed ears, pinning them between warm scalp and rough wool. "Thank you, Frank," he said.

"Is it the walking thing again, Mr. Farnsworth?"

Astonishment wiped his face clean of expression. No one at the firm knew—that he had made sure of. That had been the first priority. He had elegantly explained away his two earlier leaves of absence: everyone knew about Jane's struggle with cancer. But now he wondered: did others know the real reason, and how many? Or was it simply true what they said, that Frank Novovian in security knew everything before anyone else?

"What walking thing?"

"From before," said Frank.

"I don't know what the hell you're talking about, Frank."

"Oh," said the security man. "Never mind."

"You can go back to your post now."

"Okay, Mr. Farnsworth." But Frank kept walking beside him. "Is there anything I can do for you, Mr. Farnsworth?"

There was never anything anyone could do. Jane could handcuff him to the headboard until his wrists couldn't take another day, and Becka could feign understanding until she could flee the room again, and Bagdasarian could revisit the medical annals and run another MRI, and Hochstadt could design another pharmacological cocktail, and the Mayo Clinic could follow him with furrowed brows around the outskirts of Rochester again, and Cowley at the Cleveland Clinic could recommend psychiatric evaluation based on his patient's "health-care-seeking behavior," and Montreux's Dr. Euler could throw up his hands again, Yari Tobolowski could prepare another concoction of bat-wing extract, Sufi Regina could smoke him with the incense promises of a spiritually guided life-force energy, his channels could be reopened and his mind-body connection yoga'd and Reiki'd and Panchakarma'd until he was as one, as a rock is as one—but the goddamned thing was back. Hope and denial, the sick person's front and rear guards against the devastation of another attack, were gone.

"You can call my wife," he replied at last, "and tell her to expect a call from me."

The bodhisattva had encouraged him to look deeply into his reliance upon technology. Email and PDA, cell phone and voice mail were extensions of the ruinous consuming self. They made thoughts of the self instantaneously and irrepressibly accessible. Who's calling me, who's texting me, who wants me, me, me. The ego went along on every walk and ride, replacing the vistas and skylines, scrambling the delicate meditative code. The self was cut off from the hope that the world might reassert itself over the digitized clamor and the ego turn again into the sky, the bird, the tree.

He didn't touch mouse or keyboard, keypad or scroll button all the months of his previous recurrence, and it had thrived then, and now it was back, so so much for the bodhisattva.

II

She said his name three times into the phone, each time louder than the last. The other brokers in the open plan looked up from their preoccupations. "You have to concentrate, Tim," she said. She stood up and her chair rolled back to tap the desk behind her. The person sitting there exchanged a look with his colleague across the aisle. "What's the name of the road, can you see a name?" It was impossible for anyone to ignore her. "But

what town? What town?" She seemed to regain some measure
of control. She sat back down and issued careful instructions, as
specific as they were mysterious. "You have to call nine-one-one.
Are you listening? If you can call me you can call nine-one-one.
But if they can't locate you—Tim? If they can't locate you, you
have to walk into that subdivision. I know you're tired but you
don't have a choice if they don't know where to pick you up. Move
away from the main road. Are you listening? Move into the neighborhood. Go to the first house and ring the doorbell. Stay awake
until somebody opens the door. If nobody opens the door, go
to the next house. You tell them to call nine-one-one. Then
you can fall asleep. Somebody has to call nine-one-one before
you fall asleep. I know you're tired, I know you're tired, but are
you listening?" She stood again. "Tim, are you awake?" She
waited for him to reply. "Tim, wake up!" Everyone was silent.
The only sound in the office now was of telephones allowed to
ring. "Go into the subdivision! I will find you!"

He walked from the main road to the subdivision. His body
trembled with cold. It had let him know, five minutes earlier,
that the walk had come to its end. He wore his suit coat backward, the back in front, which did better against the wind, and
his hands were wrapped in plastic bags. He had swooped down
during the walk and plucked them from the icy ground, one
hand in a black plastic bag and the other in a white one.

The first house was circumscribed by a chain-link fence. He
forced the latch up and stumbled to the door. He tried to think
of what he might say. The right idea wasn't coming. The words
behind the idea were out of reach. He was at one remove from
the person who knew how to form ideas and say words.

He fell to his knees before he could ring the doorbell. He put his bagged hands on the storm door and rested his head there. The metal was cold against his cheek. He fought with angry determination for two or three seconds. If he could defy the tidal fatigue, his body wouldn't win, and he might still learn that someone had discovered him and would see him to safety.

She made calls from her desk, starting with the easternmost hospitals and moving west. She left her name and number in case he should be admitted later. She was not unfamiliar with the patient voices of the operators, their assurances that she would be contacted immediately should his name appear in the computer. Colleagues came up to ask if everything was okay. Sure, sure everything's okay. You've done this yourself, right—searched random hospitals for the one you love? Again she stared at the blank wall of explanation. She could have asked have you ever heard of...but there was no name. She could have said it's a condition that afflicts only...but there were no statistics. "Everything's fine," she assured them. She turned back to the phone and dialed another hospital.

The call came in around five, perfectly timed for rush hour. Better late than never. Better than going to identify his body at the morgue. Still, she was angry when they told her he had been admitted two hours earlier. Nothing like wasting time making fruitless calls when she could have been on her way. That was always the impulse when she finally located him: *I have to get to him.* And when she got to him: *never let him go.*

She left the office to sit in traffic and didn't reach the hospital until quarter to seven. He was in the waiting room of the ER. She moved past shell-shocked people and children playing on the floor. He sat against the far wall covered in a blanket, wearing a black wool cap. His face was windburned that distinct pink color two shades lighter than damage done by the sun.

"Your face," she said.

"How'd you find me?"

"I made calls."

"You always find me," he said.

"It's easier when you have the GPS with you." She sat down next to him. "Where's your pack?"

"They're worried about my toes. The blisters are bad."

"Where's your pack, Tim?"

"I had just gone down to Peter's," he said. "But when I left I went in the opposite direction."

"I asked you to always have the pack," she said.

"Frank Novovian gave me his cap."

She had to remember who Frank Novovian was. "The security guy?"

"All I had to do was ask for it."

"You promised me you would carry your pack with you wherever you went."

"I just went down the hall," he said.

They drove into the city to retrieve the pack and then they headed home. She drove. He sat gazing silently out the window at the nothing scenery passing them in the night. He turned to her at last and announced that he hadn't bothered to explain to the attending doctor what he was doing out in the cold for so long.

"You didn't tell the attending?" she said. "Why wouldn't you tell the attending?"

"Those band-aid scientists," he said, "don't get to know about me anymore."

This alarmed her. They had always had faith, both of them,

in the existence of the One Guy, out there somewhere, living and working with the answer. It was the One Guy they sought in Rochester, Minnesota, in San Francisco, in Switzerland, and, closer to home, in doctors' offices from Manhattan to Buffalo. Time was, he would stop anyone, interns and med students included. Time was, he would travel halfway across the world. Now he couldn't be bothered to so much as state the facts to an attending?

"One of those band-aid scientists may have the answer, Tim. You might be surprised someday."

"What surprise?" he said. "There are no more surprises. The only way they could surprise me is if they gave up the secret recipe to their crock of shit."

They pulled off the highway, went under the overpass and down Route 22, where the stoplights and shopping centers of their life together greeted them from both sides of the four lanes. His frostbitten hands were wrapped in something like Ace bandages intended to insulate them from the cold, a pair of taupe and layered mitts.

"I don't like the way you're talking," she said.

"What way is that?"

"Without hope."

They started up the hill that led into the neighborhood, headlights illuminating clumps of days-old snow formless as manatees, dusted with black exhaust. The blacktop glowed with cold, the salted road was white as bone.

"I must be crazy," he said.

"Crazy?"

"I'm the only one, Jane. No one else on record. That's crazy."

"You're not crazy," she said. "You're sick."

"Yeah, sick in the head."

He was a logical man who believed, as the good lawyer, in

the power of precedent. Yet there was no precedent for what he suffered, and no proof of what qualified as a disease among the physicians and clinical investigators: a toxin, a pathogen, a genetic disorder. No evidence of any physical cause. No evidence, no precedent—and the experts could give no positive testimony. That left only the mind.

"I wish you would call Dr. Bagdasarian," she said.

He didn't reply, and they reached the house in silence. She took the driveway slowly as the garage door pulled up. She put the car in park and opened the door. She turned to him before stepping out. He stared through the windshield. Tears fell down his face into his day's growth of beard.

"Oh, banana," she said.

She turned in her seat and placed a hand on his chest. She felt his staccato breathing, the resistance as he inhaled to letting himself go further than he already had. He didn't like to cry. He was fighting it the way a boy fights sleep, the mind pitted against the body and proving weaker. He cried so seldom that tears instinctively sprung to her eyes, too, the way they had when she was a girl and sympathy was as natural as breathing.

That night in bed she made him an offer. She would dress according to the weather, follow him as he walked, and watch over him as he slept. To make it possible she was going to quit her job. How could she be at work with any peace of mind when he might be anywhere at any moment, lost in the city and scared as a child?

"I know you won't go back in the cuffs," she said. "So the only solution is for me to quit."

"I don't want you to quit," he said.

She had been able to take care of him when he required cuffing to the bed only because she wasn't working. Then — poof! It disappeared. Her relief was enormous. She looked back on those barren days in the bedroom with a hazy feeling of house arrest. Once or twice she drove Becka to her violin lesson after too much wine. But her efforts had been so consuming that his life, his sickness, had in many ways become her own, and until she started selling real estate, she was at sea.

"We don't need the money," she said.

"But you enjoy your work. You've made a life for yourself these past couple of years."

"You'll find this hard to believe," she said, "but you and Becka, you are my life."

He was quiet in the dark. A peeled, flat moon cast some light through the bedroom's open windows, just enough to make their breath visible. He was on top of the bed; she huddled beneath the covers. "Why would I find that hard to believe?"

"Because your life is your work."

"Is that what you think?"

There was silence. "Listen to me," she said. "You need someone to watch over you. You're going farther away than ever before."

She had no idea, *no idea*, how badly he wanted to consent. He was scared. He wanted someone to safeguard him.

"It's too much to ask," he said. "I don't want it to be like last time when I recover and go back to work and you get depressed."

"I wasn't depressed," she said. "I just had a hard time finding my old self again."

"It's too much to ask," he repeated.

And she was silent then because she was relieved.

12

Mike Kronish appeared in Tim's doorway. Even from that distance the man seemed to hover. Proximity to him felt like sudden contact with a grizzly bear risen up on its hind legs. His broad suited figure was an American corn-fed miracle. He made his own weather in hallways and conference rooms and was legend for screwing paralegals.

Kronish was the managing partner of the litigation department, a five-year position to which he'd been elected. He assigned new business to the other partners, set policy for the department, and ran the caucuses and litigation committees. He also served internally as the voice of the firm. There were no official hierarchies among partners at Troyer, Barr, but the managing partner had certain political obligations that involved keeping important matters under control. "Knock knock," he said.

"Hey hey," said Tim.

Kronish came in and sat across from him. A delayed tide of aftershave, masking any hint of flaw, floated over the desk. "So let me just come right out with it," said Kronish. "R.H. called. He's unhappy."

"He called you?"

"You missed a meeting with him yesterday."

"No, no," said Tim. "I talked with Peter. Peter should have met with him. Where the fuck was Peter?"

"Tell me, Tim."

"What?"

"Who's the partner on the case? Is Peter the partner?"

"And whose case is it, Mike? If I want Peter to take the meeting."

"Your case, your case. But when I get a call—me—from the client."

"Then if it's my case, I take the meeting or I tell Peter to take the meeting."

Kronish pinched his nose twice quickly and then resettled his hand on his folded leg. He sat back in the chair. A moment passed.

Kronish was famous inside the firm for once having billed a twenty-seven-hour day. This was possible only if you plied the time zones. Kronish worked twenty-four hours straight and then boarded a plane for Los Angeles, where he continued working on West Coast time. When he filled out his time sheets later that week, he rightfully attributed more hours to that day than technically possible. This made Tim want to leap across the desk and eat his lucky, healthy heart. "Fucking guy needs a babysitter," he said, breaking the silence.

"Fucking guy needs an acquittal," said Kronish.

"Which is my entire fucking point as to why I wasn't in that meeting. Why am I working this hard? And it wasn't a meeting, it was a hand-holding. Look, Mike, butt out, with due respect. I can handle my client."

"You know all he brings in on the corporate side."

"I need reminding?"

"So you skipped the meeting to work the case?"

"Butt the fuck out, Mike."

There was a momentary stare-down between the two men. Then Kronish's eyes wandered. Tim followed them over to the wall, where the backpack leaned. "What's with that?"

"What?"

Kronish gestured with his chin. "The backpack."

"What, it's a backpack."

"Have I seen you walking the halls with that?"

For a moment he thought, I'll just come clean. I'll show Mike *The New England Journal of Medicine* article and I'll detail the frustration of fighting the label of crazy and I'll say, ultimately, Mike, they don't know if it's a medical condition or a psychiatric disorder. I'll be honest, and Mike will respond in kind with a show of sympathy he's never demonstrated because we are both human beings slated to fall ill and die. "All right, all right," he said. "Look." He was quiet, letting the moment build. "We've had some bad news."

"Who's 'we'?"

He took a deep breath. "Jane's cancer's come back."

Kronish's demeanor changed. He leaned forward in the chair and steepled his hands as if to pray, never letting his eyes stray from Tim's. Soon he wore a duly woeful and theatrical frown. "Shit," he said.

"Yeah."

"That is bad news."

They sat in respectful silence.

"Anything the firm can do?"

That's what he wanted to hear. He let the pause linger. "Just let me work my case."

Kronish put up his hands. "Your case," he said.

He left soon after. Tim realized that Jane's supposed cancer in no way explained why he should be carrying a backpack around the halls of the firm. Kronish, with his shrewd legal mind, should have seized on that. Maybe he had by now. The strands of his story were easy to take apart. But for the moment, Kronish had only heard the word *cancer*. Everything else went out the window. That was the power, the enviable, unlucky power, of a fatal and familiar disease.

13

Overcast was riveted to the sky as gray to a battleship. The footpath of the Brooklyn Bridge matched the color of the day, as did its intricate spiderwebbing metalwork. He went up the incline and under the first arch. The East River was scalloped white from the wind as it coursed south into the harbor. Believing he was alone, to vent his anger he cried out into the consuming gust, only to turn the corner of the arch and find two bundled lovers taking self-portraits. Startled, they backed up against the brickwork to give him a wide berth.

The path flattened out between the first arch and the second. He became aware then of someone keeping pace with him. He thought nothing of it until the man looked over and said, "Aren't you the attorney defending R. H. Hobbs?"

He turned. Where had the man come from? He looked behind him. The picture-takers were gone.

"Excuse me?" he said.

"Am I right? You're the man defending R. H. Hobbs."

That someone would address him out of the blue halfway across the pedestrian walkway of the Brooklyn Bridge was surprising. That that same someone identified him as R.H.'s attorney was alarming. The murder had been mentioned in the papers once or twice, but nothing since the early days. The case lacked a celebrity pedigree, and Tim felt sure that no one outside the legal world would have recognized the lawyers involved.

"Do I know you?"

"Oh, I doubt that," said the man.

He was about Tim's height, of a slim build under the winter layers. He was dressed in a camel-hair coat with collar raised. Out of it blossomed the black folds of a cashmere scarf covering his neck. An enormous sable hat was perched on top of his head. The fur quivered in the wind like a patch of black wheat. He had a long pale solitary face, too pale to grow whiskers, bloodless in the cheeks even on so cold a day, with a dimple in his potbellied chin and a long pinched nose that accentuated the bone in the middle, as prominent as a knuckle.

"How do you know me?"

"I followed you from midtown," said the man. "You work in midtown?"

"That doesn't answer my question," he said. And then: "You followed me all the way from midtown to the Brooklyn Bridge?"

"It's a beautiful day for a walk."

"No, it's not," he said. "It's well below freezing. What are you doing following me?"

The man continued to keep pace a little too close for comfort. "That was one vicious murder," he said. "Stabbed his wife like she was a piece of art. Almost beautiful, looked at in a certain light. But monstrous for sure. How can you defend a man like that?"

"Who are you? I'll call the police."

"Have you seen the crime-scene photos? Very premeditated cuts. He didn't just pound away, not after the first couple of stabs. He is one sick bastard, your client."

"I will call the police."

But he hadn't even taken out his phone. He was afraid the man might swipe at his hand. He didn't want to lose the new BlackBerry as he had lost the old one. He would need it to call Jane when the walk ended.

"And why Staten Island?" asked the man. "Why dump her body in that old Staten Island landfill that's been closed forever?"

"Who are you?"

"Your client lives in Rye. Why go all the way to Staten Island?"

"How do you know what you know?"

"Want to know what I know?" the man asked. "What I really know?"

The man came to an abrupt halt. Tim was forced to keep moving. They were quickly separated by a number of paces. He turned his head and watched the man recede. The man looked surprised that Tim would continue walking.

"Don't care to know?" said the man.

"What do you know?" Tim hollered.

"Your client's innocent, Mr. Farnsworth," he cried above the wind. "R. H. Hobbs is an innocent man."

The man removed a Ziploc bag from his coat. Inside the

clear bag sat a butcher's knife. The man held the bag up by the seam and gently shook the knife inside the bag. Then he turned and walked away.

14

The cemetery had been retired under a white sheet. Darkness now settled over it like dust. A black Mercedes threaded its way through the maze of winding streets.

Jane followed the Mercedes in her car. She pulled up to the curb and stepped out. She hurried through the snow.

He was lying on a cleared bed of granite. He sat up at her touch with a mortal start, as if she had jolted him out of another dimension. His eyes darted wildly in the holes of his ski mask. His unsheltered sleep had put him again at the mercy of an unknown world. He felt the approach of some violent reckoning.

"There was a man on the bridge," he said.

"What man?"

"He knew who I was."

His attention was drawn away by the slamming of a car door. He watched a man in a long charcoal wool coat approach them slowly through the crusted snow. Even from so far a distance he could make out those familiar Picasso features—the skewed nose, the plump lips, one eye bigger than the other.

"What is he doing here?"

She was also watching the man come forward. "I called him."

"I said no doctors."

"I know," she said.

"He can't help me, Jane."

"How do you know that?"

"None of them can help me."

"Hello, Tim," said Dr. Bagdasarian.

They sat in the doctor's warm Mercedes as halos of glowing halogen began to shine from the lampposts across the cemetery. Tim disliked Bagdasarian the least of all his doctors. He had been the recipient of many funny looks over the years, but Dr. Bagdasarian's was due to the fact that he was born that way, not because he questioned Tim's sanity or doubted the severity of his suffering. One look at Bagdasarian and the assumption was that God had deprived him of all beauty and vanity so that he could better dedicate himself to the puzzle of men's afflictions. The doctor was learned and eloquent with his singsong accent and carried the aura of a polymath.

Yet Tim was not pleased to see him. Before he got sick, he was under the illusion that he needed only to seek help from the medical community, and then all that American ingenuity, all that researched enlightenment, would bring about his inalienable right to good health. At the very least, he thought, there would be one person, one expert in the field, to give him some degree of understanding, solace and action. But by now he had abandoned his search for the One Guy. The One Guy was dead, the One Guy was God, the One Guy was an invention in the night when he was bottomed out and desperate to believe in something. He was sick of searching for the One Guy and sick of having his hopes dashed. He would not let himself believe in the One Guy anymore.

And anyway, who the fuck needed the One Guy? He was still

alive, wasn't he? He could beat this thing on his own, couldn't he? Fuck the One Guy. Fuck the One Guy's answers and the One Guy's hope.

Bagdasarian spoke over their heads for twenty minutes about advances in brain imaging technology. He discussed radioisotopes and motion degradation and atomic magnetometers. Considerable progress had been made, he said, since Tim's last extended medical examination. In fact there were some very cutting-edge developments that allowed a clean image of the brain to be taken *in situ*.

"In other words," the doctor said excitedly, "in other words, we no longer require complete immobility, you see. We can capture what's happening in your brain *when* you're walking, at the very moment it's changing. In neurological circles, this is extremely significant. No one dreamed we could be where we are at this moment for another fifty, sixty years. I know some who said we would never get there. But it's true. We no longer need to lay you out on a slab and push you inside a tunnel to get a very good idea of what's going on inside your head."

To his dismay, as he listened to the doctor, he couldn't prevent a little bit of renewed hope from belly-flipping inside him.

"What does that do for me?" he asked.

"What does it do?"

"Where does it get me? Does it get me a diagnosis? Does it get me a cure?"

"Well," said the doctor, "no, not a cure, certainly. It is only a tool, but a more refined tool than we've ever—"

"Not interested."

"Not interested?" said Jane.

She hung between the two men in the backseat. Tim pivoted to look at her.

"Why would I do that to myself, Janey?"

"Do what?"

"Allow myself to hope again, when it's really only another opportunity to be disappointed?"

"How do you know you'll be disappointed when you haven't tried it?"

"You just heard the man. It's not a cure, and it's not a diagnosis."

"But," said Bagdasarian, "it still might be of some comfort to you, Tim."

He turned back to the doctor in the dim light.

"I know how you've struggled to validate your condition," said the doctor. "I know you've fallen into depression because no empirical evidence has emerged to exonerate you—I use your word, which I have remembered many years—to exonerate you from the charge of being mentally ill. You hate it when people say this is something all in your head. You place great importance on having your condition regarded as a legitimate physical malfunction, something that members of the medical establishment like myself must take seriously. That is the very prerequisite of a real disease—that it's taken seriously. We have a few new tools to do that now—possibly, possibly. Wouldn't it be satisfying to prove to the world that your unique condition is as you insist it is, a matter of organic disease, and not something—a compulsion, or a psychosis—for which you, for personal reasons—and perfectly naturally so, Tim, perfectly naturally—feel you must be ashamed of? Wouldn't that be, in its humble way, some measure of progress?"

Bagdasarian was good. Tim could feel himself getting sucked in again. "What would I have to do?"

The device Bagdasarian had in mind would be a prototype made to order. As such it would not come cheaply. Because his

was a disease of one, they did not have at their disposal pre-
fab medical supplies. Tim told him not to worry about money,
they could afford it. In that case, the doctor resumed, he would
approach one of the two private biomedical firms he knew capable of engineering the kind of thing he had in mind, an ambula-
tory helmet of sorts. It would take snapshots, so to speak—some
before he walked, some during his walk, and some after. From
that they would be able to reconstruct a full picture of what was
happening inside his brain during a typical episode.

"I'd have to wear this device before walking?"

"Yes," said the doctor. "To get the before-and-after story,
you'd need to wear it day and night."

The doctor had spoken eloquently and empathetically of
Tim's despair. Why should it be so important to him to prove
that he was suffering from a legitimate medical disorder and not
a mental illness? He didn't know, except to say that it was. It
meant all the difference in the world somehow not to be lumped
in with the lunatics and the fabricators. He wanted to prove it
to Jane, who needed no proof, and to Becka, who looked at him
suspiciously, and to the medical establishment, who made a cot-
tage industry out of dismissal, and to people at the firm who
might doubt him with a lawyer's inborn skepticism. Most of all,
he wanted to prove it to himself.

But the doctor had stopped speaking, and Tim recalled
the many tests he'd already endured, the hard exam beds and
cold paper gowns, and the thousand times that hope had belly-
flipped inside him before. And he thought about Troyer, Barr.
There was already a backpack over his shoulder when he walked
the halls. What would they make of him on the day he showed
up wearing a made-to-order brain helmet?

"I'll have to think about it," he said.

"You'll have to think about it?"

He turned back to Jane. "What if he doesn't succeed?" he asked. "I get my hopes up again and nothing comes of it. What then?"

"But this is what you've wanted from the very beginning," she said. "Proof. Evidence."

"Where's the guarantee of that?"

"And what's the alternative?" she asked. "Give up? Lose hope?"

"I'm sorry," he said to the doctor. "It's something I'll have to think about."

"Perfectly understandable," said Bagdasarian.

15

She ran into the grocery store to pick up dinner. She was waiting at the meat department for the butcher to come out with her veal chops when she turned and saw the man standing next to her. Her heart leapt.

It was a girl's heart. She couldn't explain what made her, even now, forty-six and twenty years married, want him. He was in a suit and tie and overcoat and his designer eyeglasses marked him as a man who loved jazz and art magazines. He went to the gym and pressed weights and his lovely sweat dripped down his neck. He couldn't be a day over thirty-five. It was unkind of the universe to make a man so finely match her ideal of physical beauty

and to place him a few feet from her at the moment she was trying to buy veal chops for her family. If she inched a foot closer
to him, people passing by would think they were a couple. If she
inched over, people would think they had a place in the city set
high above the noise where music played across the open loft and
the walls were hung with contemporary art. Maybe he had two
kids, maybe he abused cocaine in club stalls—she didn't know
the first thing about him. It only made her want him more. She
kept desire down and kept it down because of vows and obligations and an entire moral structure that could not collapse at the
sight of one man in a grocery store, but it had collapsed.

She couldn't recall the last time a person affected her so
painfully. He turned to her and she quickly lost her nerve and
faced the meat again. She turned back eventually. He was still
looking. He smiled at her. It wasn't one of those firm-lipped hel-
los with a polite little nod. It was a smile with locked eyes. He
was flirting. She wanted to cry out. She wanted to wrap his tie
around her hand. She wanted contact information.

What was it? Something encoded in her genes? Something
reaching all the way back to the primates? The body talking.
She disliked it intensely. The man's smile was a totally negating
force. It stirred complete abandon in her. It tapped into what
was reckless and selfish. She saw herself stealing out of the store
with him and getting into a different car and being driven past
the car she shared with Tim where he sat in the passenger seat
with his eyes closed, listening to public radio. A different life, a
totally different life. How easy it would be. They would arrive at
the man's place and she would never leave. Give him to me and I
will change. I will see the point again. I will discern the code. I
will laugh into the pillow at my unbelievable luck. I will inhabit
a bed for hours with a fullness I thought gone forever. I will

not look at anything as a chore again. I will smile unprompted. I will be in love. I will have boundless energy. I will not complain. Get me out of my life and I will wax again. I'll make trips to boutiques in SoHo and pick out garter belts and babydolls, and as the clerk wraps them in tissue, it will take every possible restraint not to cry out with happiness.

The calls in the middle of the night, the long car rides out to God knows where. The worry, the frustration, the uncertainty, the sacrifice. Let Becka pick him up from now on. Make him take cabs.

She left the meat counter and walked to the far end of the store. She walked down the wine aisle. She chose the most expensive bottle. She left and then returned to the aisle for a second one.

"Where's the food?" he asked.

She shut the door. "The line was too long. I thought we could pick up something on the way."

"I was looking forward to veal," he said.

She set the two wine bottles in back.

"You could buy wine but not veal?"

"I bought the wine at the liquor counter. There was no line there."

"You couldn't buy the veal there, too?"

"You know, it really pisses me off that you won't let Bagdasarian try to help you," she said. "With the exception of me, he's the only one who hasn't accused you of being crazy. I mean, he's gone out of his way to argue that this is a real disease, and now he has something that might offer some evidence, some hope, to do for you what you've wanted, what you have searched and

searched—what you have *begged* for, Tim—he says to you here
it is, possibly, maybe, can't guarantee it, but hey, it's more than
we've ever had. Good news, right? Exciting stuff! And you look
away and say, let me think about it? What the hell is wrong with
you? How many times—"

"Hey," he said, "where is this coming from?"

"How many times have I sat with you in waiting rooms?
How many specialists have we seen? I have flown to Ohio, to
Minnesota, to California, to The fucking Hague! to be with you
while you track them down. All the big names, all the experts.
I have been there. Do you remember the chart, Tim? The log?
What did you call it? Every day. Every day we recorded what
you ate, what you drank, how you slept, how many hours, on
and on…when you had your bowel movements, what change
in weather that day, the temperature, the barometric pressure,
for fuck's sake. What else? Every insane insignificance! I kept a
map full of pushpins! Here's where you walked to on Monday.
Here's where you walked to on Wednesday. I listened to your
rants, your rage, your frustration—"

"Can I get a word in?"

"And after all my struggle and all my patience, you can't
make one—more—fucking—effort?"

"Don't you understand that if he comes up empty, I'll want
to kill myself?"

"You said you'd never do that."

"But I would want to, Jane."

"So that's it? That's the final word?"

"I said I would think about it."

"And I get no say in it? After everything, I get no say?"

"It has to be my decision," he said.

"Don't think I don't know why," she said. "You'd have to

wear that helmet at work. Don't think I don't know that's your thinking."

She threw the car in reverse, then suddenly slammed on the brakes. She had come close to hitting a mother and daughter as they passed by.

They drove home in silence and did not stop for dinner. On their way up the drive, they saw the lights from Becka's Volvo coming down. The two cars edged into the snowy margins. They rolled down their windows.

"Where are you going?"

"Nowhere."

"Where are you going, Rebecca?"

Becka turned impatiently to look through the windshield and then back to her mother. Tim leaned into Jane to better see his daughter. "I have a show," she said.

"This is a school night."

"School night? Are you serious?"

"Where's the show?"

Becka unclipped her seat belt and pivoted around to the backseat, where her guitar case lay. She straightened herself and held a flyer out the window. Jane took it and read. Then she passed it to Tim without looking at him.

"It's not an open mike?"

"I just gave you the flyer, Mom."

Tim was reading the flyer. "This has your name on it," he said through the window.

"It's just around here," she said. "Not like in the city or something."

"Why didn't you tell us about this sooner?"

"Because I didn't want you *coming*," she said. "Besides, what were the chances of that anyway? Can I go now?"

Jane made her promise to be home by one and Becka continued down the drive. Jane pulled into the garage, reached in back for the wine and stepped out. Tim was still reading the flyer when she entered the house.

16

R. H. Hobbs was a stormer. He stepped out of the car before the driver had a chance to open the door and he stormed through the lower lobby and up the escalator to the mezzanine. He stood at the elevators making the people around him nervous. He was the first in and somehow the first out, after the women. He stormed through the glass doors into Troyer, Barr's reception area and drummed his fingers on the front desk. The receptionist took his instructions, picked up the phone and silently urged it to ring faster. R.H. was this way even when he didn't have a murder indictment hanging over his head. While waiting for one of the team's associates to show up and lead him back, he tried sitting on the sofa, but then stood and walked over to the window. He vigorously shook the change in one of his pockets while peering out the glass. His gaze failed to alight on anything so he took his hands out of his pockets and ran them over his slick, brutally dyed hair, smoothing down his widow's peak as he walked back to the receptionist to ask her how much longer he was going to have to wait. He had been there just forty-five seconds. The receptionist picked up the phone to make another call when Tim appeared.

"Holy hell, look who it is," said R.H. "An attorney I used to know. I wonder how I might retain his services."

"How are you, old friend?" said Tim.

"Looking at jail time," said R.H. "You might have heard."

R.H. extended his hand. Tim's hands were badly frostbitten but he didn't feel he could deny him. He fought the urge to cry out as R.H. squeezed and pumped.

"Maybe I'm just being a prima donna because my life is on the line, but would it kill you to return my calls?"

"I've not been as attentive as I've needed to be, R.H.," he said, leading his client out of the staid lobby into the firm's quiet interior. "But I haven't neglected you, despite how it might appear, even as I've had to deal with Jane's upcoming surgery."

"Uh-huh," said R.H. "And what kind of cancer is it?"

"I'm afraid it's spread. It doesn't look good."

"I'm sorry to hear that. Why are you carrying that backpack?"

"This? Doesn't it make me look like a schoolboy?"

"And you're wearing snow boots. Why are you wearing snow boots?"

"There is a funny story about these boots, R.H. You'll get a kick out of it."

Suddenly R.H. stopped. He turned to face the wall. One of his knees buckled. Tim thought the older man was having a heart attack. But then R.H. covered his eyes with his hand and tucked the other hand under his arm and began to cry. He looked a little like the disgraced Nixon. His crying built to a steady heaving through thick nostrils. "Why is this happening to me?" he asked, struggling to breathe. "I swear to God in heaven I'm innocent."

Tim pivoted in front of R.H. to shield him from hallway onlookers. He placed a hand on his shoulder. He didn't know what to say.

"I'm an innocent man."

Tim kept his hand there until R.H. pulled out a handkerchief and began to collect himself.

They were arrayed around the conference room table. Peter, the senior associate, had before him the manila envelope that contained the sketch of the man Tim had encountered on the bridge. To Tim's annoyance Mike Kronish had asked to sit in on the meeting. A secretary put her head in to inform the four men that the detective and the assistant district attorney had arrived.

"We'll let you know when to bring them in," said Tim. "Thank you."

After the door closed Peter opened the envelope and set the sketch before R.H. Tim had sat for an hour with one of the freelancers from the courthouse and considered it a good likeness.

"I don't recognize him," R.H. said within five seconds.

"Now, just take your time, R.H. Look long and hard. Clear your mind. There's no pressure. Take all the time you need."

"This is the man who showed you the knife?"

Tim nodded. R.H. focused on the sketch again.

"I could stare at this picture until Judgment Day, I still wouldn't recognize him."

"Are you absolutely sure?"

"Well, Jesus Christ," said R.H. "I sure the hell wish I did."

The secretary ushered in the lead detective and the assistant district attorney. Detective Roy had a pack of cigarettes in the front pocket of his buttondown. He had the fissured skin of a veteran smoker, as if someone had come along and smoothed out the crumpled ball of his face. He filled the conference room with his smoker's stench and the impertinence of a hostile witness mocking his interrogator. The assistant district attorney was a short, stout woman who upon sitting down declared her hope that no one here was wasting anyone's time.

Tim pushed the sketch across the table to Detective Roy. The detective pulled it toward him slowly with all the indifference in the world. He puckered his lips as he looked it over and swished air between his two front teeth, disrupting the room's silence. He passed the sketch to the assistant district attorney who, before looking, lifted her eyeglasses to her forehead, where they sat well perched.

"So he stops you," said the detective, "he tells you your client's innocent, he shows you what he claims is the murder weapon, and then he walks away."

"That's correct," said Tim.

"Well, ain't that just fucking bizarre-o, hey?" The detective turned to the assistant district attorney. "Isn't that bizarre-o, Thelma?"

"Pretty bizarre," said Thelma.

"And where again?"

"Just outside the office here. Right as I was leaving for the night."

"And when?"

"Last week. Tuesday. No, Wednesday."

"Uh-huh," said the detective. "Hey-ho. Hundred percent

bizarre. Thelma? Bizarre?" The detective turned once again to look at Thelma.

"Does your client recognize the man?" she asked Tim.

"Sure the hell wish I did," said R.H.

Tim reached out and delicately touched R.H.'s arm. "Let us do the talking," he whispered. And then, more audibly, he said, "He does not. But that has no bearing on whether or not this man is somehow involved with the crime my client has been accused of committing."

"You didn't try to, I don't know…take the knife away from the man? You say he had it in a Ziploc bag. He wasn't brandishing it?"

"It was inside the bag."

"And you, what—you just looked at it?"

"You're asking why I didn't try to take the knife away from him?"

"Well, if he wasn't brandishing it."

"Yeah, why the hell didn't you try that?" asked R.H.

Tim attempted to touch his arm again, but R.H. pulled back.

"Couldn't you have at least swiped at it?"

Tim directed his answer at the detective. "When you are approached by a complete stranger who brandishes a knife that may be a murder weapon, your first instinct is not to try and take it away."

"Maybe not *your* first instinct," said R.H.

"Fair enough," the detective said to Tim.

"During the course of your investigation, Detective, did you have a suspect, or perhaps interview someone, who looked like the man in that sketch?"

Detective Roy smiled. He looked directly at R.H. "We only ever had one suspect, Counselor."

The room turned silent.

"Did you interview anyone who looked like that man?"

"What are you asking us to do, Mr. Farnsworth?" asked the assistant district attorney, whose glasses remained on her forehead.

"Look into who this man might be. He had the murder weapon."

"Alleged murder weapon."

"Fine, alleged. All the same, that's not your everyday occurrence, I think you can agree."

"Oh, for sure, for sure," said the detective. "Bizarre-o indeed."

"Why does he keep saying that?" asked R.H.

Tim had to reach out again. The detective and the assistant district attorney quietly conferred.

"Sure, why not," said the detective as he stood and put a fresh cigarette in one corner of his mouth. The cigarette bobbed up and down as he spoke. "Terrorism, murdered police, getting guns out of the hands of children. We got all the time in the world for this shit."

The assistant district attorney returned her glasses to her nose, and they departed.

Tim had had to excuse himself directly after the meeting to visit the men's room. He returned to discover Mike Kronish inside his office with R.H. Sam Wodica was there, too. Wodica was the firm's managing partner, overseer of all its departments, perched on the final rung of the invisible ladder. Wodica resembled an aging surfer. His sandy-blond hair, suntanned complexion and year-round seersucker had a way of disarming jurors.

They expected him to pour sand out of his shoes during closing arguments and then invite them all to the bonfire afterward, which went a long way toward winning them over.

Kronish's elbow was on a bookshelf and Wodica's ass was in Tim's chair, gently swiveling. Their unexpected presence gave the office a charge. Tim had walked into a voluble silence.

"Oh, I'm in your seat," said Wodica, standing and gesturing for Tim to sit in his own chair.

Do you expect a goddamned thank-you? he wanted to say.

He walked around the desk as Wodica retreated to the wall. Tim set the backpack in the corner. He sat down. He looked directly at R.H. and said, "What's up?" R.H. stared at him but remained silent.

Kronish spoke. "R.H. is worried that because of Jane's health, Tim, you don't have your head in the game."

"I feel for you having to deal with she has cancer," said R.H., "but I'm looking at some serious consequences if things don't go my way. They'll take my fortune and I'll rot in a cell, or I'll just fucking die who knows, so I need to know. Do I have your undivided attention?"

Tim looked across the desk directly into R.H.'s heavy-hanging eyes, ignoring the two partners, and said, "There's nobody that can try this case like I can."

"Everybody here knows you're working this case hard," said Wodica. "R.H. doesn't see it like we do, day in, day out. So he just asked that we talk this through."

"If he saw what we saw," Kronish added, "he'd know he doesn't have a worry in the world. Basically we're just here to clear up a minor communication problem."

"My guess is he needs to hear more often from you is all. He needs to hear from you every day the way he did before Jane fell ill and then he won't have any worries."

Tim did not once look at his colleagues. His eyes remained fixed on R.H. The room fell into silence and he said, "I'm the man who's going to get you acquitted."

R.H. peered back with an expression even more despairing than his breakdown in the hall. He craned his neck to look at Kronish and on his way back to Tim glanced briefly at Wodica. "You fellows figure this out on your own," he said. He stood and buttoned his suit coat. "But for fuck's sake, figure it out and figure it out quick, because I'm not going to jail for something I didn't do."

Tim rose. "I'll walk you out."

"No, sit," R.H. demanded. "And do not stand until you figure this shit out. I can damn well find my own way out."

"Twenty million dollars," said Wodica after R.H. had departed. "I could give two fucks if the man rots in jail or spends the rest of his days eating buffet in Miami, but this firm cannot lose the twenty million a year he brings in on the corporate side."

"And who the fuck found that money?" asked Tim. "Who the fuck, who the fuck's client is that? And you two come in here—"

"He asked us to."

"—and interrogate me? Lecture me?"

"Where have you been, Tim?" cried Kronish. "We lied through our asses just now. Where have you been?"

"And now you're going to tell me I can't take a day off?"

"If it were only a day!"

"Goddamn right you can't take a day off when you're in the middle of a case like this," said Wodica. "What's going on?"

"She's dying!" he cried. "She's fucking dying, gentlemen!"

This quieted them momentarily.

Wodica, who was good with transitions, sighed with the right mix of compassion and concern. "Well, that's a problem," he said.

"Should you go home if that's the case?" asked Kronish. "Take a leave of absence?"

"Mike can take over for you," said Wodica. "Peter will get him up to speed. R.H. will be in good hands with Mike."

"She doesn't want me to take a leave of absence," he said. "It's very important to her that we preserve the routine. Otherwise the disease wins. That's what she says."

Kronish and Wodica exchanged looks.

"Fuck you both," said Tim. "This is my case."

He returned to the men's room. He locked himself in a stall, hung the backpack on the metal hanger affixed to the door, and took a seat on the stool. He untied the laces of his boots with stiff and unhappy fingers and removed two pairs of socks from each foot just as he had done fifteen minutes earlier.

The sight was the same. The little toe on his left foot had mummified. It frightened him no end, how easily it might be snipped off with a pair of scissors and he would feel no pain.

Later in the day it fell off on its own. He felt it moving around inside his sock. He shut the door to his office, removed his boot and retrieved what looked like a giant raisin. He crumpled the toe up in a clean piece of paper and threw it away in a trash bin.

17

What they used to call soul. What they used to call spirit. Indivisible, complete, that thing made of mind, distinct from body.

He thought he had one—a soul, a spirit, a nature, an essence. He thought his mind was proof of it.

If mood, facial expression, hunger pain, love of color, if everything human and happenstance came not from the soul, the core of self, but from synapses firing and electrical signals, from the stuff in the brain that could be manipulated and X-rayed, what could he say about himself with any degree of certainty? Was mind just body more refined?

He refused to believe that.

He stopped that night at the security post. Frank Novovian leaned against the backrest of his stool, his arms folded over tie and blazer. With his prune-bag eyes he presided over the building's calm comings and goings. Tim put both forearms on the marble post.

"How did you know about my walking, Frank?" he asked.

Frank unfolded his arms and set his hands on his thighs. He was hesitant. His initial silence seemed to allow him time to work out some internal calculation.

"You don't remember the girl, Mr. Farnsworth?"

"The girl?"

Frank told him the story. Tim had appeared one day at the security post and asked Frank to follow him out. Frank thought he detected some panic in his voice. What transpired was a preview of the events from a few weeks prior. Frank caught up with Tim halfway across the lower lobby and followed him through one of the revolving doors. It was a hot summer day. Tim turned to Frank and told him that he couldn't get back to his desk. Frank mistook him to mean he had some pressing engagement and needed someone to convey a message for him or run an errand inside the building, but as they continued to walk and talk, Frank understood that the situation was more complicated. "Help me to stop walking," Tim said to him. City life swirled around them, car horns, snatches of conversation. Tim asked Frank to grab his arms, tackle him, hold him back somehow. "I'm sorry, Mr. Farnsworth," said Frank as he tried to keep up. "You can't stop walking?"

Neither of them saw the little girl. She broke away from her mother and went sidewise straight into Tim. The impact of his leg threw her to the ground. He skittered to avoid stepping on her and had difficulty regaining his balance. Everyone—Frank, the girl's mother, bystanders—stopped, some to stare, others to bend down to the girl who, after a second of stunned silence, began to wail on the sidewalk. Tim kept walking.

"You looked back at me terrified," Frank told him. "And I looked at you wondering why you weren't stopping. I mean, you'd told me you couldn't stop. I just didn't understand until then that what you meant was, you really couldn't stop."

"I have no memory of this."

"I remember it like it was yesterday."

"But we've never talked about it."

Frank shook his head.

"You just believed me?"

"You would have come back to make sure that girl was okay if you could have," he said.

He had moments of doubt, yet he always returned to the belief that he was sick in body and not in mind. But for whatever reason his memory of knocking that little girl to the ground had been erased. Could anything in his mind—indivisible, complete—be erased, or otherwise go haywire? What confidence did that give him in the permanent thing called the soul?

Tim thanked him and turned to leave. Then he remembered that he had something of Frank's. He pulled the wool cap out of his coat pocket.

"I owe you a hat," he said.

Frank took the cap.

"I can't thank you enough for that. It saved my life."

"Anytime, Mr. Farnsworth."

18

He was prodded awake by a billy club. He sat up in the leather seat and blinked down at the cop, who stood on the blacktop at a defensive angle. He was shining the flashlight in Tim's eyes. Tim had no idea where he was. The cop asked him to step out of the vehicle. Softer security light streamed through the broad windshield. The steering wheel in front of him was a big round toy. The van or truck had no door. He stepped down the single stair as the cop backed up to keep some distance. There was another cop on the other side of him with his hand at his holster. The three of them stood between the truck he'd slept in and another just like it. It said Utz Potato Chips on the side. A foggy memory of having slipped inside the fenced lot when there was still a little daylight remaining now returned to him.

The cop asked him what he was doing there. He said he didn't know, which was the undeniable truth, but the cop didn't care for honest answers.

He had been in the middle of witness prep. There was nothing more important prior to jury selection than readying R.H. for the possibility of putting him on the stand. It would not be without risk but Tim was leaning toward it. He thought it would be good to let the jury hear from the man directly. How many times had R.H. said he had nothing to hide? His protestations of innocence would be genuine, and therefore well received. But it would require damn good coaching. Tim considered it one of the more purely enjoyable aspects of going to trial. He was prepping his witness and loving it. Then he walked out.

By now he figured Peter and probably R.H. himself had alerted Kronish to his abrupt departure. There had been no incoming call that might have explained it, no urgent message. Tim just grabbed the backpack and fled. Kronish had probably marched the episode down the hall to Wodica. How was he going to explain this one? They were lawyers, these fellows, A-game litigators with suspicious dispositions and the professional training to detect a wide array of bullshit. Jane's cancer wasn't going to take him much further.

For the first time since this latest recurrence, Tim didn't want to return to the office.

At the station, the lieutenant apologized for any rough treatment. Government trucks were parked in that lot and there was always the fear of terrorists.

"Terrorists?"

"Who knows," said the lieutenant. "By the way, you ever try a sleep clinic? My brother-in-law walked in his sleep terrible. He went to a sleep clinic in Boston and now my sister tells me you can't get that son of a bitch out of bed with a Hyster."

"I'll have to try that," said Tim.

Outside the station he called Dr. Bagdasarian and got his service. He told the woman it was an emergency and she woke the doctor up. When he came on the line, Tim told him that he wanted to give the new technology a try. He no longer thought he had anything to lose.

"Just out of curiosity," said Bagdasarian. "What made you change your mind?"

He told him nothing about walking out of witness prep or the increasing challenge of explaining himself at the firm. He just wanted something to show people, he said. He wanted to return to the firm with evidence that he was not crazy but sick, deserving of understanding, even sympathy. And he was doing it for Jane. He had to recognize that his sickness was not his alone. She had followed him down the dark and narrowing tunnel. How could he abandon her at a possible point of light?

He waited on the bench to be picked up. He waited and he waited, never having waited so long.

She pulled up and he got in. On the drive home he told her where he'd woken up and about the Utz trucks and the lieutenant who told him to go to a sleep clinic. "Like we haven't been to sleep clinics," he said.

Jane didn't respond.

"Jane, are you listening?"

"I'm listening."

"You haven't said a word."

"It's three in the morning," she said. "I'm tired."

During his last recurrence he had agreed to go into hand-cuffs not only to save him from such episodes as being arrested in a parking lot three villages over from his own, but to spare her calls from arbitrary places at all hours, the chore of picking him up that grew more draining as the days and weeks passed.

"I called Dr. Bagdasarian," he said.

She didn't respond.

"I can't keep waking up in potato chip trucks."

"No," she said. "I guess you can't."

They drove in silence the rest of the way home.

19

Dr. Bagdasarian removed the improvised device from a small shopping bag. Tim held it in his hands and said noth-ing, for there was little to say about a common bicycle helmet. It had been retrofitted to perform an extraordinary purpose and manufactured exclusively and at great expense, but he wondered how such an everyday object could serve to advance an under-standing of his mystery. He doubted it could, and with that doubt, as he placed it on top of his head and buckled the chin strap, futility made off with his heart. The biomedical firm had installed sensors up and down the helmet's foam-cushion lining. The wireless device that captured brain activity clipped easily to a belt. This silly and makeshift heroism of Bagdasarian's, which he had encouraged in a moment of vulnerability, was all just so much overreaching, and nothing brought that home more than the snug feel of the chin strap pinching his skin and Jane's sudden laughter at the sight of him across the table. He would try it, he would wear the helmet and hope for the right reading, but this felt like the last possible desperate grasp before the root to which he clung gave way and he plummeted down the sheer cliff. He had gone from MRIs and the Mayo Clinic to a trial made possible by sporting goods, with no guarantee of a success that was itself of questionable value. No diagnosis, no cure—what was the point again? Jane continued to laugh in a tenderly mocking way, tickling the doctor into a smile, but Tim despaired and felt the urge to cry. This was it, this little piece of medicalized headgear, and beyond it, he saw the hell of a permanently compromised life whose once-healthy past tormented him as the plain earth does a man passed over by the grace of God.

"Will it work?"

"We'll find out," said the doctor. "But remember to keep it on at all times. And you should also shave your head. It will read better that way."

He sheared the bulk of his hair with clippers, then let the mirror guide him as he ran the blade over his knobby bumps. Creamy water dripped from his chin. The stark pale surface that emerged startled him. He didn't know he had this look, hiding all this time beneath a civilized trim. He was menacing or ailing or just hatched from an egg.

He dressed and strapped his skull into the helmet and joined Jane in bed.

"I'm happy you changed your mind," she said.

He was thinking about the consequences. He could not go in to work now, and he didn't think it was an equitable trade-off, his life in exchange for a shot in the dark. But the choice had been made, and so it had to be said that above all, above living itself, he just wanted some measure of understanding, some small answer that might stand in for the clarification of all the mysteries in the world.

"I don't have much confidence that it's going to tell us anything."

"Maybe that's for the best," she said.

"How's that?"

"You won't feel disappointed if it comes to nothing."

He turned to her in bed. "I want to say something," he said. He looked at her with a quiet, shamed temerity. "I know we haven't had sex in a long time."

She was silent. There was still the silence that an unexpected swerve toward sex in a conversation could provoke, even after twenty years married.

"And I'm sorry, banana," he said. "It just lowers my libido. I don't know why."

"It's okay," she said.

"Walk walk walk walk walk," he said. "And then it's the last thing on my mind."

Time passed. She changed the subject. "The doctor thinks you should be on an antidepressant," she said.

"When did he say this?"

"When I walked him to the door."

It was true he was depressed. Depression followed in lock-step with each recurrence, a morose inwardness with which he tyrannized whatever room he happened to drift into and glaze over, waiting for the next walk to take him. But it wasn't a permanent, abiding depression. Sadness always gave way to a bout of pugnacity in which he thought again, *I'm going to beat this thing*. He was tough and he was special and he had inner resources, he had many things going for him, and others had seen much worse, time was precious and things happened for a reason and there was always an upside, and it only took a good attitude to fight and win and nothing was going to stop him and tomorrow was another day.

Then suddenly he rose off the bed. He grabbed the pack on his way out. Eventually she leaned over and turned off the light.

Better luck next time, she thought in the dark. Better luck making the stars align. Wouldn't it have been a luxury to have some crystal ball into which a diviner gazed to map for the young couple their future in sickness and in health, the specifics therein. This one—pointing to the man—is no good for you. Not too far down the line, sweetheart, he will break, and you will be left carrying the load. And a heavy load it will be. Abort the union now while you still have the chance, or accustom yourself to the short end of the stick. Because *a failing body* is no grounds for divorce. A failing body and not even your own becomes your personal cross to bear and how fair is that? How desirable?

She hated these thoughts. They stole over the better part of her in the weakness of the night. She was waiting in half sleep for the phone to ring. She hated herself for imagining the concept of *medical prenuptial*. You are free to go if he turns too human too quickly. If his body derails, save yourself the grief and heartache of being nursemaid and watchman. Take intact your health and your future and go. You have a life to live. Unburden yourself.

20

A few weeks later he lay on the sofa, watching reruns of shows he'd only heard about. He watched *Oprah* and info-golf and C-Span and *Seinfeld*. He flipped channels to avoid commercials. Commercials were poignant reminders of what a waste of time it was to watch TV. He didn't feel his life wasting away so much when he was inside a show, but when the show's spell was broken by a message from the sponsor he was quick to change the channel. Changing channels distracted him almost as much as being inside a show.

He thought about the case and the man on the bridge. He returned to the day of their encounter and replayed events. He called Detective Roy to see what progress he'd made in tracking the man down, but there were only so many ways the detective could express his skepticism, sarcasm and apathy. Finally he told Tim not to call anymore. He would call if he had news. When Tim called anyway, the receptionist sent him directly to the detective's voice mail and the detective did not call back.

Kronish took over the case. He supposed Peter would do his best to get Kronish up to speed, but the trial was soon to start and there was no way Kronish could learn everything. They thought Jane was in her final days.

Sometimes he walked around the house with the chin strap dangling.

Becka called to him from upstairs. It was the summer before her first semester at college and she was home during the day. He was sleeping off a walk in a gas station bathroom when she took the stage to receive her high school diploma. She called out to him as she made her way through the house. She appeared at the foot of the sofa. "Dad!" At last he looked at her. "Didn't you hear me calling?"

"What is it?"

"Phone for you."

"Who is it?"

"Mike Kronish."

"Tell him I'll call back," he said.

She reappeared a little later, holding out the cordless. "Dad, I don't answer this phone," she said. "I only answer my cell."

"Who is it?"

"Someone named R.H."

"Tell him I'm at the hospital."

"The hospital?"

"Tell him I'm at the hospital and just let it ring from now on."

He discovered watching TV on DVDs, which eliminated the commercials, and after that he rarely went back to cable.

When the trial began, he called Fritz Weyer, an old friend and former associate who had moved to a corporate investigations firm some years ago and now did occasional work for Troyer. Tim explained over the phone that he was calling on his

own behalf and not the firm's and asked Fritz if he'd mind stopping by to discuss a few things. Fritz showed up in the afternoon and asked about the shaved head and bicycle helmet. Tim
mumbled something about a mild case of vertigo and Fritz didn't
pursue the matter. He asked how Jane was doing, which seemed
a pleasantry more than anything, so Tim presumed that he knew
nothing about her fatal cancer and answered that she was just
fine, selling houses and enjoying life. Jane had brokered the deal
for Fritz and his wife when they bought their house in Scarsdale,
and now the two couples went out from time to time.

They sat down at the kitchen table across from each other.
Tim began with a vague description of his personal health problems, quickly segueing into his leave of absence, his abandonment of his client at the moment of trial, and his misgivings
concerning the readiness of the defense team. The associate, he
said, was a moron, and the partner was ill informed. He wanted
to track the trial as it progressed by getting the rough transcripts
each day, but he was more or less confined to the house and
needed someone to get the roughs for him. Fritz said he could
get the roughs, no problem, but he was a senior investigator at
an expensive firm. Tim would be paying a lot of money for what
was essentially a courier service.

"That's fine, I don't mind paying. I need somebody I can
trust. I want to know when they fuck up. There are going to
be fuckups and I have to catch them before they turn fatal. I'm
the only one who can try this case and you understand now that
that's not possible, so having the roughs every night and reading
through them is really the only way I can keep up with what's
going on."

"Done," said Fritz.

"There's something else."

He brought out a copy of the artist's rendering of the man he encountered on the Brooklyn Bridge. In some way or another, he told Fritz, this man was connected to the murder of R.H.'s wife. He might even have the murder weapon in his possession. Tim believed R.H. was innocent but that he might nevertheless be sentenced to a punishment he didn't deserve. His fading hope was that Fritz might find the man in the sketch.

"This is all you got?" said Fritz.

"That's it."

Fritz made a fleeting face of doubt, big eyes and a twisted mouth, and then took a deep breath. "That's not a whole hell of a lot, Tim."

"I know."

"I've got people at the NYPD who will let me have a look at the case file," he said. "But this, man…" gesturing with the sketch, "this is thin. I'll be looking for one man among eight million."

Tim asked him to do the best he could.

21

Jane woke Becka up before she left for work and Becka hung around all day while her dad watched nonstop television in his bicycle helmet. Her mom paid her as much as she would have been paid at Starbucks or wherever, and now she didn't have to get a crappy part-time job for the summer. She just had to hang around waiting for him to leave and to follow him if he did. Her mom hadn't quit her job to follow him around but she still picked him up and took care of him when she wasn't working. But she still wanted someone to look after him during the day, so when the summer came around, she offered to pay Becka to keep an eye on him.

"How come he doesn't just hire somebody? Like a bodyguard or something. It's not like we don't have the money."

"He doesn't want that."

"Why not?"

"He's too independent."

"He doesn't seem independent when he calls you at three in the morning and you have to pick him up in Queens."

"Do you want the job or not?" asked Jane.

Her mom told her not to be too obvious about it, because it was more or less like she was babysitting him. And it was a little weird to babysit your dad, the man who makes you do chores and punishes you and tells you over and over again all the ways there are to be happy. He told her about more ways to be happy than you could ever try out even if you had twenty lives. But watching him was better than some crappy part-time job. Except that, day after day, he stayed on the couch and never moved. The whole point to the helmet was to record his brain waves or whatever, the whole point to babysitting him was to follow him wherever he went, but he wasn't going anywhere but the couch and his brain waves weren't doing anything but watching TV. Becka still thought her dad was mental. She didn't want to think of it that way but who ever heard of what he had? Not even the Internet.

She couldn't be downstairs with him all the time. Sometimes she took little breaks, as you would at Starbucks or wherever, and went upstairs to lie on her bed or check her email or play the guitar. She checked on him from time to time to make sure he was still there. Sometimes she found him dozing on the sofa with the bicycle helmet gone a little cockeyed. She thought if he wasn't mental he was at least really strange.

One morning she woke up and he was sitting on the edge of her bed holding her DVD box set of the first season of *Buffy the Vampire Slayer*.

"Can I take this?" he asked.

"What for?"

"To watch."

"You?"

"There's nothing else."

He took it away with him, and a few minutes later she headed downstairs in her hoodie, David Bowie tee and black sweats, on her feet a pair of Sylvester the cat slippers, a holdout from childhood, in which she shuffled across the kitchen floor. Her father was in the middle of the first episode. She put two Pop-Tarts into the toaster and fixed herself a cup of coffee with cream and sugar. She placed the Pop-Tarts on a paper towel and walked over to the recliner and sat down. She ate her breakfast during the concluding five minutes of episode one and the opening minutes of episode two. She had seen the episode a thousand times but happily watched it again, surprised to be watching it with him and pleased to be getting paid for it. At one point he said, "What'd she just say?" and she repeated the line for him, and then they sank back into silence.

He forwarded through the opening credits and they watched the next three episodes. When they were through she got up to use the bathroom. He got up to change discs. She came out and he was waiting for her before starting the next episode. It was a favorite of hers and she wondered how well she knew the lines so she decided to repeat out loud a brief exchange between Buffy and her friend Willow, which caused him to look over. She continued to repeat their lines perfectly all the way to the opening credits and he continued to look at her as the theme song came on.

"My God," he said. "How many times have you watched this?"

They finished another episode. Around one, he asked if she wanted lunch. They ate their sandwiches in front of the TV and when they were through she took the plates without disturbing him and put them in the dishwasher. She returned to the recliner as he got up to resettle the bedsheet under him and fluff up his pillow and then he started another episode.

"How many do we have left?" he asked.

"Like, five," she said. "But I have the second season upstairs."

"How many seasons are there?" he asked.

"Seven," she said.

They repeated the routine the next day and the day after that. She watched the show, but she also watched him watch it, looking for signs of his nodding off or standing up. But he did neither. Except to replace the DVD or work the remote, he remained on the sofa. When he got off the sofa to replace yet another disc, she finally asked him, "What made you want to watch *Buffy*, Dad?"

Growing up, she had had all the posters on her walls. She bought every offer of merchandise, the comic books and the novelettes and the magazines, the T-shirts and patches, the notebooks, pens, and pencils. She belonged to the fan clubs and ordered autographed eight-by-ten headshots of the actors. He once sat on the edge of her bed when she was in the eighth grade and asked if there was anything, anything at all, that he could do to make her happy, and she said the only time she was maybe happy was when she was watching *Buffy*.

"I was curious about it," he said to her now.

Within the week they had finished the second season. He asked her if she had the third. Between the third season and the fourth he didn't need to ask. She just got off the recliner and brought the next season down from her bedroom.

They were in the middle of the sixth season when he unexpectedly sat up mid-episode and turned away from the TV. He looked straight ahead, toward the fireplace. He set the remote down on the coffee table. He unbuckled the chin strap and peeled the bicycle helmet from his shaved head. It was startling to see him bald. It was almost like he suffered from a real disease like cancer or something. He placed the helmet and its portable device next to him on the sofa.

"Should you really be taking that off, Dad?" she asked.

"Why am I not walking?" he asked, more to himself than her. "Where has all the goddamn walking gone?"

It was the very thing she had been asking herself for weeks.

22

Mike Kronish drove to the courthouse every morning with R. H. Hobbs in the back of a tinted SUV. He reassured his client, who had taken to calling him at home late at night, about the previous day's proceedings, and then prepared him for what would likely happen during the day ahead. The driver let them off at the foot of the courthouse steps, which they climbed in the hundred-plus heat. By the time R.H. entered the grand echoing foyer and joined the line to go through security, perspiration was pouring down his face and he was panting. Mike Kronish had started to fear his client wouldn't make it through trial without suffering a heart attack. He had appealed to the judge to give them a continuance on that basis, but the judge ordered a physical and reviewed the results and the motion was denied. He would grant it, he told Kronish, when R.H. was admitted to the hospital for chest pains.

They made it through security, where the marshals took away their cell phones and BlackBerrys, and they entered the courtroom together. The judge began the day's proceedings promptly at nine thirty. Kronish and his client walked through the gate separating the gallery from the well at exactly twenty-two after. Peter was already present, managing the work of two junior associates and three paralegals. They were assembled now no differently from the way they had been every morning since the trial began, with one exception: to the right of Peter in Kronish's chair sat a man in a gray suit with a bicycle helmet on his head. When the two men came into view, Tim turned and greeted them. He stood up and shook hands with Kronish and R.H. awkwardly, with his left hand. Though it was now summer, the effects of Tim's frostbite lingered. Kronish asked him what he was doing there.

"I've just been getting the rundown from Peter," he replied. "I'm ready to help any way I can."

Kronish set his briefcase on the table. "What do you mean, the rundown?"

"I'm all caught up. Peter and I talked."

"About what?"

R.H. interrupted them. "I thought you were supposed to be at the hospital," he said. "If it was important to be at the hospital, why aren't you at the hospital?"

Tim didn't look at R.H. He looked at Kronish and reiterated that Peter had caught him up and that he was ready to get to work. He also wanted Kronish to know that he'd been reading the transcripts nightly and, frankly, no disrespect intended, they could use his help. Kronish did not want R.H. to know that they had just walked in on the greatest breach of professional protocol he could remember in all his years as a trial lawyer, but he was having difficulty seeing straight. He asked R.H. to have a seat.

"Why is he here?" R.H. demanded. Tim's reappearance could mean only one thing to R.H.—that his trial was going worse than he suspected, and that they had had to call a man away from his wife's deathbed in order to salvage it. "Where were you three weeks ago?"

"Have a seat, R.H.," said Kronish.

"Why haven't you been here from the beginning?"

Kronish gave Peter a look and Peter understood immediately. Peter jumped up, took gentle hold of R.H.'s arm and
started coaxing him into his chair. R.H. went reluctantly.

"What is he doing here?" he asked Peter.

Kronish would have preferred to talk to Tim privately, away
from R.H., the prosecution team, and all those looking on from
the gallery, but the judge was expected in less than five minutes
and would not be pleased to find the defense team's lead counsel
absent from the courtroom. He remained standing, as did Tim,
and spoke to him in a soft whisper.

"What the hell? What the fuck? What the fuck what the
fuck what the *fuck?*"

"Hey, Mike, go easy. I'm here to help."

"Help how?"

"Any way I can."

"There is no way you can."

"Come on, Mike. I was the architect of the strategy, Peter's
got me all caught up—"

"Fuck caught up, Tim! We're three weeks into trial. You're
the architect of a strategy that's radically changed. Do you not
see? Do you not understand the delicate dynamic? Look at the
man. Look what you've done. The fucking protocol, man!"

"Hey, Mike—"

"You arrogant bastard," said Kronish. "This has nothing to
do with R.H. and everything to do with you. And why are you
wearing that fucking helmet?"

"Read this," he said.

He handed Kronish a photocopy of an article from *The New
England Journal of Medicine.* "John B." was the pseudonym the
authors had assigned him. The article detailed his condition and
debated its causes. The psychiatrists believed his situation came

from a physical malfunction of the body, something organic and diseased, while the neurologists pointed to the scans and the tests that revealed nothing and concluded that he had to be suffering something psychological. Each camp passed the responsibility for his diagnosis to the other, from the mind to the body back to the mind, just as they had done in private over the course of his endless consultations.

Kronish flipped through the pages he had been handed. "What's this?"

"I'm John B.," said Tim.

"Who?"

"The subject of that article."

Kronish looked at him in disbelief. "Are you unaware of the fucking protocol, man?"

Just as he said this, the judge walked through the chambers door and the marshal called out for all to rise. Kronish was caught holding the article Tim had given him.

"Please be seated," said the judge.

When Tim sat down, Kronish realized he intended to stay. He had no choice but to sit as well, if he wished not to draw attention to himself. As he did so, he considered rising again and asking the judge for permission to approach. He would ask for a fifteen-minute recess in which he would take Tim outside the courthouse and beat him behind a dumpster. But he preferred not to request permission to approach because R.H. worried about conversations he didn't participate in. He was also loath to ask the judge for a recess before the day had even begun. Kronish was momentarily paralyzed. He was never paralyzed. He turned to Tim, who was sitting next to him, awaiting the resumption of a trial he'd been absent from since day one.

"Take that helmet off," he whispered.

"What?"

"That goddamn bicycle helmet on your head. Take it off."

"I can't."

Kronish stared. "Take that ridiculous fucking helmet off your head, Tim, before the fucking judge notices."

"I won't," said Tim.

For a moment of blinding discomfort, the two sides of Kronish battled for primacy—reason, which knew any sudden movement would be bad for his client, and rage, which wanted to rip the helmet off Tim's head and Tim's head with it.

"When I get back this evening," he said, "I'm calling an emergency caucus among the partners and I'm recommending that you be stripped of partnership."

"I have a right to be here," said Tim.

"You have no fucking right to be here!"

"Does the defense have something it would like to share?" asked the judge from the bench.

Kronish stood. "No, Your Honor."

Members of the prosecution were peering over. Kronish heard the strokes of a sketch artist behind him and felt the gallery looking on.

"Is that Mr. Farnsworth?"

Tim rose. "It is, Your Honor."

"You have arrived at your destination, Mr. Farnsworth," said the judge. "Why are you still in your helmet?"

"He's not staying, Your Honor," said Kronish.

"I am staying, Your Honor," said Tim. "I have not yet appeared before Your Honor during these proceedings, but I would like to request permission to appear now."

As these words were making their way to the judge, Tim

turned, grabbed his backpack, and began to walk out of the well.

"On second thought, Your Honor," he said, turning his head around to address the judge as onlookers, seated on both sides of the gallery, watched from their wooden pews.

"What is going on here?" asked the judge.

Tim walked past the marshal and pushed the door open.

"Mr. Kronish, what is going on?"

Kronish had his back to the judge. He was watching Tim Farnsworth walk out of the room. Then the door swung shut and he turned around to face his inquisitor. He opened his mouth, but nothing came out.

He woke up in a booth at a KFC in Queens. He lifted his head off the table. A napkin stuck to his face. Becka reached out for it, straightening his helmet in the process.

"What are you doing here?" he asked.

She had followed him from the courthouse steps across the Brooklyn Bridge. He shed his suit coat and his buttondown in the heat without stopping, without the least concern for how he looked to those he passed: a crazy man possessed. She picked up his discarded clothes and followed him into the heart of the borough. She trailed behind him, ready to seize on his first false move, at any subtle sign of fakery, but he never halted, he never paused. The city was a wading pool of cement heat. The buildings bleating with glare, the sidewalks pulsing with sunlight. The bus exhaust and the interminable miles made the long walk unbearable. But he never stopped. She watched him slog inside the KFC and collapse.

Now she looked at him with tears in her eyes. "I'm sorry I didn't believe you," she said.

23

Wildfires burned across several square miles, closing highways and forcing evacuations. The rainless summer and the
wind and the lightning had turned the brush border between
counties into kindling. Flames left charred contrails in the land
resembling the scars of comets running aground on the face of
the earth. Emergency workers had corralled most of the fire
into containment lines where they starved the blaze of the fuel it
needed to burn. They called in backfire experts, leased Helitack
helicopters, scheduled twenty-four-hour water drops to keep the
fires from destroying forest preserves and the shockingly close
residential homes. Golf courses were used as termination points
in an art new to frightened cities that had just barely adjusted
to the flash floods of a swift and freakish spring. Disaster once
confined to the west had migrated, a wayward animal confused
by scrambled weather. Reservoirs were poisoned. Pockets of fire
continued to glow but eventually the expressways were reopened
and most residents were invited to return.

He reached around the back of her neck and collected her
hair into a ponytail as she eased into him. Their mouths met
and pressed into each other. He cupped the small of her back
in his hands and turned their bodies over and laid her down on
the field. He removed her pants over her shoes, too impatient to
bother with the buckles. She felt all along his lean walker's body,

the legs that were all muscle now and the torso that had slimmed down to the ribs as if he were a boy again. He took both her hands and stretched her arms as far as they would reach across the switchgrass as the hard soil began to skin his knees. They interlocked their fingers and squeezed as if to prevent death from separating them and they stared at each other under the smoke-fogged sky. They required almost no movement to be stunned again by something they had done so often, that had grown stale in the months before his recurrence but that now felt like the first time between them. They could smell the burn in the air and feel the heat on their faces. They were near a slowly dying outcrop of fire being tamped into embers by barely audible voices. Cows sauntered before a wooden fence in the distance.

They lay afterward, two bodies humming in a field. He felt bad that he had not been able to last. It had been a long time and after a minute or two there was no stopping what had taken over.

"It's almost worth waiting when it's like that," she said.

"I'm sorry I didn't last."

"That's the downside."

They buttoned and zipped and got to their feet. They began to walk through the field to the car, tall steps through the high grass. It occurred to him that they were leaving too quickly. He wanted to reclaim that spent urgency, the irrefutable proof they both felt in their bodies that they needed each other for life. Had such a long and arduous walk out here to the middle of nowhere, had the task of picking him up, which made his sickness seem to her but a common irritant of clocking miles in the sleepiest hours, really been the occasion for the best sex they'd had in years?

"We should go back," he said.

"Back where?"

"Back there."

She looked behind them and saw only the fenced borderland and dry expanse of grass. "What for?"

"To get that back."

She seemed to get his meaning. "It wouldn't be the same."

All at once she jerked away. She did a kind of stutter-step, shrieking, and ended behind him gripping his arms with her claws.

"What is it?" he cried.

"A snake!"

He stopped still and held her behind him. He looked down at the grass. "I don't see it," he said.

"How could you miss it?"

"Well, it's gone now."

"It's not gone. It's just ahead of us. Ahead of us is not gone."

"It's more scared of you than you are of it," he said.

"You talked to the snake?"

"Want me to carry you out, banana?"

"I don't like snakes," she said.

She walked the rest of the way with a mix of trepidation and resolve, eyes frozen to the grass, feet choosing the least dense spots. They climbed the wooden fence. The car was waiting for them on the far side of the road. A sign in front of the fence said No Trespassing—Stony Hold Farms.

They drove out of the back roads, past the same fire-damaged landscape she had followed him into. They entered an area more densely populated by single-family residences and there saw exposed houses flaking with ash, cul-de-sacs with pitted cars more fitting the scenes of a riot from a troubled city. Porch pillars burnt down halfway turned ranch houses into small sites of ancient ruin. Most of the houses stood unmolested. The individual damage seemed arbitrary, or perhaps singled out by an inscrutable fate.

"It's even worse than what you see on the news," she said.

"What do you make of it?" he asked.

She drove in silence before answering. "It's either the world just doing its thing," she said, "or something we've never known before."

They drove a long time. He sat in the passenger seat with the helmet on, the monitor in his hands, wondering what it might have recorded over the course of a walk they were driving miles to erase.

24

"Nothing," said Dr. Bagdasarian. "I'm sorry, Tim."

The scans had revealed nothing. That was neither positive proof of mental illness nor the negative confirmation of a medical disease. It was more of the same, exactly what he feared — greater inconclusiveness, additional absence of evidence, the final barrier removed from boundless interpretation. He was anything anyone wanted him to be — a nutcase, a victim, a freak, a mystery. He'd known to expect it from the moment he took the bicycle helmet out of Bagdasarian's hands, yet the disappointment, so familiar, felt brand-new. He had no idea to what extent he'd allowed his hopes to rise once more. What a fool he was, an inveterate and self-punishing fool. He felt Jane and Becka looking at him. He turned to them and smiled.

The doctor made an effort to qualify these indeterminate test results. He cautioned again that the device was a proto-type, that the sensors picked up only neural activity, and that a second-generation helmet might be made not only to improve the sensitivity of the readings, but to include electrical and hor-monal changes, the flow of blood and other biological currents. He suggested they go back to the drawing board for a better device.

Jane shook her head. "This has been a mistake. I'm sorry I encouraged it." She turned to her husband. "Tim, I'm sorry," she said. She reached out for his hand.

"We've come this far," said Bagdasarian.

"No, Doctor, thank you," she said. "I think we're through."

Tim turned to her. "Why not give him another shot?" he asked. "See what improvements can be made?"

That night he went down to the basement after Jane and Becka had fallen asleep. He sat on the weight bench and put the barrel of the gun inside his mouth. The cold metal made him salivate. He angled the barrel up toward his brains.

He had told Dr. Ditmar, the psychologist beloved by *New York* magazine, that he would prefer the diagnosis of a fatal disease. Ditmar bluntly stated that he was being excessive and naive. Compare his situation to someone with Lou Gehrig's, Ditmar suggested, dead within three months. Wasn't it better to be on a walk than in a grave? "No," he said. "I'd rather have something I understand." To which Ditmar replied: "Do you think you'd understand Lou Gehrig's?"

He had perfect conviction that killing himself was not only

justified now but necessary, that the relief of death was the only reply to the torment of a life that had to be lived as a lost cause, and his mind told him to pull the trigger. But his body, which spoke a persuasive language of its own, singular, subterranean, objected with the most fundamental repulsion, and while he sat with the gun in his mouth, nearly gagging on the barrel, these two opposite wills worked to gain the better of each other in a struggle so primitive that it could not be named. And finally he removed the gun and set it back in the standing toolbox behind the blunt hammers and screwdrivers and returned upstairs. He lacked the courage and the will—although perhaps he had astonishing amounts of both and was simply defeated again, if barely, on a playing field most people never realize exists until the final days and moments of their lives.

25

Mike Kronish wouldn't even deign to pick up the phone when he called. Sam Wodica broke the news. The caucus had convened, a vote had been taken, and his partnership was thereby revoked.

"It wasn't just your appearance at trial, Tim," said Wodica. "Your wife?"

"She's not dying."

"No shit."

He thought he should have been present for the caucus. He should have been allowed to defend himself. They were lawyers. Weren't they familiar with due process?

"Does R.H. know about my wife?"

"For fuck's sake," said Wodica. "You don't just want us to lose the revenue? Let's open ourselves up to malpractice, too?"

"I don't see how what I did constitutes malpractice."

"Just what the fuck did you do, Tim? Huh, please allow me to ask. Just what the fuck did you do?"

It settled in, the enormity of a crumbling life. Twenty-one years. The firm had been a second home. Now Frank Novovian would not even be required to greet him. Maybe Frank would look at him and say, "I'm sorry, Mr. Farnsworth. I'm not allowed to let you up." And he might say, "Twenty-one years, Frank."

He and Wodica briefly discussed R.H.'s conviction. The only good news was that New York State didn't allow the death penalty. The presentencing report was due in a few weeks, and then R.H. would be sent off. How would R.H. have fared if Tim had been able to see his case through to the end? If Tim had been allowed to finish the pretrial preparations, to help in jury selection, to argue and object? He was certain that right now they would be celebrating R.H.'s acquittal.

He called Detective Roy from time to time, and Fritz Weyer to see what progress had been made on his end. Fritz had calls in to friends at the department and one of his guys searching databases for a possible match on the face in the sketch. Maybe they'd get lucky.

26

He was at the firm again, dressed in suit and tie and standing before his fellow partners. R.H. was there, as were Jane and
Becka. He had to campaign for his job. He said he should not be
blamed for R.H.'s conviction because R.H. was guilty. Detective
Roy began to applaud. Tim looked at R.H. sitting at the defense
table, attempting to conceal his weeping. He approached R.H.
and whispered to him, "Don't worry, I know you're innocent."
R.H. thanked him. The assistant district attorney who had tried
the case was now itemizing all of the infractions Tim had committed: the internal lies, the false statements to authorities, the
unprofessional conduct. She concluded with a passionate plea to
the jury that they expel him from the firm. The judge stood up
and poured sand from his shoes. It was Sam Wodica in a black
gown and sun visor. He peered over to the other partners in the
jury box and gave them a big thumbs-up. Jane was at the defense
table comforting R.H. Mike Kronish entered the courtroom
and tried to yank Tim's pants down. Tim grabbed at his pants
to keep them up because he did not want his pants to go down
when he was fighting for his job. But Kronish was strong. He
wanted everyone to see Tim with his pants down. Tim tried to
push Kronish away but Kronish was now on top of him on the
courtroom floor in front of Judge Wodica while a sketch artist

documented the scene. Kronish gripped the back of Tim's neck to make it easier to take his pants down. Tim lost track of the people in the room because his head was pinned to the ground and little courtroom rocks were digging into his skin. He was trying to swat Kronish away. It was hard with Kronish on top of him. It was only when Kronish succeeded in getting his pants down and exposing Tim that Tim woke up and realized that his pants were really down and that his head was pinned against crumbling blacktop.

He was in Newark behind a boarded-up Safeway. Shattered glass and strewn garbage were illuminated by a single security light off in the distance. Some encampment of derelicts was living out of an abandoned semitrailer.

He used both hands to try and pry the man's grip from his neck but the angle was awkward and the man punched him in the head with his one free hand. Tim's skull dug into the blacktop. In the stunned minute that followed, the man got Tim's pants off entirely. Tim swiveled under him, so that he and the man were face-to-face. A terrible burn had melted the man's eye into his cheek and shriveled his right ear. Tim reached up and grabbed his neck. He dug his fingers into his windpipe as if to pull it out and at the same time grabbed hold of the man's balls and squeezed, and the man's horrible animal noises careened off the side of a dumpster. Tim kept squeezing while struggling to his knees. He got to his feet and kicked the man in the head as if punting a football. The man's head hit the side of the dumpster and he fell back on his knees. Blood poured from his nose like some weak fountain. Tim could have walked away then but he couldn't stop. He took up an empty forty-ounce bottle and beat the man over the head. The man's blood jumped out of him and splattered the pavement. Tim fled without his pants.

He waited for Jane to pick him up in a public park full of dead trees and flitting shadows, in the dugout of a baseball diamond where trash had accumulated ankle-deep. He followed the car as the headlights turned in the parking lot. He crept out across the shadows. He hurried toward her in his underwear.

She saw him coming across the dead field and opened the door. "Where are your pants?"

"Stay in there."

"Is that blood?"

"Not mine," he said. "Janey, get back in."

He stepped inside the car and they drove out of the park.

She put his bloodied clothes in the washer and then walked up from the basement. Over the kitchen sink she opened a bottle of white wine and poured herself a glass, drank it down, and poured herself another. She took the second glass and the bottle over to the kitchen table. It was two thirty in the morning.

He came downstairs after his shower in sweatpants and T-shirt. He saw how tired she was. The bags under her eyes had never been more pronounced. He was ruining her.

"I can't keep doing this to you," he said.

He saw it written on her face. She had had enough. No one could blame her.

She poured herself a third glass. "Sit down next to me," she said. He did as he was told. "You're going farther and farther away. You call me, it's midnight, you're in Newark. In Newark with the murder rate and the ghosts drifting across the street."

He mumbled a tired apology.

"Listen to me," she said, finally feeling the effects of the wine. "You've lost more weight. You're depressed. You ran out of that dugout naked, blood all over you. If the walking doesn't kill you, something else will. Is that how you want to go?"

"What's the alternative?" he asked.

"I'm quitting my job. And you're going back in the cuffs. No more midnight trips to Newark. No more somebody else's blood."

27

They say it takes a long time to really get to know somebody. They say a good marriage requires work. They say it's important to change alongside your partner to avoid growing apart. They talk about patience, sacrifice, compromise, tolerance. It seems the goal of these bearers of conventional wisdom is to get back to zero. They would have you underwater, tethered by chains to the bow of a ship full of treasure now sunk, struggling to free yourself to make it to the surface. With luck he will free himself, too, and then you can bob along together, scanning the horizon for some hint of land. They say boredom sets in, passion dissipates, idiosyncrasies start to grate, and the same problems repeat themselves. Why do you do it? Security, family, companionship. Ideally you do it for love. *There's* something they don't elaborate on. They just say the word and you're supposed to know what it means, and after twenty years of marriage, you are held up as exemplars of that simple foundation, *love*, upon which (with sweeping arms) all this is built. But don't let appearances fool you. That couple with twenty years still fights, they still go to bed angry, they still let days pass without—

The trouble with these cheap bromides, she thought, is that they don't capture the half of it.

He spent an entire day walking, only to arrive at the back of a grocery store. He woke up to a man attempting to rape him in his sleep. He beat that man to within an inch of his life.

When that's your husband, who's the right counselor to see? What episode of *Oprah* will be most helpful?

She would have liked to know if the man he beat was dead or alive. She didn't ask and he didn't offer. He just said, "It was in self-defense, Janey. I did it in self-defense."

She would have liked him to show some greater agony over the beating and less certainty that he had done what needed to be done.

But then she hadn't been there. How could she know what he needed to do, any more than he could know what she needed to do?

Which was, simply put, to leave him.

I dare you to leave him.

The timing was right. Becka had started college. She made good money on her own. She was still beautiful. She could start over. She had half a lifetime remaining.

The alternative to leaving him was sitting at his bedside for who knows how long, waiting on the whim of an unpredictable illness to lift, at last, and allow them to resume some measure of real life.

And what if it didn't lift? And what did real life mean but the struggle to get back to zero?

Did she need him? She didn't think so. Was there really only one person for you, one man, *the one?* She didn't think so.

She would sit with him if he was wasting from Parkinson's.

If he was wasting from cancer or old age, she'd sit with him. If he just had an expiration date, of course she'd sit with him.

But this thing, this could go on forever. Is that how she wanted to spend her life? Tethered alongside him to that bed...

I *dare* you.

She pulled the cork out and filled the glass and downed it quickly. She needed a second one and poured it out and drank that one at the table waiting for him to come downstairs. He shuffled into the room.

"I can't keep doing this to you," he said.

He looked contrite and sad and ten years older. He was thin and desperate and as needy as a child. She poured herself another glass.

"Sit down next to me," she said.

28

Bagdasarian came in and removed two toes. Tim screamed despite the anesthetic that dulled what surrounded the dead nerves and he thrashed futilely against his restraints. After fierce refusal he had capitulated again to being so narrowly confined, and now it felt like waking inside a coffin six feet under. He cursed the doctor angrily and his curses were mixed with personal insults aimed at the doctor's ugliness and his medical impotence and the recklessness with which he offered hope to the sick. Dr. Bagdasarian said nothing but commented to Jane, who stood horrified in the doorway, that Tim was very lucky to suffer only the loss of two more toes, and that the absence of gangrene was nothing short of a miracle. Tim continued to scream, and his screams could be heard beyond the window, picked up by the breeze and spread throughout a neighborhood that otherwise knew only calm and prosperity.

Jane saw the doctor out. Before leaving he gave her two letters. He explained that the first was a letter to Tim from a friend of his, a renowned neuroscientist who had authored many books on medical curiosities. He said she might even have heard of him. The second was from a woman from an institute. The doctor didn't know what to make of it. He told Jane that she'd have to decide for herself.

Dr. Bagdasarian reached out gently and put a hand on her shoulder. "Try your best that he doesn't forget what it means to be human," he said.

"I'm trying," she said.

He opened the door. They shook hands and she thanked him. "You've been so helpful," she said.

Dr. Bagdasarian smiled. "I've been no help at all."

She walked through the house to the kitchen. She read the letters at the table. The first, from the neuroscientist, was a letter of introduction. She recognized him, as Dr. Bagdasarian had suggested she might, having read his articles in popular magazines. He explained that part of his goal in life was to give voice to strange cases. In his letter he wrote compassionately and without condescension, and she thought how heartened the letter and its tone would have made Tim even a short time ago. The second letter was from the executive director of something called the Endocrine Disruption Prevention Alliance, a loose affiliation of science groups based out of Milwaukee, Wisconsin. The writer introduced herself and explained that Tim's condition had come to her attention.

...and I am one-hundred percent certain that the cause is endocrine disruption, a phenomenon that results from the intake of chemicals extremely hostile to the human endocrine system. These chemicals, released in huge quantities into the environment, can fundamentally change how an individual functions, how he or she thinks, even—as in your case—moves. Here is the frightening truth: clinical trials have proven that a chemical agent no bigger than two benzene rings, or one-trillionth of a part of the human body (to put that in perspective, that is one second over the course of three thousand centuries) can take total control over our bodies. I am writing to you today to educate you, but more importantly to persuade you that your condition is caused by—

She stopped reading.

There was a time when receiving a letter like this one, no matter how odd its message, would have restored their faith in a flawed system. He had been forced to seek out the opinion of specialists, who sent him on to other specialists, who made him stand at the mercy of ever-more-refined specialists, who referred him to the specialists they most admired. Now a specialist was coming to him. The executive director of a medical alliance was telling him once and for all what ailed him. "Endocrine disruption." It would not have mattered that he had never heard of it before. It would not have mattered if the science was debated, if the evidence was still outstanding, if the experts had been debunked. He would have been instantly on the phone. He would have flown anywhere, stayed any length of time. And she would have been there beside him.

Now she walked the two letters over to the sink and disposed of them in the trash.

THE HOUR OF LEAD

I

Tuesday morning he returned to work and read over the motion for summary judgment he'd written for the Keibler case. He'd started it the week before, wary at first. Typically you wait for a partner to assign the motion. But five days ago he found himself clearing through a thicket of case documents and juggling a few arguments in his head, just for the fun of it. When he began the outline, a certain heat flashed across the desk, and it jolted the small office with an iridescent energy, a magnetic field inside of which he moved throughout the day. By the time he began to write the introductory paragraph, his mind was alight with radiance.

Outside the window, bees were trying to get in, a dozen or so sideswiping the pane, for reasons you had to be an expert on bees to understand. He thought they should be long dead, or still hibernating in one of their combs, if hibernate was what they did—anything but dipping and hovering in the wintry light so many floors up. Outside the window, the city stretched north before him with its sleek towers and squat, box-top buildings of different sizes and shadows, all bound by the two rivers whose edges were just in view. He had reconciled himself to no longer having a view of the park, just as he had reconciled himself to the smaller office, the scarred desk, and the downgraded chair. The amenities mattered less now. He had not bothered to bring in the canted standing globe or the Tiffany desk lamp or the degrees and certificates that had adorned his previous office. The bareness of this new approach suited his austerity of purpose. He was there to work, and when work was over, to leave the office and resume life.

He stood up to get a better look at the bees. They were really winding back and slamming themselves against the window. He thought they must be knocking their little bee brains out. They hit and rebounded and fluttered up and returned to hit the glass again. Maybe they were in the very process of dying. Or maybe they were just doing what bees did when they got separated from the hive. Did they travel in a hive? Or was that called a swarm? He knew so little about bees.

He returned to his desk. There were problems with the draft, gaps in his argument, a few structural missteps. He spent the next hour patching things up and the following hour doing a cite check. He thought he'd print out the draft and read it at his desk a final time and then file it away in a drawer before doing the work that had actually been assigned to him. He had not been asked to write a motion for summary judgment. By doing so he was disrespecting the protocol and flouting the conditions of his employment. He wrote it as a kind of hobbyist, with the greatest purity of intent. Millions of motions had been written over the course of the law's centuries, but they had been written with a court in mind, objects of utility and persuasion, while it was possible that until today, not a single one had been composed for the simple satisfaction of the writing itself. He had spent hours working on it over the weekend, happy to have it as a distraction. The house could be a thundering vacuum of quiet when there was no one there to rifle through a kitchen drawer or to lay out the makings of a sandwich on the counter.

He left the office and walked to the printer. He didn't want the printout sitting in the tray because he had not been authorized and he did not want Peter to think he was ignoring protocol. No one had even discussed the need for a motion for summary judgment in Keibler, at least not with him. But the time would come when submitting a motion for summary judgment would be the right strategic move. Then Kronish and Peter would get together to decide who to assign it to. Probably that kid Masserly. He was Peter's favorite. Masserly would probably be asked to write the motion.

On his way back to the office Peter called out to him. Masserly was in there, sitting across the desk from Peter, probably not even thirty yet. Just a second-year associate, Masserly, but already with that air of entitlement that some junior associates acquire when they sense they are favored by one or another partner. His skin was dry and pink and flaked at certain termination points like his receding hairline and the curves of his knuckles. When Tim thought of him abstractly, he was reminded of one of those children who age rapidly and prematurely and die as old men at thirteen. Today he was wearing a pink buttondown with white collar and cuffs, silver cuff links winking from the armrests of the wing chair, and a long paisley tie draped down his shirtfront like a silky tongue. Every layman's idea of the asshole lawyer. Peter offered another iteration in his blue pinstripes and bow tie. He should have worn knotted ties if he was going to let his gut go like that. As it was, with his belly drooping low and prominent, his neck appeared to have hold of a water balloon. A festive spirit animated the air between the two men. Tim held the printout close to his body. There were bees just outside Peter's window, too.

"Masserly doesn't know about the walking," Peter said to him.

Tim stood in the doorway and said nothing.

"No, seriously. I just asked him and he said he'd never heard."

"I doubt that," said Tim.

"Tell him, Masserly."

Masserly turned. "Never heard."

"It's sort of a private matter."

"Private matter? You were profiled in the fucking *New England Journal of Medicine,* for Christ's sake. He used to carry a copy of it around with him," Peter said to Masserly, "to prove to people he wasn't nuts."

"That's not why I carried it around."

"He'd come in here with a bicycle helmet on his head, wearing a backpack."

"I'm sure he's heard this from somebody, Peter."

"And he'd walk around like a schoolkid heading out for the bus. They were doing some kind of experiment. What was the point of that experiment again?"

"What's the point of bringing it up?"

Peter shrugged. "We're just talking. He showed up to court like that once. Judge comes in and he won't take off the bicycle helmet. He's got the chin strap all buckled in, wearing a suit. Judge asks him what's with the helmet. You should have seen Kronish."

"You can read about it in the *New England Journal,*" Tim said to Masserly.

"I've never seen Kronish so pissed. I was just an associate then. I didn't say a fucking word, did I, Tim? Did I say a word to you about that bicycle helmet? Not one fucking word."

"You were a saint."

"Hey, Tim, don't be angry. We're just talking here. Uncontrollable bouts of walking. Masserly, you gotta read the thing to believe it. And then you still won't believe it."

Tim wondered who had championed Peter for partnership. Was it Kronish? Personally he had not thought Peter had shown himself to be partnership material. Peter worthy of partnership at Troyer, Barr? He didn't think so. "I'm going to get back to work," he said.

"Wait, wait. I mean, it brings up questions. For instance, for instance. What would have happened to you if you had been blindfolded?"

"Hey, Peter. Have you and Kronish talked about a motion for summary judgment yet?"

He preferred to keep a low profile, but suddenly he was unable to hold back. Who had championed that bow-tied twerp to be a Troyer, Barr partner?

Peter cocked his head. "In what case?"

He damn well knew what case.

"Do you guys have any idea who you might assign it to?"

"A motion for summary judgment in what case, Tim?"

"The Keibler case."

"Keibler?"

"I was just curious if you and Mike had discussed who you might assign it to."

Peter looked over at Masserly. "Who in their right mind would submit a motion for summary judgment in Keibler?" he asked the kid.

2

He had complained of brain fog. Neither Jane nor Becka understood what brain fog was but neither did they disbelieve he was suffering from it. He had earned the right to say he felt a certain way and to be taken at his word. He said he felt mentally unsticky. The description was unhelpful, but he insisted that he suffered from a lack of mental stickiness. His nerves felt "jangly." He told Becka to imagine a guitar whose strings had all gone slack. The image was vivid but she had trouble applying jangly to her own nervous system. The physical pain was easier to describe, but this, too, he did in a private way. His muscles felt hyperslogged. His left side was floaty. Some days his breathing was all bunched up. They could only approximate for themselves how those words made him feel when he translated them into metaphor, as with the guitar strings, but he insisted on identifying them in these nonmedical and not very useful ways because to him there was no adequate substitute. They offered the most precise descriptions, the ones that aligned best with his inner experience of being.

"So when you say all bunched up," Becka had asked him, "you mean to say you can't catch your breath?"

"No," he replied. "I mean to say my breath is all bunched up."

Jangly, hyperslogged, all bunched up—he spoke a language only he understood.

They read to him through the brain fog. He favored history and biography. He was worried that without stimulus he would shed IQ points as if sweating them off into the bedsheets. Not long after his sequestering, Jane had purchased a hospital bed with retractable sides and Velcro restraints at the wrists and ankles, an improvement over the headboard and handcuffs. Together with the bedpan and the bottles of skin ointment and antidepressants and the general stagnant smell of antiseptic and body sweat, the bed transformed the guest room into something out of hospice care. He was in one long nightmare of walking now: walk, sleep, wake up, wait for the next walk. His feet convulsed rhythmically against the restraints. Becka was narrating the Senate exploits of Lyndon B. Johnson when she discovered that he could fall asleep even as his body continued to walk.

"Dad," she said. She shook him and he came to. "You fell asleep."

"It's hard to concentrate through the brain fog."

"But you never stopped walking," she said.

She thought that was all the evidence anyone would ever need to prove that what afflicted him was not "all in the head." His body was not his own if it continued to labor without his conscious input. But he no longer seemed interested in debates. What caused it, mind or body, what it should be labeled, organic disease or mental illness, fell second to his immediate concern.

"You can't let me fall asleep like that."

"Why not?"

"Wake me up if I do it again. Keep me up, Becka. Keep reading."

The next time she came home to relieve her mother, he stopped her before she could even start to read. "This isn't working," he said. "Get my things together. Unstrap me."

"No," she said.

"This room is death, Becka. Let me out."

"It will run its course. You have to be patient."

"It would have done so by now, goddamn it. Let me out of here! It's death in here!"

How easy it would have been to leave the room and plug his screams with headphones. He was locked away as well as any lunatic on suicide watch. But with her mother gone and she alone to care for him, abandoning him was not an option. Her three or four days with him were always a rigorous and continual effort to keep him focused, somehow keep him connected.

She bought an iPod and filled it with music. "I want you to try something, Dad."

"Where is your mother?" he asked.

"I don't know."

"Where does she go when she leaves the house?"

"I don't know."

"You're lying."

"Stop straining your neck. Relax."

She placed a noise-canceling pair of headphones over his ears, hopeful they would eliminate the rustle of his legs as they struggled against the sheets. Then she introduced him to some of the music that had been her own solace for as long as she could remember.

3

He had sat before the panel trying not to cry. Whatever you do, don't cry. Just keep talking. His desperation was like a pheromone secreting itself into a room full of wolves. He appealed to them on the basis of over twenty years of impeccable service and the many millions of dollars he'd made the firm. You thankless sons of bitches! he wanted to scream. You ruthless bureaucrats! You'll all get sick one day, too! This flinty nerve vied in him against total supplication. Oh, please, please take me back! Grant me the full measure of life again. On hand and knee, peering up at formidable and unmoving faces: I will be good, will do as told. No more breakdowns, promise, promise.

"Tim, I think we've heard all we need to hear," said Kronish.

He was jabbering on, making a case for himself, trying not to cry.

"Tim, Tim—"

He stopped talking.

"We've heard enough, thank you. I'm sure we're all very happy that your health has returned. Now give us some time to discuss the matter and we'll have an answer for you in a couple of days."

Enough time had passed that his worst transgressions had faded and his earlier reputation had somewhat revived. They agreed he deserved an audience, and he made a decent case for what he had to offer: expertise, years of loyal service, a good legal mind. Still, they voted not to reinstate his partnership in light of his professional misconduct. They invited him to rejoin as a staff attorney, a non-partner-track position.

In accordance with the bylaws he was still receiving his quarterly share of that business he had brought in for the firm during his partnership days. Financially he could have rejected Kronish's offer for the insult it was. But he was so grateful to be back in the world again and loved Troyer so fiercely that he immediately accepted. He set the phone down and wept. They were such fine people. They had such capacity for forgiveness. It would be fun to be a staff attorney.

4

One of the first things he did after he returned to Troyer was invite Frank Novovian to dinner. He wanted to express his appreciation for the time long ago when Frank walked down the street with him on a cold winter day and gave him his wool cap.

Frank sat on his stool at the security post as still as a pond frog. He looked up from a bank of security monitors as Tim approached.

"Mr. Farnsworth, how are you, sir?"

His tone was flat and affectless and he did not smile—-admirable qualities in a man in charge of building security.

"Frank, we'd like to have you over for dinner, you and your wife."

The invitation caught Frank off guard.

"I'm afraid I don't know your wife's name," said Tim.

"Linda."

"Jane and I were thinking Saturday, if you and Linda are free this weekend."

Frank reached around to scratch at a shoulder blade, stretching his suit coat taut. He had added bulk since Tim's departure. Tim wondered how the blazer didn't rip down the back. "We're pretty free, I think, Mr. Farnsworth. What's the occasion?"

"You can call me Tim, Frank," he said. "I'm not a partner anymore."

"If you work for Troyer, Barr, Mr. Farnsworth, I call you by your last name, partner or no partner. It's a policy not too many others take seriously around here, but that's them."

Tim nodded. "All right. But will you call me Tim if you come to my house for dinner?"

Frank thought about it. "If you let me bring the wine," he said.

"It's a deal, then. Saturday?"

"Saturday," said Frank.

Frank took off his Yankees cap the minute he stepped through the door, placing it inside his winter coat in which Tim could picture him clearing his driveway of snow. A vivid image of

Frank's neighborhood came to mind: many houses set close together, metal siding, small backyards separated by chain-link fencing. There was a dog barking and minivans were squeezed into tiny driveways.

In the doorway, Frank lifted his head and looked around the house, as if standing at the start of a guided tour. Out from his post now, he had loosened up and began to praise Tim's house. He offered Tim a six-pack of bottled beer and introduced his wife. Linda was smaller than Frank, an Asian woman with dark bangs, thick eyeliner, and a wide and pretty smile. Tim had expected a heavily primped Italian with a Bronx accent. Tim took their coats, and Linda offered him a bottle of wine.

"I really mean it, Mr. Farnsworth. This is one hell of a house."

Tim considered reminding him that they had a deal—he was Tim tonight, not Mr. Farnsworth—but he thought calling attention to that fact might embarrass Frank. He decided to let the matter resolve itself. He moved them inside and Frank thanked him again for having them over.

"This is one hell of a nice room," said Frank once he had situated himself on the sofa. "And I bet that thing gets great reception."

"Try it out," said Tim, handing Frank the TV remote. "My wife's just in the kitchen."

"Can I help?" asked Linda.

"Whatever it is," said Frank, "smells delicious."

"You can help by telling me what you'd like to drink," said Tim.

Linda looked at Frank.

Frank looked up at Tim and asked, "What are you having?"

"I thought I'd start with one of your beers," he said.

"Me, too, then," said Frank.

"I'll have a beer," said Linda.

"Three beers, then," said Tim, "coming up."

He walked in and found Jane sitting at the kitchen island. She was peering into her wineglass as if in search of fish.

"Jane?"

She turned to him slowly. She looked at him and then lifted the wineglass. She inadvertently clinked her teeth against the glass, making a ringing sound and causing the liquid inside to break like a golden wave and splash her face. "Mmmm," she said, setting the glass down and reaching precariously over the kitchen island for a napkin. She sat back heavily on the stool and wiped away the wine.

"Banana?" he said.

"Hmmm?"

"How many glasses of wine have you had?"

She didn't answer.

"Tonight, too? It had to be tonight, too, Janey?"

"Mmmm," she said, getting off the stool. "The lamb." She walked to the oven as if through water. With the oven door open she stood again and turned around, peering across the kitchen. "The hot mitt go?"

"Let me do that," he said, taking the hot mitt from her hand.

"I got drunk," she said.

"I noticed," he said. "When did that happen?"

She reached out for him. She was wobbling and he held her in his arms trying to contain her. "On and off in the bathroom," she said.

He returned to the living room with beers and Frank announced that he wanted to make a toast. "To your house," he said. They all clinked frosted mugs and drank to Tim's house. Then Tim broke the news that Jane wasn't feeling well and had gone upstairs to lie down. She might be out for the night. Frank and Linda expressed concern.

"We should go then, maybe," Linda said to Frank.

"No, please," said Tim. "I'd hate—"

Jane walked into the room. "You must be Hank," she said.

Tim turned around as Jane came forward to shake Frank's hand. She tripped on the rug, steadied herself and looked down at her feet. Then she turned and left the room.

All three of them stared with great stillness at the doorway. Tim stood. "She must be feeling better," he said to his guests. Then he almost collided with her as she came back in. "I forgot my drink," she said, flicking spilled wine from her hand as she transferred the glass.

"His name is *Frank*," he whispered fiercely.

As they ate appetizers, Tim and Frank made small talk about TVs and appetizers in general and then, for some reason, and for a long time, Chex Mix in particular. He didn't want to talk about Chex Mix. He wanted to share with Frank, a man who could be trusted, the physical and psychic toll of all his recent months in the room.

"Yorba Linda," he overheard Jane say to Frank's wife. "Where Richard Nixon was born."

"Yorba Linda?" said Frank's wife.

"Because I was thinking, *Linda, Linda,* because of your name, and then I thought, Yorba Linda."

Her lamb managed to be edible. By then she wasn't saying

much. She had sunk down into herself far below the frequency of conversation. Tim took charge of the ordeal by summoning his resources as a former Troyer partner and bored his two guests all night with stories of famous cases. They listened politely while sipping their wine. When the monologue was over, they left.

5

He left Peter and Masserly and returned to his office. The motion for summary judgment in the Keibler case was still warm from the printer. He sat down behind his desk and opened the bottom drawer and filed the motion away just as he had planned to do. He tried to recapture the purer impulse that had prompted him to write it and the nourishment the writing itself had offered him during the long and lonely weekend. But now only the sad diminishment of the final product's destiny meant anything to him. Into the drawer, what a waste. Peter and Masserly together couldn't formulate half as cogent an argument against the plaintiffs in Keibler if they spent six months knocking their simian brows together, and he'd done it in a weekend. It pissed him off, Masserly's sense of entitlement and Peter's unmerited partner status.

He shut the drawer and then rested his arms on the desk and looked through the doorway, burdened and discontented. He tried to think an appropriate thought, something ennobling and proud. Staff attorneys are people, too, he thought. Then he thought, Oh, fuck that.

He took the motion with him down to Mike Kronish's office. Empty. That was a good thing. He didn't think he could do it if he had to hand it to Kronish in person. He set the motion on Kronish's desk and wrote a quick note. He departed with renewed hope and a bad case of butterflies. He was halfway down the hall when he started fretting that he'd done the wrong thing.

6

Twice a day during his time in the room they unstrapped one hand and turned him to prevent bedsores. They did this when he was sleeping. They applied antibiotic ointment to the backs of his legs where the skin had rubbed away.

Becka unstrapped him one night and walked around the bed for the ointment when he grabbed her hard at the wrist with his one free hand. She let out a startled cry.

"Don't unstrap me again," he said, his grip tightening.

"You're hurting me, Dad."

"If you unstrap half, I will unstrap the rest."

He let go of her.

"I won't make it," he said. "I'll walk out and I won't come back."

They had to find a new way to prevent bedsores. Bagdasarian prescribed a liquid sedative they administered by needle, which toward the end, when he was more or less incoherent, was no longer necessary.

7

Within the hour he was refreshing his inbox every ten seconds in expectation of an email from Kronish. He was watching his phone for it to ring. By half past eleven the wait was killing him and he had to leave. He programmed his office phone to forward all calls to his BlackBerry, and he strode down the hall toward the elevator, wary of being seen.

Frank Novovian stood at his post in the lobby like a raw blister. Coming in or going out, he tried to avoid Frank at whatever cost, but there was little maneuvering with the security man so close to the escalator. He often hid himself in a pack of lawyers but it wasn't quite lunch hour yet and he was alone. Frank looked up as he approached, and they locked eyes.

"Hey, Frank."

"Mr. Farnsworth."

"Getting some lunch," he said. "Can I pick you up something?"

"My wife packs a lunch for me," said Frank.

"She does?" He casually walked over to the security post.

"Every day."

"That's nice of her. How's she doing?"

"Loves her new job."

"She changed jobs, did she?"

"Well, same job, different bank."

Tim had not recalled, perhaps had never known, that Linda worked at a bank. "Good for her. Wish her luck for me."

"And how's your wife doing these days, Mr. Farnsworth? If you don't mind me asking."

Tim lowered his voice and peered at Frank across the lobby post.

"Let me tell you something," he said, almost in a whisper. "I sure appreciate your discretion on that subject."

He nodded to Frank to lend his words some definitive thrust of body language, as if he had actually told the man something about how Jane was doing. Then he drummed his knuckles on the marble counter.

"Now I'm going to get something to eat," he said.

He checked his BlackBerry going down the escalator and all across the lower lobby. Jane was fine. Jane came home from the treatment center tomorrow. But Tim didn't know what business that was of Frank Novovian's.

8

Jane was asleep on the chair next to the bed. He called out to her and she stood up and turned on the lamp. His eyes adjusted, and he saw that it wasn't Jane but Becka. She waddled back to the long-suffering La-Z-Boy and flopped down on it as if she were stuffed with plastic beans, invertebrate and sprawling. The jaunty springs died quickly. Her settling might have indicated a day's honest labor, the spent effort of a middle-aged waitress come home to her lonely recliner, but she was instead a young student exhausted by the inconvenient hour and the simple upkeep of this arid and stuffy vigil she brokered when her mother was not around.

"Becka," he said, "where does she go?"

Becka yawned and shook her head. "I don't know, Dad. If I knew, I would tell you."

"I don't ask her," he said.

She yawned again.

"You're tired," he said. "You should go to bed."

She didn't move. He watched her closely. It wasn't morning as the clock determined it but it was morning to him—the one time in the cycle when for an hour or two he was capable of engaging as nearly a full human being again. If she stood and walked out of the room, kissing him good night before she left, he would lie awake in the dark, and his desire to engage would give way to despair. He had to have this one hour.

"Have I ever told you the story of Lev Wittig?" he asked.

She raised her head off the back of the chair and looked at him with heavy eyes.

"Lev Wittig was a partner at Troyer, Barr," he said. "Tax partner from Connecticut. Family man, went to Yale. Dullest man you will ever meet. And ugly. He had a neck on him. The largest continuous piece of flesh I've seen on a human being."

She rested her head on the recliner's gold velvet arm. That chair belonged in a different house, in an alternative family history in which festive struggles were ones of car troubles, bill paying, and who controlled the remote. He looked at his daughter over the edge of the hospital bed. Poor girl, middle of the night, she was so tired.

"But this man Lev Wittig was really a genius at tax," he said. "You don't find many of those. Some of the most effective structures currently in place that keep the really big corporations from paying federal income tax were devised by Lev Wittig. You do that at Troyer, Barr, and there's no question you make partner. Do you want to hear this?"

"Sure," she said.

"You're not just taking pity on me?"

"Taking pity on you?"

"It's so late."

"Go on with your story, Dad."

"Okay," he said. "Lev Wittig. He brought in so many clients, made the firm so much money. But you know what some of our partners are like. Just dull, dull, dull. So rich, so dull. And a guy like Lev Wittig, ugly, too. Rich, dull, and ugly. Now, that's a powder keg. Are you sure you want to listen to this?"

"Why do you keep asking me?"

"I'm saying if you have to go to bed I'll understand."

"Dad, I'm up, I'm listening."

"I bet you could unstrap me," he said. "For an hour. I'd be fine."

"No," she said.

He sank down into silence.

"Dad?"

"I feel like talking," he said.

"So talk."

He remained silent another minute. "Lev Wittig. He throws all his energy into becoming the tax king of the world, and after twenty years, he's at the top of his game. It's never going to get any better. He's sitting on more money than he knows what to do with, and he's a powerhouse at one of the city's most prestigious firms. Then he starts to feel age creep up on him. He turns fifty—this is what happens when you turn fifty, you feel age creep up on you. And something in Lev sort of breaks, where he says, if I'm going to work this hard and make this much money and be this good at my job, I'm gonna do whatever I goddamn well want to do. And so he sets forth to do what he wants to do."

"Which is what?"

"Indulge his sexual proclivities. Which is what all of them want, basically. Are you up to hearing your old man tell you the story of someone's sexual proclivities?"

"Is it going to make me uncomfortable?"

"No," he said. "It's too weird."

She motioned for him to continue.

"Okay, so he wants to indulge himself, so he finds a guy in Chinatown. Who knows how he finds him, but Lev Wittig's got money, and when you have money, you can always find a guy. This guy specializes in smuggling exotic animals out of China, Africa, wherever, for people in the city who want to own them as pets and can bear the cost. And Lev Wittig can bear the cost."

Becka lifted off the arm of the chair. "Where's this going?" she asked. She curled her legs under her so that now she sat as if meditating.

"Now, the other thing you have to know is, Lev's sick of having sex with his wife. And you can't really blame him, because Lev Wittig's wife, let's just say, is a brutish woman. Mustache, thinning hair. And he doesn't want to do it anymore."

"How do you know?"

"He told me. He told everybody. I was just an associate when all this was going on, but he told me how sick he was of having sex with his wife and I didn't even work in tax. At major firm functions, he'd tell entire groups of people. We'd all be in a circle, you know, everybody dressed up, drinks in hand, and he's telling it like it's a courtroom anecdote. But he was Lev Wittig. He practically wrote the tax code."

"Still gross," she said.

"But the truth of the matter is this," he said. And he paused, but not for too long. He wanted to build tension but he didn't want her losing interest. "Under certain circumstances, he can still have sex with her."

"How do you know this?"

"Under very particular circumstances," he said, "he can still do it."

"Which are what?"

He paused again, longer this time. "There has to be a snake in the room," he said.

"What?"

"He can't get an erection unless there's a snake in the room."

"Are you serious?"

"Swear to God."

"And how do you know *that?*"

"It came out at trial."

"What trial?"

"Just listen. The guy he hooks up with in Chinatown, at first this guy doesn't even have to go outside the country. He has a three-foot rattlesnake from Arizona delivered to Lev at the firm. It comes in a box. Inside the box is the cage, and inside the cage is the snake. There are feeding instructions. Do you know what certain types of rattlesnake do to your respiratory system?"

She hugged her knees. "Are you kidding about this?"

"So Lev takes the snake home," he said, "and he tells his wife that if she wants to stay married, if she wants to keep the family together and the house and all that, from now on she'll be having sex with a snake in the room." He paused, letting that sink in. He had gained confidence that she wasn't going to leave the room until he was through. "I'm going to go out on a limb," he said, "and say that that one comes as a shock to old Mrs. Wittig."

"You think?"

"But it's a fantasy he's had for years and he's not going to suppress it any longer. This is what he tells her. A snake in the room gets him excited. So he puts the cage up in one of the guest rooms and he tells her that he's going to let it out, and she can either be in there already or come in after, but either way, they're going to have sex with the snake on the loose. So she goes up to the guest room and she sees the snake in the cage and she comes back down and opts for the divorce."

"Which is the only sane thing to do," she said.

"Thank you for listening to me," he said.

"Is that it? Is that the end of the story?"

"No."

"So why are you thanking me?"

"I just felt like thanking you."

"Dad," she said, "finish the story."

"So what does Lev do? Despite the threats and manipulations, he can't really do much of anything except move out, given what she can now testify to at family court. So he moves to an apartment near Central Park, and that's when he starts to hire the prostitutes."

"To go with the snake?"

"He's got the money," he said, "and he wants what he wants."

"Who *is* this guy?"

"Lev Wittig. Wrote the tax code. Dullest man you'll ever meet."

"*I'm* not meeting him."

"He tells them a little fib about how everything must be absolutely dark or he can't, you know, perform, and then they go into the bedroom, and this is exciting for Lev because there's a snake present."

She squirmed and shuddered audibly and gathered herself closer, holding her legs tighter.

"And here's the thing. Each time, it has to be a different snake. That turns out to be part of the kick. The guy from Chinatown brings Lev cobras and vipers and green mambas, I don't know what all. Not good snakes to have around."

"Define a good snake," she said.

He held up an index finger to indicate that her point was

well taken. His hand went only so far because his wrist was held tight to the side of the bed. "He gets good at handling them. He's got equipment, you know, the boots and the gloves, and he has a pair of snake tongs that allow him to get the snake in and out of the cage, and when that's done, he puts the cage in a box and walks to the park, where he lets it go."

"Lets it go in Central Park?"

"Rare and extremely venomous snakes."

"I can never go there again," she said. "I can never go to Central Park again."

"And this keeps up until one night, one of the girls goes into the room and walks toward the bed and steps on the snake."

"Oh, my God," she said. "What happened?"

"The girl died. I don't imagine she was in very good health to begin with. Now, say what you will about Lev, he does call nine-one-one, and he tells the EMTs exactly what happened, and there's the snake right there in the cage, and the snake tongs, and the snakebite on the girl's thigh, so they call the cops and he gets arrested."

"I can't believe you knew this man."

"These are the people I work with," he said. "I saw him one last time, before he went to prison. It was just before his trial. He was out on bail. He went from office to office explaining why he'd done what he'd done. Not in a contrite sort of way. Sort of mystified, and sort of looking for understanding. Because he was not the only rich, ugly partner at Troyer, Barr known to indulge himself. And I remember I ran into him in the hall and he pulled me aside. I had just made partner. And he wanted to know if I'd heard the story. So I said I had. And he just looked at me with his bug eyes and his big neck and basically said I'd do the same thing one day. Just wait, he said. He basically cursed me with his own fate. Then he said something like, 'This has been my cross to bear my entire life. I don't want to fuck unless there's a snake in the room, and I just love to fuck.'"

Becka sat in the chair hugging her legs and shaking her head.

"Can you believe that?"

She continued to shake her head. The story was over. What, he wondered, would they do now?

"Are you tired?" he asked. "Do you want to go to bed?"

She suddenly yawned as if in answer. He had to think of something.

"Do you know Mike Kronish?" he asked.

"The name's familiar," she said.

"You've met him," he said. "He's the managing partner for litigation."

"What animal does he have to have in the room with him?"

"Listen to this," he said. "Will you listen to just one more?"

She let her head fall back, but her eyes stayed open.

"So Kronish makes it a policy as managing partner to personally interview every candidate for hire, which is a pretty arduous task when you consider how many people we look at in any given year. But this is a legendary control freak, even worse than me if you can believe it. And he tells every candidate a little autobiographical story, which I can confirm is true because I was on the plane with him right after it happened. He tells it so that the incoming class of associates understands his personal idea of an exemplary Troyer, Barr attorney, and the story goes something like this. Kronish worked on a case, a very famous case involving the government's attempt to break up a big tech company for what it considered antitrust violations, a case that went on for several years. Part of that case took place in California, where one of the tech company's competitors had brought suit against it. And Kronish, who had just made partner, worked the case, so he had to be in California for trial prep. Now, he said he intended—although I sort of doubt this—he intended to fly back to New York a few weekends every month, you know, to spend time with his wife and kids. He had two boys, they were, like, six and eight at the time, maybe eight and ten. And for about two years, except for holidays, Kronish never made it back home. So the boys would come out to visit, and their mom would take them to Disneyland and the beach, and more frequently than not, they'd return to New York after an entire week's visit having seen their father literally for a dinner or two at the hotel restaurant. So when the case is over—we won, by the way—to make things up to the boys he says to them, okay, you and I are going to spend an entire week at the house in the Hamptons, just you and your mom and me, and we're going to catch up on lost time. So one Friday they drive out to the Hamptons, and that very night, that Friday night, Kronish gets a call from an important client. And this client says to him that while Kronish has been in California saving the tech client's ass, another partner at Troyer has been fucking up his own impending trial, and with only two months to prepare, the client's considering defecting to another firm unless Kronish, and yours truly, step in personally. So Kronish, in the Hamptons with his boys less than twelve hours, calls his driver to turn around and pick him up. He tells the boys that he has to fly to Houston that night and won't be able to spend the week with them after all. And the boys' hearts—now this according to Mike himself—the boys' hearts break. Tears, tantrums, everything Kronish detests about children. So he hands them off to his wife and goes upstairs to pack his things and then comes back down and waits for the car outside the house. The driver comes. Kronish gets inside. And then one of the boys breaks free of the house and runs toward the car. Not a tear on this boy's face. He promises never to cry ever again if Kronish will just stay. He promises no more crying, and Kronish can see his little face quiver, but he doesn't say a word to the boy, he just rolls up the window and tells the driver to drive. And the kid just bursts into tears behind the tinted glass while Kronish heads off to Houston. And he tells me on the plane later that night that if the kid hadn't cried as the driver started off, he would have considered staying. It was like a test, he tells me. Personally I doubt that. But that's the story he tells me on the plane, and it's the same story he tells every member of the firm's incoming class, and he tells it to crowds of people at firm events and to clients so that everyone knows what he considers to be his idea of client commitment. And what is the first thing you see when you walk into the man's office? You see an eight-by-ten glossy of him and his family on the wall next to his law degree. They're grown now, those boys. They call Mike 'Uncle Daddy.' Now, I dropped the ball with you sometimes," he said to her, "but I was never as bad as that."

"You never dropped the ball with me, Dad," she said.

"In high school," he said. "I let you down."

"I was an asshole in high school."

"I was an asshole from nineteen seventy-nine onward," he said.

"I've been an asshole my whole life."

They laughed. Then the unsettling silence set in again, and he had to try to think of another story.

9

His return to the firm, his steadiness behind the desk, his palpable sense of day following uninterrupted day gave him faith that it would hold. His time in the room was over. Twenty-seven months and six days of profitless labor had passed. He had endured as a half-wit, the scale of life diminished to a light fixture. Elation followed by delicate readjustment. He remembered the first time stepping out onto the lawn, etiolated, held upright on trembling legs, blinking in the awesome sun.

He walked the halls more often after his return. There was always someone to say hello to in the halls, and he liked to stop with a cup of coffee to look out at the views he had seldom noticed before. He watched taxis taking their slow, toylike turns around corners, and tugboats drifting down the great river.

From time to time he'd want out of the office as out of a catacomb, just so he could breathe fresh air and feel the sunlight on his face. How long would this reprieve last? He lived in constant fear of a recurrence, as if he were an immigrant living in the country of his dreams whose fickle authorities could nevertheless decide without warning to take him into custody, nullify his freedom and dispatch him to sorrow and dust.

On one such outing, he encountered an eclectic group of people stretching around the corner of a gray concrete building, as ornate and generic as a reconstituted bank. They were assembled single file and waiting to enter for a mysterious purpose that made passersby look twice, wondering what they might be missing. He'd seen such lines before but had never cared. Now he slid between two car bumpers, crossed the street and approached the last man in line, and, like a tourist new to the phenomenon of anonymous city gatherings, asked him what was what.

"Casting call."

"For what?"

"Movie."

Move on if you don't know, the man's curt reply seemed to say. *We don't need the extra competition.*

But he stayed put just for the thrill of it, doubtful he'd last so long as to actually enter the building and find himself in front of a casting agent, but feeling nothing else pressing. Or trying his best not to, anyway. There was some busywork waiting for him back at the office, but nothing exciting. Soon a small gathering had accumulated behind him. He felt the interloper. Never took an acting class in his life. Never sat for a headshot or waited tables for crap pay or suffered the heartbreak of losing a part on the final audition. So this was the subculture, so often talked about but so often scattered, invisible as bedbugs, of the struggling actor. With the rest of the artists, together with the immigrants, they carried the city on their backs. Eating like hell and suffering miserable colds, serving your ahi tuna, reciting Shakespeare in the shower. Directly behind him stood two girls: one Latina with hoop earrings and curls stiff and frozen and black as tar, and the other dressed, improbably—although nothing was improbable here, if you just looked around—as a princess, a jean jacket thrown over a strapless white gown of silk and organdy that flared widely at the skirt, a silver spangled tiara in her hair. Must be auditioning for princesses, he thought.

The Latina said to the princess, "Why he think he can do me like that? I been good to him, girl! And then he treat me like some ho, like I don't even go to church and shit."

"Have Manny whoop his ass," said the princess.

"What I'm gonna say to Manny gonna make him whoop his boy's ass like that?"

"That he been saying shit."

First the acting subculture, then the subculture of women who did not get the respect they deserved from men whose asses should be whooped by Manny. He strained to recall a single exchange—on the street, from the next table over at a restaurant—overheard in all the years he had lived in the city, within the inescapable nexus of babble he had sat in most of his life, and not one came to mind. Not one. Had he never unplugged his ears of the self-involvement that consumed him about work, when he wasn't sick, or about sickness, when he couldn't work? Had he never listened?

Later that day he overheard another conversation after ordering food from the Kebab King. The Kebab King was a white portable plastic hut parked down one of the numbered streets in the Forties. Laminated articles stuck to the side of the cart proclaimed the Kebab King the leader of street-vendor cuisine. The menu consisted of three items—lamb, chicken and falafel—spelled out on the front of the hut. He asked for a lamb kebab and gave his money to a small woman wearing a white double-breasted chef's jacket and a pair of latex gloves. The Kebab Queen, maybe. The Kebab King was in a similar jacket and had his back to her as he tended to diced meat on the sizzling grill.

Tim waited for his order with great anticipation. He was much hungrier than he thought, and this was something he had wanted a long time. There were entire walks whose source of bitterness was not the pain, nor the mystery, nor the ruination, but the simple fact of passing a vendor's cart as it issued the agonizing aroma of unattainable meat. Walking hungry with no way of stopping played tricks on the mind, as those who die in deserts know when they mistake sand for water. He had fixed for hours on images of charred shanks turning on a spit over a flickering fire and of tearing hocks of roasted meat directly from the bone, blisters of blood sizzling on the surface of the skin. There was nothing civilized about him then. Just the instinct, primordial and naked, for food and fire.

The woman handed him the tightly foiled sandwich with a ration of napkins, and he realized he had no patience for taking it back to the office. He stood against a brick wall and, out of the way of foot traffic, tore away the foil at one end. The sandwich was hot as ore in his hand. His first bite of meat and juice and yogurt sauce and onions and diced pickles nearly made the deprivation of such a thing worth it. The sandy pita was a fullbodied pleasure. He took large bites that forced him to chew dramatically. He was eating the steam itself.

He ordered a second kebab and walked over to the courtyard on the avenue side of the street. There he sat on a smooth roseate ledge that sloped gently toward the sidewalk and watched the other lunchgoers who sat eating around a decommissioned fountain among the tall buildings. As he ate he overheard two men talking. He had passed them on his way to sitting down. They were just on the other side of the ledge from him, reclining against the wall. They were homeless, or lived in a shelter or in the tunnels, and they each had a bottle in a bag within arm's reach. One of them owned a wheelbarrow, which had been pushed sideways against the wall, out of the way. It was rounded over with clothes and plastic bags, partially bungeed with a blue tarp. Tim stopped chewing to listen. They were speaking English, but he could not understand what they were saying. He got only the tone of complaint. He understood that the speaker had been wronged in some way, and that the injustice was more than just a minor slight. But as for the words themselves…

"They corset cheese to blanket trinket for the whole nine. Bungle commons lack the motherfucker to razz Mahoney. Talk, knickers! Almost osmosis for the whole nine. Make snow, eye gone ain't four daze Don."

"Uh-huh," said the second man.

"And sheer traps ton elevate the chord dim. Eyes roaring make a leap sight socket."

"Uh-huh."

"Sheeeeee-it," said the first man.

Then they fell into silence.

10

On the day he set the motion on Mike Kronish's desk, he found himself in Bryant Park at lunchtime. He walked up to a kiosk where he purchased a turkey wrap and then made his way toward one of the green tables laid out in the shade. Under his feet, he sensed the final crunch of fallen leaves. He was mistaken—it was the opposite season for turning leaves—but he was too preoc-cupied to notice. He had but one thing on his mind: had Kronish seen the motion, and if so, what did he think?

He sat down, brushing off the table a languid-moving bee, and unsealed the sandwich from its plastic-wrap cocoon. He kept his eye on the BlackBerry. The day had acquired an edge of cold, but there were still plenty of people about, as if defiance could force spring to act appropriately. He paid no attention to their conversations. From the first bite of his sandwich to the last, he ate mechanically and without pleasure. The ache in his jaw told him he had finished. The duty of lunch had been acquitted. Shortly after, as if his stare at the mute BlackBerry all at once exerted an actual force in the world, Mike Kronish called. He recognized the number lit up on-screen and his heart began to flutter. His heart had done the same nearly twenty-five years earlier when, as a junior associate, a call from a senior partner, no matter how insignificant, was a mortal quest to prove one's competence. He answered reluctantly in a voice he did not recognize. "Hello?"

"What's this you put on my desk, Tim?"

"Who is this? Mike?"

"This motion for summary judgment. You write this motion?"

"Did you see that? I left that on your desk."

"Who wrote it?"

"I did."

"What for?"

"Oh, because, did you read it?"

"What would I do that for?"

"What for?"

"Who in their right mind would submit a motion for sum-mary judgment in Keibler?"

"Because the strategy."

"What strategy?"

"I've been following the case, Mike. I know it back and front. We both know sooner or later."

"What do we both know?"

"Sooner or later, you'd want a motion for summary judgment in Keibler and there's nobody can write that motion like I can."

"First of all," said Kronish. He paused to clear his throat. "One, perhaps you don't know Keibler like you think you know Keibler. Keibler comes down to credibility disputes, and no judge is going to grant summary judgment when there's a credibility dispute. Two, if you know Keibler, you know the Ellison deposition, and if you know Ellison then you know no, no motion for summary judgment. Three, Second Circuit last year heard Horvath, which is Keibler if you switch the Swiss concern for an Israeli, and the Second Circuit said no, in such cases, never summary judgment."

"I forgot about Ellison," he said.

"And Horvath?"

He had never heard of Horvath. He must have been out of commission when the Second Circuit decided Horvath. "I forgot about Horvath," he said.

"Just switch the nationalities with Horvath and you get Keibler, and now there's precedent not to grant summary judgment in such cases. So what strategy are you talking about?"

"I was thinking there were differences between the two."

"Four, you don't work on my team, Tim. You do and you don't, you understand?"

"Mike," he said.

"You hear what I'm saying, Tim?"

"Am I going to be a staff attorney for the rest of my life if I stay at Troyer, Mike? Or is there some way that I could get my old job back? I'd like to get my old job back, Mike. I'm healthy again. I've got credentials, I've got experience. I just want to know it's something possible."

Kronish's silence on the other end was a torment.

"You say you know Keibler, is that right?"

"Back and front, Mike."

"Not if you're writing a motion for summary judgment you don't," he said. "Let's stick to the game plan, Tim, okay?"

He sat for a long time at the flimsy green table in Bryant Park. He wasn't disappointed. The more he thought about it, the more he was relieved. He recalled the old bodhisattva he'd seen years ago who had warned him against too much focus on the incoming message. He had given over his entire morning to waiting for word from Mike Kronish about a motion he'd never meant to show anyone, whose purity was now compromised. A morning of utter anxiety, stealing right from under him the pleasures of the day. His anxiety had taken him out of the world when one of the things he was trying not to forget, as the memory of his time in the room faded and his old ambitions and preoccupations reasserted themselves, was how to remain in the world. Giving that motion to Kronish and awaiting word of his benediction by way of the BlackBerry had thrust him into the ether of anticipation, a cyberstate where time passed unattended and the world, so long denied during his recurrence, was discarded for the dubious reward of a phone call or email that couldn't arrive soon enough and would deliver only grief when it did. He had to have resolve. He couldn't let himself get bogged down again. Jane was coming home tomorrow. She needed his help. How could he give her the attention she deserved if Kronish

had called and made him a partner on the spot? He'd be check-
ing his BlackBerry five hundred times a day. What kind of life
was that?

As these thoughts came over him, he started paying attention for the first time that day. The wind had picked up and
he suddenly felt his frostbitten nerves start to ring in their
sheaths like cold bells. The neutered sun cast shadows and just
as quickly took them away. My God, he thought, it was already
half past one.

He stood and began to walk, once again crunching his way
through dead leaves, but now, his attention restored, he saw his
error. They weren't leaves at all but rather a thin blanket of dead
bees. He lifted his feet as if to avoid stepping on them, but they
were everywhere. They thinned out only when he reached the
street. He looked back in amazement—at the hundreds, the
thousands of delicate brown and yellow carapaces. In a city of
odd sights, it took the prize.

II

Not long after his return to Troyer and on the heels of inviting Frank to dinner, he visited R.H. in prison. It was the one
thing he wanted to do least and the most pressing of all the
business that had awaited his recovery. It did not go well.

The prisoner, stripped of suit and tie and looking old beyond his years, did not speak. For the longest time R.H. simply remained silent behind the wire-reinforced glass that separated them. He wore an orange jumpsuit with short sleeves. Tim saw the hair on his arms, prominent swirls of gray hair that had been covered over by bespoke suits for all the years he had known him. This small laying-bare pierced his heart. Another notice-able change had taken hold of the hair on R.H.'s head. The dye had washed out, leaving the hair a dull gray. It wavered thin and airy like a loose clump of field pollen. With a regal reluctance R.H. picked up the phone. He held it to his ear and stared at Tim with a kind of catatonic intent, sitting forward and say-ing nothing. Tim began to speak. Trying to interpret how his words were being received, he was not encouraged. Was R.H. angry at him past reclamation, or was he simply traumatized by his circumstances beyond the niceties of human interaction? He found he had no choice but to put the question out of mind and persevere, knowing that such perseverance was itself a kind of penance.

He admitted that Jane was not ill and never had been. He had lied about her sickness to cover up his own. He had fallen ill just prior to the trial, and the instinct that came naturally to him as a man too proud for his own good was to cover it up. Cover up all hint of weakness, cover it up or he was finished. Essentially, though it was not the first time he had struggled with this particular illness, he was scared out of his wits: scared of failing R.H. at a dire moment, yes, but most of all, scared of losing control over his professional life. Scared for himself first, R.H. second. It was important for him to admit that now.

"I had an option," he said, as R.H. bore two clean holes through the glass with his silent and inscrutable stare, holes that at any moment might begin to smoke. "I could have recused myself from the start and thrown all my efforts into helping Mike Kronish take over the case. Would that have gotten you an acquittal? I don't know. Could I have gotten you an acquittal if I had stayed healthy? There was a time when I thought I knew the answer to that. But the truth is, I don't know. I have learned to have less conviction."

He believed that R.H. was innocent of killing his wife, but the man on the other side of the glass, almost waxlike in his stillness, staring at him with cold, flinty eyes, *that* man seemed capable of killing.

"You had him," he said.

"What?"

R.H.'s head did not move. "You had him."

"Had who?"

"The man who killed Evelyn," he said. "You had him."

"Are you talking about the man with the knife?"

"You had him."

"Do we really know," he said, "can we say with absolute certainty that that man is the one who killed her?"

"You had him and you let him go. He was right there in front of you and you let him go."

"At the time, R.H., I didn't know—"

"The one guy who could have exonerated me," he said. "You let him walk away."

"I think maybe you're putting too much faith in—"

"You should have grabbed him," he interrupted with a rising voice. "Why didn't you grab the son of a bitch? He's the only one who knows who did it. *He* did it! And you let him slip through your goddamn fingers! Why couldn't you grab him?"

R.H. didn't seem to give a damn for his confession of lies and failures. He blamed Tim for one thing and one thing only.

Now it was like an obsession that he had been waiting years to unleash. Tim could hear him just as well through the glass as through the phone.

"Answer me!"

"I think you might be overplaying that man's role. No one knows for certain that he killed her."

"He had the murder weapon."

"It may have been the murder weapon."

"May have been? May have been?"

His loud voice attracted the attention of the guard standing against the wall. "How could you let him go? How could you walk away? He was my one hope! And you let him go!" He stood up. He screamed into the phone, "You let him go!" He began to beat the glass with the phone. "You let him go!" The guard rushed over. *Thump!* "You let him go!" *Thump thump!* The guard grabbed him from behind and lifted him into the air. The chair went flying as the old man kicked out his legs. One of the kicks landed on the glass. He hung on to the phone as long as he could, until the cord snapped and he and the guard went sailing. "You had him!" he cried through the partition. He threw the phone at the glass as the guard dragged him out of the room. His cries grew more muffled. "You had him! You had him! You had him! You had him!"

12

When did she go from someone who liked a glass of wine with dinner to the woman with the lights blazing at four a.m.? Trying to do the bills totally blasted. Her nice quiet life had been stalked from behind by alcohol. Who would have guessed? If you were predisposed, or had the gene, or lacked some inner resource, you had to be vigilant or you went down. Four in the morning and she was digging through her purse for a Newport. What was that? She was not that woman. But she was. Oldest story there is, total cliché. Except when it's your life. When it's your life it's not a cliché, it's real life, real everyday life, just drunk. It came up from behind her and knocked her to her knees. She never expected it, but that's what happened, it came up from behind. Being a drunk was simple. It was an accident you caught sight of in the rearview mirror, and the car you saw was your own. The intersection where the accident happened, it was the very one you were approaching. When you turned from the mirror to the road in front of you—BAM! you got hit again. And then, once again, you were looking back at it. She was supposed to be on guard her whole life against alcohol? Who knew.

But it wasn't an accident. She was making choices, even if she didn't know it.

She called Becka during his time in the room and said, "You have to come home now and watch your father. It's your turn, it's time." Like he was a baby and not her husband. Like Becka had made the vows and not her. Becka didn't understand. "Why, do you have plans?" She had no plans. She hadn't had plans for months. She hadn't seen a movie, she hadn't talked to friends, she hadn't been to the dentist. She wasn't going outside to collect the mail. Becka got the mail when she came home. Becka was the one who had to drag her by the hair to see Dr. Bagdasarian. Jane kept thinking, when did *she* become the parent? Becka told her to put the wine down and get in the car. She had called from school to make the appointment. The doctor took one look at Jane and said she was in the dictionary under *depressed* and wrote her a prescription. She didn't need a prescription, she needed a life. She needed to start over again with new teeth and fresh underwear. But of course she took the prescription. If it came from a pharmacy and modified behavior, there had to be some merit to it.

But a month went by and she was still calling Becka. "You have to come home. I have to drive." And Becka said, "Drive?" "Yes, drive." "Drive where?" Drive where—what sort of question was that? When you're driving just to drive you don't know where. You're just driving. She shrieked that into the phone. If she shrieked, if she called late at night, if she cried, if she made several calls in the same hour, Becka came home and she was able to drive. In the magazines and the newspapers, those people, they had such inner resources. Meeting adversity head-on and all that.

Her first time driving, she made it to Stamford, Connecticut. That wasn't even an hour away. She thought she'd stop at the Bennigan's for lunch and then she'd keep driving north. She walked in around lunchtime and the tables in the dining room were full so she took a seat at the bar. She was just going to fuel up before hitting the road again. But she got drunk instead. She was at the bar throughout the day. The daytime bartender switched with the nighttime bartender and she was still there. She finally asked the nighttime bartender to call her a cab. She was drunk and tired and didn't want to have to walk out to the parking lot. She thought there might be some way to convince someone to carry her. But when the cabbie showed up and the bartender said, "Your cab's here," she got off the barstool and grabbed her purse and walked out on her own. She got inside the cab and didn't know what to say. "How about a hotel?" she finally said. The cabbie drove her to a Holiday Inn and helped her inside. He helped her check in and then he helped her to her room. She woke up around noon not knowing where she was. She woke up, she knew it was a hotel room, but she didn't know in what city. She walked down to the Denny's for some coffee and when the coffee started to take effect she remembered the Bennigan's. She went back to the Holiday Inn and asked for a cab. It was the same cabbie from the night before. She didn't remember him. He said to her, "Back to the Bennigan's?" She asked if he ever took a break from driving and he told her that he was doing twenty hours a day so he could pay to pull a tooth.

He drove her back to the Bennigan's. They drove through the lot but she couldn't find her car. The cabbie called a friend of his at the municipality and sure enough her car had been towed. Cars weren't allowed to stay overnight in that lot. The cabbie offered to help, but she thanked him and paid him and went inside to think. It was lunchtime. She ordered a drink and then she ordered a second one. The daytime bartender gave way to the nighttime bartender, and she was drunk a second day at the Bennigan's in Stamford. She was there another five or six hours until Todd called her a cab. Todd was the nighttime bartender. When the cab came, it was the same driver. She couldn't believe it. She drank through his night. He was getting at most three hours of sleep a day, trying to earn enough to pull his tooth. But was he fleeing *his* responsibilities? Was he getting drunk in *her* neighborhood Bennigan's? People have such inner resources. He said, "Back to the Holiday Inn?" She went back to the Holiday Inn. Same woman at the check-in counter, same room from the night before. The next morning it was the same cabbie. "Back to the Bennigan's?"

She asked him to help her get her car out of hock. Then she drove home. It was Monday, and Becka had already missed her first class of the week. That was the first drive she took.

She needed a place like Stamford if she was going to run away from her self-respect. Stamford was the perfect place to feel shameful. She didn't want too much luxury around to remind her that she could afford not to be unhappy. She liked sitting at the Bennigan's. She was attracted to it because it was just another chain in another strip mall. If it had been a real bar, the people would have been too real. It would have been the same bartender every time, the same regulars, a home away from home. But after two or three months she never saw Todd again. During her time there, there was Renell and Deirdre and Eva. There was Jerry and Ron. They knew her but they didn't. People came and went. It was all very anonymous, perfect for getting shitfaced. The Holiday Inn was perfect for the same reasons. She got a room first so she could park the car and then she'd call Emmett. Emmett was the cabbie. He'd pick her up and drive her to the Bennigan's. She drank Tanqueray and cranberry juice. Then she'd call Emmett to drive her back to the Holiday Inn. He worked twenty hours a day because something was nearly always wrong. He had bad teeth and an ulcer. He had high blood pressure. There were things in the future that needed fixing and things in the past that needed paying off. He couldn't get insurance and he couldn't pay for what the insurance would never cover. She had his cell number and on the rare occasion he wasn't driving for the company he picked her up in his Chevy Lumina. He took care of her when she wasn't able to take care of herself.

"Why are you doing this to yourself?" he asked her one night after helping her inside her room at the Holiday Inn.

"My husband."

"Your husband?"

"My husband's at home. Suffering."

"Suffering what?"

"Suffering what?" she said. "Suffering what? Ha ha ha ha ha ha!" she roared. "HA HA HA HA HA HA!"

"Do you think this is helping him?" he asked when her laughter had finally died.

"It's helping me," she replied.

She failed him. She hadn't fucked anyone, she hadn't left him for someone new, but that was only because it was easier to drink. That's all. With something to take a drink from, she could find the strength to care for him most of the time. But how hard was that? He was strapped to a bed. She could walk away whenever she wanted—and she did a lot of walking away. She got used to him screaming. It got so that with enough wine she could ignore him. She did a shitty job tending to his bedsores.

She would fall asleep when she read out loud to him. She wasn't in the room when he needed to talk. She kept more company with the wine. So she never left, big whoop. So she never fucked somebody else, so what?

When she wasn't at the Bennigan's, she moved through the house. She went from room to room feeling the massive crushing weight of it. She tried to remember why they had decided that they needed so much space. To raise Becka, of course — but how big did they expect the child to be? And did they not realize how quickly eighteen years would go by? Did they not foresee how alone they would become in that oversized house? When he was sleeping or when she chose to ignore him, she wandered from room to room, counting the beds. They had a total of eight beds, if she included his hospital bed and the pullout sofa and the twin mattress in the basement. How did they ever come to own so many beds? Who were they for? She didn't know except to say that seven of them must have been for her. There was no one else around. If his parents had been alive or if her parents had been alive, if he had had brothers and sisters or if she had had brothers and sisters, but nobody had anything and everyone was dead. She could sleep in a different bed every night and never repeat beds for an entire week. He needed one specific type of bed and couldn't sleep anywhere else and she sort of envied that. She loved her room at the Stamford Holiday Inn. It was too big but it had only one bed. She could move the chair and the desk and the hutch and the other chair around the bed and the room got much smaller. She was shitfaced when she was doing the moving and they always charged her for it but it was worth it. There was just one bed and with the rearranged furniture the room was the size she liked.

One night at the Bennigan's, she counted the people at the

bar. There were three couples, her, and the bartender. That made eight total, and her mind just went from there. She stood up on the barstool, on the rungs that supported its legs, and beat the bar with her hand. That got everyone's attention. She said, "I see there are eight of us here at this bar." The people she addressed were total strangers. "Eight of us at this bar," she continued, "and at my home, I have eight beds." The bartender came over to ask her to lower her voice. She couldn't remember who exactly, Eva maybe. "Now I would like to invite every one of you over to my house," she said, "because I have a bed for each and every one of you. I want all of you to spend the night at my house. It's about twenty…about forty, it's…an hour or…don't know how far away it is…" She kept going on and on until the manager came over. He tried to get her to sit down but she wouldn't sit down. He tried to get her to be quiet but she snapped at him. "I will not be silenced!" The manager exchanged a look with the bartender. "Please excuse us," he said to the others at the bar. "I will not be silenced, goddamn it!" she cried. "I'm inviting these good people to spend the night at my *house!*" The next thing she remembered was Emmett picking her up in the women's room, where she had fallen asleep on the floor. She had rested her cheek on the toilet seat. That was the last time she was allowed back at the Bennigan's. From then on, she started drinking at the T.G.I. Friday's.

13

He did not go back to work after his lunch in Bryant Park. He stopped into a men's store to buy an overcoat and a pair of gloves to warm him as the sun waned. The day was turning steadily colder. The saleswoman cut the tags from the overcoat and he walked out wearing it. He moved along more comfortably. The luxury of being able to stop for a coat and gloves was a freedom he would never take for granted again.

He went inside a corner bar. The front window was covered with thin metal latticework befitting a hermitage or cloister. He eased onto the barstool as if it were a hot bath for sore joints. With the exception of maybe his desire for a lamb kebab, his thirst for a beer had been the greatest agony. When you wanted a drink and couldn't have one, the city turned into one long block of lounges and Irish pubs, rathskellers, beer gardens, dive bars, taprooms with a pool table in back, flickering sports bars, wine bars, hotel bars dimly lit as water cascaded down one wall, tiki bars, nightclubs and brasseries and every other conceivable watering hole, including the convenience stores where they made your beer portable with a paper sack. All of them had remained just out of reach. The people he had passed in their windows, with their coats off and half-finished pints in hand, how he had despised them.

A day laborer was drinking down the way, smoking a ciga-

rette in violation of city ordinance and talking with the bartender, who leaned in close to him. Eventually she ventured
down the bar to ask Tim what he wanted. She leaned in while
he looked over the tap. After he'd made up his mind, she lifted
off the bar as if it were a final push-up and poured his beer. It
was garnet-colored, shot through with its own light. Tiny bub-
bles made a half-inch head of foam. He put the beer to his lips
and drank.

This was more like it. This was being in the world.

When the bartender returned to see if he wanted another,
he asked her, "Have you seen all these bees around lately?"

"Bees?"

"Honeybees."

"I haven't seen any bees."

"I saw a bunch of them dead in Bryant Park just now. Do
you know if bees are supposed to be around this early in the
spring? Or if they hibernate?"

"I know nothing about bees," she said. "Steve, do you know
anything about bees?"

"Bees?" said the man at the end of the bar.

"Like honeybees."

"I know they make honey," he called down to them.

She turned back to Tim. "Charmer, isn't he?"

She drifted back down the bar.

When he and Jane talked about her drinking, they were free of
the recriminations that might have taken hold of them over some
lesser matter. This only seemed to make it harder to talk about.
A strangeness lay coiled in their domestic familiarity. They lay
in bed in anticipation of talking but remained silent for long

stretches of time, as if the subject under discussion were not the self-evident steps they would have to take to address her willful drunkenness but the unimaginable ways they might resolve his involuntary walking. They stared into the essential mystery of each other, but felt passing between them in those moments of silence the recognition of that more impossible mystery—their togetherness, the agreement each made that they would withstand the wayward directions they had taken and, despite their inviolable separateness, still remain. It had nothing to do with how age and custom had narrowed their circumstances or how sickness had shaped them outside of their control. It was not a backward but a forward glance.

"I don't want to go," she had said.

"It will go by fast."

"What will you do?"

"Wait for you. Visit you."

"I don't see why," she said.

She hated herself for having failed him. Becka had done it better, she said. He would have done it better by an order of magnitude. He interrupted her. If she was going to assign blame, he would have to take his share. He never intended to bring this on them, no, but intention, or the lack of it, could not grant a full pardon. He could not escape blame even if it was the faultless blame of being born and falling ill, blame that was also Jane's, that was anyone's, really—everyone's price to pay for being mortal.

"We'll take a vacation afterward," he said. "Where would you like to go?"

"How often will you visit me?"

"As often as they let me."

Visiting hours were from six to nine. He often left work early to spend a few hours with her before returning home.

The ring of his BlackBerry brought him back to the bar and the barstool.

From the moment Masserly began to speak, with his clown's voice that seemed to suggest the arrival of puberty any day now, Tim forgot his resolution to remain in the world and resumed a bitter longing for his old job. He didn't even mark the transition. The pockmarked bar smooth to the touch, the mahogany details, the bottles arrayed before the distressed mirror like all the king's men—they faded the moment of the phone call. "Tim, it's Kyle Masserly."

"Yeah?"

"This motion for summary judgment in Keibler."

"How do you know about that?"

"Didn't you get a call from Kronish?"

"How do you know about my motion, Masserly?"

"They gave it to me."

"They who?"

"They want me to clean it up. Not that it, you know—"

"Clean what up?"

Tim listened intently. He had his finger drilled into his opposite ear to block out the music from the bar, and for a quick second it sounded as if Masserly had hit the mute button.

"Did you just put me on mute, Masserly?"

The office ambiance came back with the kid's voice. "Yeah, clean it up. They're going to submit it tomorrow."

"To the court?"

"But like I need to do anything to this thing."

"They're going to submit that motion to the court?"

"Tomorrow. I just got off the phone with—"

He was standing now between the bar and the stool, trying to concentrate on what Masserly was saying.

"With who?" he said. "Masserly?"

"—and they love it."

"I wrote that motion," he said.

"Which is why I'm calling. You should get credit, not me."

"Kronish told me it was pointless."

"And where did you get the genius to—"

Tim thought he heard the start of a guffaw just as Masserly's voice cut out. His end had gone mute again. Or so it seemed. Sometimes lawyers made phone calls with one finger poised over mute so they could bad-mouth the opposition.

"Did you just hit mute again? Is someone in the office with you?"

"Mute? Look, I was asking where you got the insight to write a motion for summary judgment in Keibler when there's Horvath. It's genius. But you know Horvath chapter and verse the way you make implicit the differ—"

There might have been another guffaw, but the line went dead.

14

Another thing he had to do after getting his life back was tend to his ailing body. He visited the Russian and Turkish Baths on 10th Street, not far from Tompkins Square Park, where he sat in the steam room. The heat softened his bones. A bucket of cold water poured over his head reawakened dulled nerves. He liked the place, despite the fact that the other men made him feel like an anorexic. They were hunched, hairy, burly-backed men with traces of immigrant pasts who walked naked around the locker room, their taut bellies and bulby pricks too much for the rough handkerchiefs that passed for towels at the registration desk. He didn't mind. He wasn't vain. Vanity was a luxury of those exempt from the compromises of a long illness. He felt self-conscious only of his missing toes.

The entrance to the baths resembled any other crumbling red stoop in the city, with a lunette above the double doors that read Tenth St. Baths. A man came out just as he was entering and held the outer door open for him. Tim thanked him and climbed the small flight of stairs and almost went through the black door to the registration desk when he suddenly stopped. He dropped his gym bag and ran quickly back down the stairs.

He spotted the man walking east toward Avenue A. He was just then opening a translucent umbrella screen-printed with a map of the world. The unfurled umbrella swallowed up his head and shoulders.

Tim needed a better look, a clear and unambiguous look, to confirm that it was the same man he'd encountered on the Brooklyn Bridge. He ran down the stoop stairs and crossed to the opposite side of the street. It still felt unnatural to walk hurriedly with missing toes. He pressed down on their phantoms. He reached the corner ahead of the man and lingered there to see in which direction he would turn. The man waited for the traffic to clear and then walked across Avenue A. Tim followed him into Tompkins Square Park.

He kept his distance as they walked along the curving path, past benches and fenced-off trees. As they approached 7th Street, Tim quickened his pace. He walked ten feet ahead of the man and then turned and walked toward him. The man's head was downcast and buried in the umbrella. Tim realized he wasn't going to get the look he needed unless he said something.

"Excuse me."

The man peered up. Tim saw the same drawn, lonely face, the same dimpled chin, the same long pointy nose with the knuckle in the middle. The man lowered his head quickly and resumed walking.

They hit 7th Street. They walked alongside each other just as they had on the bridge. "Hey," said Tim, but the man would not be distracted again. Tim tapped his umbrella, and when that did nothing he grabbed it and held on. "Hey, I'm talking to you."

The man yanked the umbrella away. "What do you want?" he asked.

"I know who you are."

"Do you want some change, is that the idea? Well, I don't have any change to give you. You should get a job."

The man returned the umbrella above his head and resumed walking.

"Hey, don't walk away from me."

Tim had to move quickly to remain at the man's side. He looked around for others on the street with them but there was no one. The city seemed to have cleared out.

"Find someone else to harass," said the man. "I have no change for you."

"I know who you are," said Tim.

"You're obviously a lunatic."

Tim reached out to grab hold of the man's arm. With one graceful move the man slipped his grasp and retreated two paces. In the process he abandoned the umbrella. It spun like a dying top on the sidewalk. When Tim looked at the man, he saw that he was standing oddly erect, his two hands lightly fisted.

"You must stop harassing me," he cried loud enough for anyone to hear.

"You know something about the murder of Evelyn Hobbs," said Tim. "The police want to talk to you."

"Fine," the man said, again too loudly, "take the umbrella. Just leave me in peace and you can have the umbrella."

The man walked sideways toward the corner of 7th and A. He raised one hand to hail a cab, but the street was just then empty of all cars except those parked at the curb.

Tim approached him cautiously. "I'm not letting you out of my sight."

"You are a lunatic!" cried the man.

"You and I need to go to the police."

Finally a single cab appeared in the distance. The man held up his hand. "Do not come any closer," he said to Tim.

Tim took another step forward. "I'm not letting you inside that cab."

The cab aimed its way toward them. He grabbed the man just as he was reaching for the door. He got hold of his upper body and clasped him from behind in a bear hug. The man swiveled with Tim on his back and slammed him against the rear door of the cab, knocking the wind out of him. He had a raw vital power all out of proportion to his pale demeanor. His struggle was a practiced struggle, his resistance a trained one. Pinned against the cab, Tim gasped for air. The cabbie stepped out but then stood there frozen, staring from the open door. Tim told himself he just needed to hold on until someone called the police. The police would take them in, they would identify the man, they would finally have the man in custody. But then he was lifted off his feet and lofted into the air, thrown right over the man's back, and landed hard on the curb. He lay, stunned, half on the sidewalk, half on the street.

The man hovered over him and grabbed his jaw like an angry mother. He got close and looked him in the eye. "You forget me now," he whispered, "or I will kill your wife and daughter. Do you understand?"

"Yes."

"Forget me."

"Okay."

Tim stared up at the dense sky for he didn't know how long. Only his eyes moved, blinking involuntarily when a raindrop landed close by. Someone finally came over.

"Where'd he go?" asked Tim.

"Are you okay?"

"Where'd that man go?"

The stranger looked up. "What man?"

In the days that followed, Tim reengaged Fritz Weyer. Fritz showed the sketch to the guys who ran the baths. No one recognized the face. Tim told Fritz to keep searching. He was confident the man lived in the area. He said nothing about the fact that he and the man seemed to be the only two people in the entire city at the moment of their encounter.

15

The details of the Ellison deposition came back to him, unbidden, while he sat at the bar, and he couldn't see any reason why it precluded summary judgment in Keibler. The credibility dispute issue was highly debatable. And as for Horvath, whatever that was, there was always a way around precedent.

But was someone in Masserly's office guffawing at him?

He was on his way back to the office to find out when his cab slowed for a light. He peered over at a garbage truck, where a man in corn-colored gloves was just then stepping off the truck's ledge. From the street corner the man dragged one of the city's green mesh bins over to the truck's hopper and tossed it in, shaking it twice with quick indifference before returning it and resuming his weary perch on the ledge.

As Tim watched him, he thought despite all that man must see of the city on any given day, he probably noticed none of it. He put in his eight hours of garbage and went home. His memories were of stench, stickiness, weighty bins. That was no way to live. If you want to do it right, he thought, you have to get down on your hands and knees and crawl inch by inch across the earth, stopping occasionally to touch your cheek to the ground.

So then what was he doing in a cab?

"Can you let me out here please?" he asked the driver.

He paid and stepped to the curb. He was still far from the office. He stood on the street corner in his new coat and pulled his gloves tight. He watched the people passing by on the opposite side of the street, the cars thundering past, the unyielding permanent motion of the city. He stood absolutely still. The first of a spring snow was beginning to fall. It collected on his shoulders. The wind bum-rushed him from the west, filling his eyes with tears. He squinted and took a close look at a building across the way, the three whipping flags mounted above the revolving door, the green scaffold poles. A cluster of exiled smokers hovered around the entrance. Closer by, pigeons cooed and balked. A stout Hispanic woman in sandwich boards stood on the street corner mutely passing out flyers for discount men's clothing. Metal burned bitterly from a pretzel vendor's cart.

Maybe they let him return not because they were generous, but because they were cruel. They knew the greatest way to punish him was not to freeze him out forever, but to put him within reach of real work every day and then to deny him and deny him.

He walked down to the West Village. He sat for a spell on the stoop leading up to a brownstone. The sun had fled from the block and was rapidly disappearing from the city altogether while casual flakes drifted in the air. The exposed brick, the cement stairs, the small ironwork gates, the tin garbage cans, the protective grilles overlaying the windows of the garden apartments—all radiated a falling night's cold. The cars parked along the curb were naked and cold.

A woman emerged from a brownstone across the street. She was accompanied by a couple. The three of them stood on the stairs a moment before shaking hands and saying good-bye. The woman remained on the stoop and looked in both directions as if expecting someone. He noticed a For Sale sign posted on the brownstone.

He walked across the street and introduced himself. He told the woman he was a partner at Troyer, Barr. Quick to recognize the name of the firm, she immediately invited him in. She was trim, smartly dressed, and full of rehearsed speech. They entered the parlor-floor apartment. He walked to a recess of windows where he admired the view. The woman stood behind him, in front of the fireplace. She broke her monologue occasionally to say, "Let's see... what else..." He stared through the darkening glass as it began to reflect more of his warm and motionless silhouette than the stuff of the outside world.

"Would you mind turning off that light?" he asked.

The woman walked to the kitchen, her shoes clapping against the hardwood floor. The room fell into darkness, and his reflection in the window faded. Outside, lit windows made a lambent patchwork in the brownstones across the street. The buildings were built of white brick and red brick and the brick of fall colors. Residents walked down the street toward home as softly as the falling snow. He resolved to call Kronish. They weren't going to let him back in. And what did it matter anyway.

"It's a wonderful street," he told the broker.

16

Jane came out into the light and stood abreast the long white columns of the porch while he walked down the stairs and placed her bag in the trunk. The fickle temperature had risen overnight and the day was warm and bright. They left the facility down a dusty lane overhung with trees just coming into leaf.

"Would you like to take a drive?" he asked.

"Where to?"

"I don't know," he said. "I just wasn't sure if you wanted to go home right away or if you'd like to be out in the world. You haven't really been out in the world."

She didn't know how to tell him that she didn't want to go home. She wasn't sure she was ready to leave the facility. She lived among flowers and courtesy there, among the firm and guiding voices of the counselors, surrounded by nicely groomed lawns. She was cut off from temptation, unburdened by compromise and guilt, and there she had only one room with one bed, her life stripped down to the simplicity of self-survival.

"A drive's a good idea," she said.

"It's a good day for one."

"It's nice to feel the wind coming in. I haven't been in a car in a long time."

"Are you happy to be going home?"

She didn't answer.

"You can be honest."

"Yes," she said. "Very much."

They avoided the highways. They took the numbered routes that turned into streets with names whenever they entered one of the small towns. They stopped at a state park and walked from the parking lot down a footpath to a flowering lake and stood at the edge a few feet from the still water and listened to the silence.

"Let's jump in," he said.

"I don't have my bathing suit."

"We'll go naked."

"In the middle of the day?"

"Who's looking?"

She peered around and saw no one, no one on the water itself or on the far shore. They walked up into the woods a few feet and took off their clothes and hung them from a tree and then ran silently into the sun-skinned lake, which was much colder than either of them anticipated when they were taking its temperature with their fingertips.

"Christ, oh Christ," he said. He reached for her in a panic of cold, and she was eager for him. They fought the water in a firm embrace, turning in circles and chattering and rubbing each other's bodies with their hands and wondering how much longer they could stand it. "It's kind of torture."

"Bracing," she said.

"Stupid."

"Your idea," she said.

"Really stupid. Are you ready?"

"We just got in."

They raced back to their clothes. He dried her off with his undershirt and stopped to kiss her breasts. Her red nipples had hardened and dimpled from the cold, and with her hand on the back of his head, she pressed his hot mouth tighter. He got down on his knees and pushed her gently against the tree. She spread her legs and dug her backside into the rough bark and gripped his hair between her fingers until she came.

Inside the car again they blasted the heat. "I've missed that," he said.

"*You've* missed it?" she said, touching her flushed face with both her hands. Then she burst into laughter.

They drove along the water, past seaports and tourist spots that had been battered the week before by the season's first hurricane, which came earlier and hit stronger than anyone could have forecasted. The harbors and beaches had been damaged, and as they drove along they got a glimpse of a stretch of expensive beach homes, one of which had been cleaved on one side by a schooner.

They got on the highway that led home and he drove past the exit. "You just missed the exit, Tim."

"Are you going to go back to work?" he asked.

"I don't know," she said. "Why?"

"Just curious."

She didn't want to go back to work. She supposed it was the best way to spend her time, that it was an honorable distraction from the many hours in a day, and that it gave her life continuity and purpose. But the truth was she didn't want to do anything. She couldn't explain why, but she was nearly completely absent of any assertive sense of what she wanted to do with herself. She didn't mind that they had missed the exit. They could keep driving forever.

"I probably will," she said.

"If you do go back," he said, "I have a listing for you."

"A listing?"

"Will you do me a favor?"

"Are we driving into the city?"

"Be honest with me. Do you really want to go home?"

"It's probably the last place I want to go," she said.

"Why didn't you say so?"

"I'm supposed to be happy to be going home, aren't I?"

"Not if home makes you unhappy."

When they reached the city he parked in front of a fire hydrant and threw on the hazards. He didn't step out immediately. She was taking her cues from him, so she waited, watching him. He turned and announced he'd quit the firm. He had presented his resignation to Mike Kronish the day before, only to learn that staff attorneys didn't need to formally resign. They just needed to give personnel their two weeks' notice. Hearing the news, she felt something for the first time.

"They were never going to let me back in," he said.

"You thought they would?"

"Didn't you know that's what I was hoping for?"

"I didn't understand how you could do it if you weren't a partner," she said.

"Well, I couldn't." He opened the door. "Come on."

They stepped out. He had a key to the front door of a brown-stone she had never seen before, and he had the key to the parlor floor, and when he opened the door to the empty apartment he said, "We don't own it just yet."

She hung in the doorway. He stepped inside and leaned his back against the wall to look at her.

"What's all this about?"

He motioned for her to follow. They walked through the apartment. It was a tenth the size of their house in the suburbs. It had charm and character and windows full of sunlight, hardwood floors and a remodeled kitchen, and a restorer's touch around the woodwork. It had an antique chandelier and claw-foot tub. He led her to the far room.

"This is the bedroom," he said. "It's the only one."

She walked around the empty room. "What would we do with all our stuff?"

"What do we need stuff for?"

"And what happens when Becka comes home?"

"We give her the sofa."

"What if she wants to move back in after college?"

He looked at her. "We're talking about Becka here," he said. "Have you met Becka?"

"Good point."

"Here's the point."

"What?"

"Only one bedroom," he said. "Only one bed."

FIRST CHILL, THEN STUPOR

I

They woke that morning in the bed that had contained them like a miracle for another night. Four years had passed since her return. Any predawn stir in those days that rustled the bedsheets put the one on guard that the other might be ready to rise and start the day. But if neither of them opened their eyes to look at the other, that was a sign that sleep was still irresistible in the lengthening hour, maybe because of the lengthening hour, and they drifted back to sleep. They dozed in and out like that most mornings, half-conscious of the clock and of the other.

She woke in the bed alone and had no memory of his having left the room, and this surprised her. In the daze of half sleep she was vulnerable and for an instant she felt that bottomless fear. She got out of bed quickly and put on her robe and slippers and carried her reading glasses out of the bedroom, through the apartment into the kitchen, where the smell of coffee made her both instantly comforted and more alert. She went up to him without speaking and put her arms around him from behind as he read the newspaper.

"I was scared when I woke up," she said. "I didn't hear you get out of bed."

"Why were you scared?"

"I don't know," she said.

The kitchen at that hour was a place of drift and small preparations. The milk and the sugar bowl and the jars of jam and the butter dish were laid on the counter, and when the toast popped up they dressed it, and when their coffee ran low they refilled it. She preferred a delivered paper, in part so she could do the crossword but also for its fresh inky smell, second only to coffee as an announcement of a new morning. She liked the physical touch of the pages and the sense of fullness that having it all in front of her gave her, a containment of the world. He ate his toast and she peeled a tangerine and they talked of what they were reading, sharing parts the other had not yet gotten to. They added a little commentary if something seemed outrageous or, more common, all too predictable, and sometimes one of them reached across the counter and briefly touched the other, as in good morning, and smiled, and then went back to reading.

At some point one of them got up and started to put the lids back on the jars and to move the dirty dishes into the sink, and the other, not to be hurried, finished whatever article had been started before standing and replacing the lid to the butter dish and collecting the crumbs off the countertop and moving them to the garbage below the sink.

"Do you have a showing today?" he asked.

"Too many," she said. "Although look at that."

He peered out the window. "Another beautiful day," he said.

"If it keeps up—"

"Let's hope it keeps up."

"Then we can do something this weekend."

A few years prior he had found a job as an adjunct professor teaching a class on mediation at Columbia, and now she said, "You have class today?"

"At three," he said.

He rinsed the dishes and placed them in the dishwasher and heard the water going as she prepared to take a shower.

He was back at the counter looking at the Internet when she came in dressed for work. She told him the tub was still leaking and now seemed to be draining slowly, and he said, "The one-two punch."

"Let's just call a plumber," she said.

"Where do you want to have lunch today?" he asked.

Later that day at an early lunch they talked about what had transpired since breakfast, which was nothing, really, but they still talked as if they hadn't seen each other in a while. They had lived another half a day and that time had gone by without incident and they were together again, and this alone made them talkative. Then, after paying the bill, they walked to the back of the restaurant as they did once or twice a week, sometimes more, first her, followed by him, and entered the same door and locked it, and sometimes they did it with her on the sink and sometimes they did it against the wall. The illicit risk, the appeal of the fear of being suspected or caught, never attenuated or grew stale, and they knew that to make things really exciting, they needed only to change the tempo and slow everything down and stare intently at each other and stay in there much longer than anyone ever should. Then they left the bathroom just as they came in, her first, followed by him a minute later, keeping their eyes fixed on the exit until they were outside again.

"Well," he said. "That was fun."

"Have a good class," she said, kissing him modestly on the cheek.

"Good-bye, banana," he said.
"Good-bye, banana."

She troubleshot the downpour that descended on the city by slipping inside a Starbucks, where she bought a latte in exchange for temporary shelter. All the tables were full and the show of the tempest out the window was standing-room only when things really got going. Everyone watched it as they would some gripping season finale. The only sounds not of the storm were of order calls and cries from the espresso machines. Outside it was torrential. The skies were all drumspit and fury and made her feel a child's awe at the natural world, even if her view was only of stalled taxis and whipped awnings and water flowing over a slanting putty-colored pavement. She waited half an hour until the contentious storm eased back a little and she could wait no longer. Then she reentered the street with a small umbrella that went sailing in the wind and proved as ineffective against the driving rain as a kite on a string. Her heels hit every pothole and puddle and curb-hugging rapid and she felt dog-wet and slimy when she entered the lobby running woefully late.

The man she met there was an art dealer named David. David owned two galleries, one on Tenth Avenue and the other in London, and he came to her as her other clients did, by referral. He was sitting on a leather sofa under a softly lit sconce and rose to greet her when she walked in. She apologized for being so wet. He wore a tailored suit with a linen shirt, no tie and an open collar, and did not appear to have a single drop on him. She wanted to ask what portal he had emerged from, but instead they made small talk and then went up together in the elevator.

She took him around the apartment, a seven-room duplex

with a wall-to-wall view of the Hudson, a wine pantry, a professional culinary kitchen, and it dawned on her, slowly, as they drifted through the impeccable rooms filled with the occult light of a sky gone prematurely dark, and talked casually about the place, with none of the usual tension that characterized conversations during walk-throughs with prospective buyers who tended to think you were lying about every I beam and faucet—it slowly dawned on her that this man, David, was of that type, on account of his shoulders and full head of hair, his two days' growth flecked with gray on the chin, and the bright blue of his intelligent eyes, that he was of the type she found tempting. He would have been a temptation. Five or six years ago, he would have been better than a drink. If a man like David had pressed himself on her five or six years ago, she might have avoided drinking altogether.

They talked over the details of the building's recent renovation and she pointed out the best features of each room. She did most of the talking but when they turned silent again and his attention was elsewhere, she looked at him intently. He reminded her of other men she had encountered in passing, infrequently and always fleetingly, who in their wake left her feeling reckless and intense, afraid of what she was capable of. They brought out in her a longing that stayed with her for a day or two, like a particularly vivid dream, until it began to fade and was finally forgotten. As they continued through the rooms, she started to feel giddy and romantic. Just to indulge a fantasy, she pretended that they were looking at the place together, that she knew everything there was to know about contemporary art, that her name was not Jane, that she went to parties with painters and eccentrics, and that as they looked at each room, they wondered what piece would go best on what wall. Then she returned to earth, smiled at David, and told him that she would wait for him in the kitchen while he had a chance to look over the place on his own.

She was staring out at the grim day through the window overlooking the river when he came down the spiral staircase. The steps were white and curved and reminded her of the wings of a swan. She turned and watched him descend the final few steps. He clapped his hands together and rubbed them hungrily. "I'm going to put a bid in," he said.

"On the first one you've seen?"

"I love it," he said. "And I'm very impulsive."

"Well," she said, "that's wonderful."

They talked about what his initial offer should be and what she thought they could get the developer to come down to. He wanted it badly and suggested starting at the listing price minus ten percent, but she knew that the developer was having a hard time selling and suggested that he start at minus twenty and go from there. He thanked her for the advice and after going over a few more formalities, they left and she locked up.

In the elevator, he surprised her. "Remember how I said I was impulsive?" he asked.

"Yes."

"Well, I say we celebrate."

"Celebrate?"

"A drink, my treat. A deal like this can't happen every day, can it?"

"Well. Nothing is, you know, final yet."

She felt dull and sobering, having said that.

"I can promise you this," he said. "I'm buying that apartment. And at this hour—"

He moved to reveal the watch beneath his cuff. She liked

the watch and she liked the graceful way he brought it out into the light.

"—we can just avoid scandal."

For one fleeting instant, her sobriety was tested as it had not been since the day Tim picked her up from Cedarview. For one fleeting instant, her way of life, necessary for normal healthy functioning, struck her as totally life*less*, drained of spontaneity and energy and pleasure. She wanted nothing more than to have a drink with him. She wanted to get herself lost inside the darkness of a neighborhood bar, become unrecognizable to herself, gorge on the excitement of a stranger and risk everything—the languorous mornings, the illicit lunch dates, the companionable nights—risk it all for the sake of the risk itself. Then, the moment passed.

"I'm not much of a drinker," she said.

"Oh, don't make me beg," he said. "Everyone enjoys a glass of champagne."

"Especially recovering alcoholics," she said.

He leaned back in his tracks and winced. "That was stupid of me," he said. "I would have never suggested."

"How could you have known?" she said. "Don't think a thing of it."

"Dinner, then," he said.

His look was unwavering. He was so prepossessing that it didn't seem brazen. It seemed merely part of his charm that he didn't give a damn about whether she was married or not. She was flattered, mystified, exhilarated. She was also, after a moment, steady.

"I'm having dinner with my husband tonight," she said, just as the elevator dinged and the doors opened. He smiled and gestured for her to go first.

Walking through the lobby, she felt effervescent. She had shown resolve. They stepped out together onto Greenwich Street just as night was falling. She was surprised by the sudden chill in the air. "It's plummeted," she said, as her phone began to ring.

"At least it's stopped raining," he said.

"I have to take this," she said to him. "I'll just be a second."

Later she thought back on that moment, and the ironies were not lost on her. That she was with that particular man who had the power, just in passing, to make her feel restive and extravagant, urgent, fanciful, and destructive. That such a man was buying, in essence, shelter, protection from rain and falling temperatures. That Tim calling at that very moment should have driven the final stake between her and temptation.

"Tim, are you there?"

She gestured for David to give her a minute. David opened his umbrella to shake the trapped water from its folds. There was more sound on the other end than that stillborn nothingness of a bad connection, so she persisted. "Tim?"

"It's back."

She turned around and looked at David. In that moment she saw more than a temptation. She saw a life.

Hang up!

So I've had a change of heart about dinner.

Say wrong number, say...

But first take me to a bar. Order the champagne.

Say are you there? I can't hear you. Are you there, Tim?

Start from the beginning. Teach me everything there is to know about art.

Turn it off and throw it in the gutter.

Where do you think this piece should go—this wall here, or that one?

Jane? Jane who? You must have the wrong number.

Hurry, David, come to the window! Look at the storm gathering over the river.

I wouldn't want to be out in that.

But it's beautiful, isn't it?

"Jane?" he said. "Are you there?"

"Come home," she said.

2

A sudden splintering of the wind had scattered the rain like a school of silverfish. Women held their clothes to their bodies as they ran. The freak menace drove people inside, some to where they belonged, the rest to the nearest shelter. The fear was ingrained in them, bone-deep, and their reactions foretold. One or two wretches wandered around in it, indifferent to the lashings, drenched, labeled crazy to give the world its point of reference. His body moved him down the sidewalk. From the storm, the raging city edges, the clanking lanyards, the corridors of wind, the raindrops white as blisters, the windows whipping in their warped sills—from these things he had no awning under which to take cover, no deli, no lobby, no office, no Starbucks, no bedroom.

Blue security horses lay in the street. He removed his gabardine blazer and let it fall to the ground. A man came out of a doorway, one of a loose association of the ill and unkempt, and picked it up and put it on and returned to the doorway where he sheltered. The man should have followed him as he discarded the rest: his tie next; his white oxford, which he tore the buttons off and let fall some distance from the tie; his watch, which Jane had given him for a recent anniversary, sent clattering into the gutter. Rainwater backed up around the sewer drains with a gray and foamy choleric density.

His undershirt and chinos and tennis shoes were soaked through, his hair was matted and his eyes red and clenching as they struggled to make out the next step in his advance. He was trapped again in the next step, the next step and the next step. He walked across a halted intersection where the lights flashed red in both directions and long lines of cars sounded their horns down the lanes. They honked louder at his impudent passing. He paid no attention. His world had constricted. He cried out. People on the sidewalk turned.

Two pole workers were repairing a downed line at the corner.

"Did you hear that guy?"

"What was he saying?"

"Just screaming to himself."

"About what?"

"About somebody."

They stood in his wake and looked at him through the storm. He shed his T-shirt at last and flung the wet lump to the sidewalk, inviting the chill that came with the rain. Who did that? Who walked bare-chested through the cold rain? Maniacs. People at war with themselves. You saw them from time to time, wasted, psychotic, off their meds, poor naked wretches doomed to crime or death or jail or forced sedation. They tear a hole in the city for half a block until they disappear again inside the crowd.

The two workers turned back to the downed line, shaking their heads. He had not noticed them. His world had constricted to exclude everything but himself, and then was riven in two.

"You and me," he cried, "you son of a bitch!"

He woke up shivering on the wet pavement in the back of a gas station. The rain had died but the wind continued to shake water from the trees and the sky was draped in folds of purple shrouds. The trees behind the station were leftovers, demarcation points convenient to separate the surrounding developments, choked at pavement's end with crushed beer cans and soggy newspaper. The dumpster was overflowing with uncollected trash. Near one of its wheels lay an old rag. He stood and took up the rag. It folded out into a T-shirt. Though it was soaked through with rainwater, it remained stiff and required a series of shakes before he could put it on, and still it retained its bellows-like wrinkles. It was moldy and smelled of rot and advertised MasterCard, but he needed it to walk the distance up the road, past the auto-parts dealers and the fast-food franchises, so as to look present-able enough to rent a room at one of the motels. He did this, and once inside the room took the shirt off and washed it with the bar soap, scrubbing it with itself inch by inch. When he was through he wrung it out as best he could. He removed the rest of his clothes and wrung them free of the rainwater over the tub. Then he put them back on. They clung to him and that made him cold. He got under the blankets, shivering, thinking what he needed was a good fire. Instead of a fire he had free HBO.

He could still smell traces of mold on the shirt. As night fell he stopped chattering and reached for his BlackBerry.

Jane was standing with David on Greenwich Street just south of West 10th. She took her phone out of her purse and looked down at caller ID as David unwrapped his umbrella. He twirled it lightly with his wrist and the rainwater fell off in drops.

"Hello?" she said.

He kept silent.

"Hello? Tim?"

He didn't want to tell her.

"Tim, are you there?"

Jane put up a finger and smiled at David. She repeated Tim's name into the phone a third time.

Finally he told her. She was silent.

"Jane?" he said. "Are you there?"

"Come home."

The next walk took him from the motel to a Home Depot to the McDonald's to the strip mall with the Family Dollar store. He came to a stop outside a mall, specifically the long wall of glass doors leading into the Sears wing, locked that time of night. A stone ashtray and stone bench matched the plain stone arcade above the doors that extended twenty feet out toward the parking lot to keep the smokers dry and the old people safe from the treacheries of the curb while awaiting rides. He remembered all over again how pleasurable it was, arguably the most pleasurable physical experience of his life, to arrive at the end and, without giving a damn where, to lie down, the blood in his veins still walking, and to yield to the exhaustion. He fell asleep on the stone bench by a refugee tree in a metal grate and by the time mall security came around to run him off he'd gotten the sleep he needed and felt oddly cheery.

He walked to the fork in the road and went left and that road gradually curved around and followed the stucco wall of a private country club and then went up past the cemetery and a few miles later down a hill to a reservoir sitting beyond a bank of trees, which gave way to a public golf course, and then to a switching station humming menacingly behind a chain-link cage, and he continued onward to a town square, through the parking lot, and he walked the edges of gas stations hung with red and white flag bunting along another endless avenue until five miles later a writhing parabola of highway appeared and his body stopped under an overpass festooned with graffiti, where he lay down a few feet from the traffic rushing overhead and fell asleep.

He squatted at the top of the concrete ramp after waking. He could descend and go left or right or he could remain squatting. There were things he should probably do, like secure some kind of food before being forced to walk again. Usually he called Jane and she picked him up. He was either going to get picked up by Jane or from this point forward have a lot of time on his hands. He wasn't good with excess time. He stopped breathing and had to remind himself to start up again. The traffic went by him overhead and one of the things he thought of doing was climbing up and throwing himself in front of the passing cars. But that was letting the son of a bitch off too easy. He decided to call Jane.

His BlackBerry was dead. He was going to have to stop

squatting and make his way down the loose rock and broken glass scattered across the ramp to the shoulder of the highway and go back the way he came, where he would search out a pay phone.

A few miles down he found a convenience store. He went inside and microwaved some burritos. He ate outside, standing next to the ice machine. When he finished he walked over to the pay phone and pulled out some pocket change. She picked up on the first ring.

"Well, I've fed the son of a bitch," he said.

"Tim?" she said. "Where are you? For God's sake, it's been almost twenty-four hours."

The relief in her voice gave way to panic. He let her go on for a while longer. "I've fed the son of a bitch and now we're standing outside the mini-mart where I bought the burritos."

"What mini-mart?"

He didn't reply.

"Tim, come home, you need to come home, tell me where you are and I'll pick you up."

"We're feeling better," he said. "I think maybe . . . maybe we'll go over to that sporting goods store while there's still time."

"What sporting goods store?"

"Jane?"

"Yes?"

"Jane, you don't have to worry about us. We're going to be just fine."

"Are you with someone?"

"We're going to be just fine," he said. "We're going to go over to that sporting goods store and stock up on a few things."

"Tell me where you are so I can pick you up."

"That's the operator, and I don't have any more change."

"Tim!"

"Don't worry about us," he said.

He supposed that decided it: he wasn't going to be picked up. He walked over to the sporting goods store. Their winter offering was on display. They had fleece and spandex, neoprene and knit, polyester and cotton. He needed a different shirt. The one advertising MasterCard was dry now and the stench of rotted milk enveloped him. But to choose a size and a color and to do all that human business inside the fitting room was so exhausting. He needed boots and a coat as well, but that was also a pain in the ass. You had to hunt down a salesperson, give him your size, and wait for him to return from the back, where everything was kept, and then try on one of the boots — maybe both, depending on how the first one fit — and all the rest of it. What a pain in the ass. He didn't want to make the effort. He refused to. He left the store and stood outside the automatic doors, just off to the side, where he remained standing a long time.

3

She did not say, she told Becka later, "Tell me where you are and I'll pick you up." As far back as Becka could remember, that's how it was done. He called and told her where, what town, what gas station, what intersection, and then she and Becka got in the car and drove. Becka remembered the long drives. She remembered watching her mom get out of the car, walk up to him, and bend down and shake him gently. Her mom would tuck her hair behind an ear as she squatted beside him, waiting for him to come to. She remembered the car rides home, some tense and silent, others full of anguish and adult talk going nowhere. By the time she was old enough to better understand, she didn't ride along as much. They would just suddenly return to the house together, or the phone would ring and wake her up and her mom would leave in the middle of the night. Her idea of family was bound up in those car rides and midnight runs, in her mom's attempts to keep everyone together, everyone safe, and in the memory of her mom squatting patiently beside her dad as he slowly rose to a sitting position.

This time her mother didn't have the energy. She didn't want to get in a car and resume the ordeal. She told Becka about the art dealer named David she had just finished showing a listing to when she got the call and how she didn't want to leave him. She wanted to hang up the phone and start a new life. So instead of saying, "Tell me where you are and I'll pick you up," she shifted the responsibility and the struggle to him: *come home.* As if that was such an easy thing to do when you were on foot, when you were lost and hungry and exhausted from walking so many miles.

"We had our heads in the sand," she said. "We never talked about it. But I knew one day it would come back, and when it did, I promised myself I'd do it right. No drinking, no compromises. I would follow him everywhere, I would never let him out of my sight. Then he called and said it was back, and my first instinct was to abandon him."

"But look where you are now," said Becka. "Look at what you're doing now."

The two of them sat inside the lobby of a police department in western New Jersey. Behind them on the wall the authorities had posted profiles of wanted fugitives. Even in a sleepy town like Oldwick, the police station was a depot of the wayward and the deviant.

He had called Jane three times, once from a motel in Newark, once from a pay phone in Chatham, and then once from Potterstown, nearly fifty miles away. They learned these town names by taking down the area codes from caller ID and looking them up on the Internet. Eight days had passed since his last call.

"What does he say when he calls?" Becka had asked.

"Not a whole lot that's coherent," her mother replied.

The rides out to New Jersey reminded Becka of the ones she took as a kid. Except now her mother was going ninety miles an hour and they had no idea of a final destination. They just got in the car and drove, wandering around New Jersey, aimless and on edge, their eyes everywhere but on the road. Usually, as now, they ended up at one of the police stations.

An officer came out to talk to them. He took the flyer with Tim's picture and all of Jane's information and then he assured them that if anyone from the Oldwick police department ran into him, they'd contact her right away. She and Becka walked out into the start of another long night inching toward winter.

On the interstate Becka's eyes moved back and forth from the median to the side of the road, squinting for her dad through the gloaming. She gazed up underpass ramps and turned her head to peer back at the concrete pylons. She saw nothing up the exits and no human shape or color among the clusters of trees. He was nowhere. Or he was standing right at the point she had just turned away from an instant earlier. She felt the deep deficit of not being omniscient and the insecurity of human limitations that a time of crisis lays bare. They'd never find him. They had already passed him. He was standing in front of them mile after mile but they were too blind and frantic to see.

She let her eyes drift from outside the car to her mother, who was holding herself together, all things considered. Her mother's eyes were also moving from road to median to rearview mirror. Becka had her hand on the parking brake between them, and for an instant she had a familiar urge to yank it up with everything she had. They would then skid safely to a stop and take a big collective sigh and turn to each other and abruptly burst into laughter. Then her mom would undo the brake and drive them home. They would eat together somewhere in the Village and Becka would finally open up about all the boys she had had crushes on since the third grade, all the secrets and vulnerabilities that she had kept from her mom first and foremost, for some obscure reason, and her mom would be able to share a bottle of wine with her without consequence. They would embrace outside the subway station before Becka went back to her apartment in Brooklyn, where she worked as a bartender and played in a band. Once a week they would get together to do something like that, and their conversation would never, or almost never, touch upon her father, whom she had known only as either absence or sickness. They might mention him in passing with some sadness or toast him in memoriam on his birthday. They would not talk about the nights they each spent alone in their separate beds, sobbing for a memory or simply staring blankly in the dark, wondering why and never receiving an answer.

The phone began to ring on the windowsill, where Jane had not intended to leave it. She leapt up from the sofa and studied the caller ID. She glanced away, defeated. Becka listened as her mom told the party on the other end to call the main office, she wasn't showing at the moment. She had to repeat herself. "I said call the main office," said Jane. "The main office!" She paused. *"Then look it up in the fucking phone book!"*

She stabbed the phone long and hard and it issued a discordant tone change, a small chaotic noise. She walked back to the sofa.

Becka had a feeling that he wasn't coming home. She didn't know how she knew this. It was an intuition brought on by the memory of the misery he suffered strapped to the hospital bed and a certainty that he would not willingly repeat it.

"Are you prepared for him not to come home?" she asked.

"He has to come home," Jane said. "What other option is there?"

She told Becka about the man who had tried to rape him behind the grocery store in Newark. "It's not safe. There's only one place for him."

The phone rang again. Jane answered and turned to Becka, nodding. It was him. "He won't stop talking," she said. She listened awhile longer. "I can't make sense of it."

"Tell him I'm here. Tell him I want to know where he is."

"Tim? Tim, Becka's here. She wants to know where you are."

She could hear her dad's voice, muffled inside the phone, breathlessly spilling out word after word as her mom's face grew increasingly blank. She looked at Becka and shook her head almost imperceptibly. "This is what I mean," she said, and handed the phone to Becka.

"Dad?"

"—cruel, and dumb. Like those idiot kids from the high school, you see them in the movie theater, you can't understand their speech. You don't know, maybe they're going to follow you out into the parking lot and jump on your car and then pummel you to death with a baseball bat. He doesn't know reason—"

"Dad—"

"What sort of life is that? He belongs in an institution, but what institution would have him? There's nothing specially designed, there's no expert on hand. Oh, I know, they're all experts, we're nothing but a country of experts. But this one? This one's an idiot. So treat him like an idiot. I don't just mean restrain him. I mean subdue him, electrify him. Electrify him at the highest voltages, and beat him, they should beat him with batons, they should withhold food from him, starve him into submission, starve him within an inch of his life. They really should just abandon the hope of reform and work on him and work on him like cult leaders do, you know, like how political torturers do, really work him down until there is nothing left, he will never walk again, there is just a mad little smile maybe, maybe every once in a while he opens his eyes or remembers a little bit of song... *news guy wept and told us... earth was really dying... cried so much his face was wet*—I'd be happy with that," he said, and then the phone went dead.

4

You go on and on. Your one note gets repetitive, it's taxing. The crying, the lowing, the constant me me me. Do you know what you're missing? The color of birds, a vibrant spectrum. The moon. The, the... a lot, let's just say you're missing a lot. Some very interesting people, opening their eyes to the wonder

of the world, responded by taking voyages across the ocean, setting up easels on mountaintops. You, on the other hand, you
hum. You vibrate with cold pain. You moan dumbly of want and
complaint. Your steady low register, it would have driven them
mad. They would have jumped overboard if their souls had been
saddled with you.

"You are a hominid," Tim said out loud.

Food!

Thunder was rattling in the distance and the lightning cut a
vein of silver across a cloudy opaline sky.

"You have walked backward three million years. You are a
branch of ancestors fallen extinct."

Food! replied the other mutely.

"Food!" Tim cried out above the thunder.

People packing up their trunks and returning their carts
stopped to look.

Food food food! the other howled.

"FOOD FOOD FOOD FOOD FOOD!" cried Tim.

And within the minute they had walked the rest of the way
through the parking lot of the supermarket.

He waited out by the pine tree under the eerie light of dawn.
When the Dunkin' Donuts opened he walked across the street
and brought back a dozen doughnuts and set them on the ground
and ate them by the pine tree. The other stopped saying food,
food, and started saying leg, leg—but he continued to eat the
doughnuts and ignored him. One by one the bankers showed up
and filed into the bank. He crawled out from under the pine tree
and went inside. He was tightening his belt in the lobby when a
woman came forward and greeted him. He told her he needed

to reallocate some funds and maybe establish a trust. He really didn't want to deal with the belt anymore. The far notch was too tight but the near notch was not tight enough. The woman stared at him while he debated which notch. He finally settled on the near one.

He noticed an urn of coffee on a nearby table. He walked over and poured himself a cup and sat down on a padded chair with his legs outstretched. Contentment should have buffered him all around but the other kept moaning leg, leg—so eventually he pulled up the cuff of his chinos and looked at the leg. Something had torn right through. The cut was deep and clean, from shinbone to calf. He had no memory of it happening. Blood had dried down the leg. One of the bankers approached. The banker watched him, dressed in a soiled T-shirt and ripped chinos, peel the blood-stiffened sock from his skin. He looked up and saw the banker watching and clapped his hands on his knees and said, "I need to reallocate some funds and maybe establish a trust."

"It looks like you might need stitches," said the banker.

"I might go to the drugstore later," he said. "Get some analgesics."

When the banker took him back and accessed his portfolio with the various websites and passwords he'd been given, he saw an inordinate amount of money diversified across a wide spectrum of investment vehicles. This caused him to turn away from his computer screen and stare at the man across from him. His foot was perched on the edge of the desk and he was picking dried blood from his leg and collecting the flakes in the palm of his hand. The banker fished the garbage pail out from under the desk. "Do you need this?" he asked. Tim pocketed the flakes of dried blood as if they were so many nickels and dimes and settled back in the chair and looked past the banker. The banker returned the pail to his desk.

"Are those your diplomas on the wall?" he asked.

The banker turned to the wall and said they were.

"They'll come down someday," he told the banker.

When he finished banking, he walked out into a cold and still afternoon under solid ashen clouds. Cold pricked the insides of his nostrils. He wandered through a parking lot and then followed the exiting cars to the road where he walked along the curb to an intersection of three competing drugstores. He patronized the closest one. In the middle of the store he found a rack of sweatshirts. Among them was one of orange cotton with an iron-on decal of a cornucopia spilling forth with vegetables and rich with autumnal colors. It said Happy Thanksgiving. He bought it. He also bought some rope, a steak knife and a box of cookies. He threw his old belt away behind the drugstore, where his breath blew white, and with the knife fashioned a new one out of the rope.

He circled a downtown rotary. He fell asleep in the city square. In the morning he woke up to a young man squatting a foot away. The young man wore a blue polo with an official insignia visible between the flaps of an unzipped down jacket. He held a small cardboard box with a cardboard handle and fruit emblazoned on the sides. He had been trying to wake him without violating one of the first rules of training: *never touch the Client.* Sometimes the Client had bloodshot alcoholic slits for eyes and took a minute to orient himself, *in certain extreme situations, like the victim of a car crash.*

Tim clambered to a sitting position and leaned back against the gray stone of the city building.

"Good morning," said the young man. "Would you like some lunch?"

He offered him the cardboard box. When he made no move to take it, the young man said, "I'm going to leave it here," and set the lunch box just outside the perimeter of a circle of pigeon waste. "It has enough calories to keep you going for twenty-four hours." He continued to squat. "It's cold out here, you know," he said. "You're going to need more than just that sweatshirt."

"Fuck him," he replied.

The young man looked around, but there was no one else there. Finally he stood and walked away.

"Hey!"

The young man turned. The Client was holding the lunch box. "You have me confused with someone interested. Come back here and get this."

The young man returned. *If the Client refuses to accept the offered meal, gently encourage him to reconsider, while maintaining the appropriate distance. Do not insist if he continues to refuse. Always remain courteous.*

"Are you sure you don't want it?"

"The makers of our Constitution," he replied, "undertook to secure conditions favorable to the pursuit of happiness, conferring, as against the Government, the right to be left alone—the most comprehensive of rights, and the right most valued by civilized man."

The young man looked at him. "I'm not with the government," he said. "I'm with Food Bank America."

The lunch box remained suspended in the air between them. The young man took it and walked away.

Then the other started to howl with a kind of primal senescence. The pitch rose above Tim's pride and forced him to call the young man back a second time. He took the lunch box and, in exchange, offered him a hundred-dollar bill out of his wallet. The money was a condition for taking the food, which the confused young man, more than surprised by the amount in the Client's possession, finally agreed to accept, after much protest, as a donation to the cause.

On the state highway, drivers came around the bend erratic and unmindful. These were roads no one expected a pedestrian to walk down. The electricity poles all had a lean to them. A carload of teenagers passed by honking as if he were a night at the prom.

Clouds of broken granite covered the sky. He passed the Village Dodge and the Wonderland Farms Storage. He walked past rain-bleached boxes of cigarettes and what might have been the carapace of a sea turtle. He didn't believe he was anywhere near the ocean.

He stood at the customer-service desk of a Barnes and Noble waiting for the woman at the computer to free up. In the meantime he bent to a knee and gingerly untied his shoestring, which had been double-knotted and made tight by water. The blisters of frostbite on his fingertips and the lost sensation in his hands made the action crude and slow. He pulled off the wet sock and saw that his remaining toes were also blistered and his foot was as white as the pallor of his hands. Removing the shoe momentarily eased the pulsating swelling caused by so much walking. His feet were like two engorged and squishy hearts.

He rolled up the cuff of his chinos to inspect the cut on his leg. There was weeping from the abscess. A halo of soft pink tissue surrounded it. The calf had ballooned. He had been confusing its stench for the MasterCard T-shirt. He removed dirt with his fingernail—not dirt, it turned out, but a trapped bug.

"Can I help you?" asked the woman.

He sprung up. "I'm looking for a book on birds."

"Any particular title?"

"Something I can use to identify them in the wild."

Name a bird and master the world. Reveal nature's mystery and momentarily triumph over it. The fleeting containment within the mind of spotted flight, which has no name until you give it one. That was something the other could never do. He should buy a book on butterflies and trees, too. Trees would include flowers and shrubbery.

The woman stepped away from the help desk and quickly started on her way to Nature. He walked behind her with his cuff still rolled, holding his sock and shoe. It was only when she arrived at the section and turned to look at him that she saw his exposed leg, swollen like a goiter in the middle of the calf.

"Oh my God," she said.

He read books on birding in the café. He warmed himself with cups of coffee and replenished on the baked goods under the display case. Then he was forced to move as quickly as possible through the store to the men's room, where he remained a long time. A manager came in and said generally, "Is everyone okay in here?"

Eventually he reemerged. They asked if he needed an ambulance and he asked what for. He bought one of the birding books and left the store. When his walk started later that evening, he abandoned the book first thing.

Hands and feet are cold. Leg is hurting. Stomach is empty and would like some food.

He was assailed night and day by such complaints. They were crude and unimpeachable. He was accustomed to accommodating his body, so his defiance had to be deliberate, disciplined, as Zen-like as possible.

System is weak in general. Neck stiffness is never good. This dark road is scary.

He had tried to learn bird-watching because the other, despite his ability to detect light and color and movement, was too coarse for such refined activity as the appreciation of beauty and the translation of nature into names. Name a bird and master the world. It would be a victory over brute want and dumb matter.

But brute want was more powerful than he might have guessed. He knew more about case law than he did about bird-watching, so after discarding the burdensome book on birds he started reciting the better bits from famous decisions. The recitation of case law was refinement purely of the mind, many layers of sophistication above what the other could ever hope to achieve.

Fluid balance is essential to proper organ function. A fever indicates the need for medical attention. Would that not be a fine place to stop and rest?

"Law in its most general and comprehensive sense signifies a rule of action," he said, "which is prescribed by some superior and which the inferior is bound to obey."

McDonald's is quick, tasty, and conveniently located. Everyone loves TV. Discharging semen is an unbeatable sensation.

"Liberty lies in the hearts of men and women, and when it dies there, no constitution, no law, no court can save it."

Operations functioning below his reach were sending out distress signals. He ignored them as much as possible. He revolted against the disproportionate power enjoyed by chemical imbalances and shorting neural circuits. He could say the words "autonomic nervous system," whereas the autonomic nervous system just was; therefore he was superior to the autonomic nervous system. He passed the Printing Plus and Pik-Kwik and the Wing Ting. All the driveways in the subdivision had pickups and one had a Corvette. "Corvette," he said.

He climbed partway up the hill behind a Jiffy Lube, closed for the night, where he fell asleep. He woke with his head on the hard earth and for an hour or two listened to the hydraulic thunder of the mechanics' instruments and to the banter of the men at their work.

Good shoes are not simply a luxury. Funny looks from male strangers are unsettling. A change in bowel habits is cause for alarm.

Later, when the day's walk seized him, it was his turn to complain to the other. He passed billboards and stoplights and shopping centers. There were stop signs and rec centers and residential houses. There were train tracks and entrance ramps and signal towers.

"You go on and on about how cold and hungry you are," he said. "The night is long, you say. Good shoes are not just a luxury. But then you're off and there's no appeal. There's no explanation for your behavior and no memory of your complaints. Are you not still cold? Are you not hungry? What is your purpose, your aim, but to hurl us both into suffering and darkness? Speak to me! You destroy my life, you rob me of my will, you troll me

through the streets like meat on a hook. You have laid plain all
my limitations and my total illusion of freedom. To what end?
What do you gain from this?"

The other limped along steadily, saying nothing.

They agreed on one thing. If he wanted to starve the other of
all alimentation, if his only pleasure was a kind of a suicidal
spite, he did a good job with shelter and a so-so one with food,
but he failed every time to resist the call of sleep. When the
other stopped, he could have kept right on walking and driven
him into the ground. He could have drowned himself in a body
of water or thrown himself in front of a car. But he was too
exhausted. The body released him, and then he walked bare-
headed to some hovel, to some dubious sanctuary, where they
collapsed in a harmony of purpose. For a minute, he knew the
meaning of bliss: oblivion. In oblivion, they were at peace.

He came out of the men's room. The man who had been knocking
swung wide to let him pass. He left through the side door where
the drive-thru line had stalled and vomited up his lunch by the
dumpster. He wandered off to a nearby patch of frostbitten grass
between the McDonald's and the Conoco and sat down there and
perspired. The cars out on the road went by in slow motion.

He stopped in front of a display window in a downtown
district recently renovated so as to better highlight its desola-
tion. He stared through the glass of a sporting goods store at
a pitched tent with a forest-green fly-sheet. Accessories surrounded the camp pastoral—a lantern and a canteen and a fire
made of cardboard.

He lay down on a bench and took a nap. The city cop woke him by hitting his billy club against the wood.

"You got identification?" asked the cop.

He sat up slowly. He removed his wallet from the back pocket of his chinos. His insensate fingers made it difficult to remove the license. The cop looked it over and handed it back to him.

"No sleeping here."

"Do you know your right-of-public-access laws?"

The cop looked at him. "You got some place to go, wise guy?"

With a crude and mechanical deliberation he opened the wallet in his lap and removed a crisp sheaf of newly minted hundred-dollar bills and made their edges flop between his fingers. "I can go anywhere I want."

"Then get there," said the cop.

"Your concern for my well-being is touching."

The cop started to walk away.

"One might as well ask if the State, to avoid public unease, could incarcerate all who are physically unattractive or socially eccentric," he called out. "Mere public intolerance or animosity cannot constitutionally justify the deprivation of a person's physical liberty!"

He went back to sleep. When he woke up, he said no, he would not get up, no matter what, not now, no getting up, you are a fleshy weed for plucking. He said you are a feast for worms. You are a carping and hidebound bitch with your fevers and limps and predictable appetites.

Deficiency of copper causes anemia, just so you know. Which at this point is way down there on the list of concerns.

"A stench, a rotgut, a boil," he retorted aloud, rising again on the bench. A woman stood nearby walking her dog. When his voice rose up she tugged at the leash to get the sniffing dog going again. "A gaseous blowhole. You are a blind clutch and claw. Go off. Go off and leave me alone."

Can't.

"You hang on the wheel of fortune. I rise upward on angel's wings. You turn in the gyre. I dream of old lovers with youthful smiles."

Sorry, pal, we're in this together.

"Prove it!" he cried.

What is a wing? What is a smile?

"You can't be smart," he said. "Only I can be smart."

I'm evolving, replied the other.

A crane and a tractor and a few smaller excavating vehicles sat as still as a display of dinosaurs in the man-made pit behind the convenience store. He took the access road down and sat in the cabin of the tractor as he ate a pair of hot dogs. He was able to keep them down, which he attributed to the other's shrewd calculation for what nourishment a walk would require. "You are a wily cunt," he said.

On the road that led out of town, a blackbird fell out of the sky. A second bird hit the shoulder and a third one landed in the far lane, followed by the rest of the flock. They hit with heavy thuds one after the other and lay scattered like jacks on the road. Then darkness fell and he was walking again.

He skirted the edge of a copse of trees that had been corralled at their trunks by orange plastic fencing and climbed the bluff that rose over the highway and traversed that weedy expanse that offered no purpose to commerce or settlement but a clear border. When he came down he diverted away from the highway into a neighborhood of half-finished Tudor-style homes on acre plots with dumpsters in the streets full of broken Sheetrock and mounds of rose-hued stone gravel in the driveways that with their air of thwarted expectancy accentuated the abandonment of the stillborn development. The freezing rain had soaked through his cornucopia sweatshirt and made it stiff. He was chattering and perspiring and raging like the fierce storm itself at the wrongs he had suffered at the hands of the other. His threats and accusations echoed in the ghost town as the icy pellets rained down white and round as balls of salt and soon he was gone from there, and the rooftops and windows froze over with a second skin of glass, and the trees and shrubbery looked part of some crystal city.

He was under the eaves of the highway oasis when the man with the garbage bag approached. It was a black industrial-strength garbage bag so old that its pale stretch marks had started to give way to holes, especially at the gathered neck, where the man gripped it to carry it over his shoulder. He set it down and then sat next to Tim on the stone bench.

"Why your fingers like that?" asked the man.

Tim was holding his hands in his lap. His curled and rigid fingers faced upward. The blisters had disappeared and much of the surface area had turned a dark purple that faded at the tips to pitch-black. He looked down at them. They resembled a carrion bird's claws set by rigor mortis.

"He's a wily cunt."

"Who? You frien'?"

"He's no friend of mine."

"You ain't got no frien'?"

He shook his head. They sat quietly. "You got the poison?" asked the man.

The question lingered between them.

"The poison?"

The man stared at him. Eventually he nodded.

"You be all right," said the man, who looked off in the low visibility. People stood at the rear of their cars, filling them up at the Mobil station.

Before he stood again, the man said, "You oughta be thinking about getting yourself over to the shelter clinic on McAdams. Have the volunteer man check you out."

Out on the old highway a man driving home steered his clattering pickup over to the shoulder. He pulled in twenty yards ahead of Tim and spoke to him through the passenger-side window when he caught up to the truck. The belly-white clouds foretold the coming blizzard.

"You look like you're hurt," said the man. "Do you need some help?"

He stopped before the window. He felt the hot blasts from the vents. They stung his benumbed skin and he took a step back.

"You have a bad limp there," the man continued. "Are you a veteran?"

He didn't reply.

"I was Third Battalion, Ninth Marines, in the first Gulf War," said the man. "Now I help run a place, it's kind of a safe haven for us. We feed everybody, everybody gets a place to sleep."

"Do you have the poison?"

"The poison?" said the man.

He stared at him through the open window.

"I've never heard it referred to that way," said the man. "I suppose I do, even if they tell me I don't."

He opened the car door and stepped inside the truck.

"Will you do me a favor," the man asked, before he could put the car in drive, "and roll up your window for me?" He did as he was told. The man looked at his clawed grip crudely manning the handle as his stench grew strong in the cab. "Jesus Christ." The man opened the driver's-side door and stepped out. "I'm sorry," he said, with the door hanging open. "I don't mean to be rude. There's just a smell."

"That's my leg," he replied. He delicately rolled up his chinos to show the man.

"Hey," he said. "Hey, you have to get to a hospital."

He stepped out of the truck just as the man, who quickly began to roll down his window to let the air in before stepping back inside, got behind the wheel again.

"No way," he said, standing again on the shoulder of the highway. "No hospitals."

"Hey, I understand," said the man. "A hospital is not my favorite place, either. But that infection, that could kill you."

He shut the door. "No hospitals," he said through the window.

"But you're in danger."

"Nobody asked you to stop for me," he said.

Eventually he made it to the grounds of the local high school where he passed out on the baseball diamond behind home plate. He swooned in and out. He was awake for the first of the snow. He found the strength to remove his clothes so that he sat under the winter sky in nothing but boxer shorts, feeling the evaporating sizzle of the billowing flakes along his fevered body. He was euphoric with the certainty of physical death. The other had gone completely quiet. No more complaints of hunger or the cold. He had no memory of the last time it had managed to keep anything down. He was winning. He had never given much thought to heaven before, but now he was certain it existed. Without God, the body won, and that couldn't be possible. He was one thing, his body a different thing altogether, and he was willing a separation, in which he went off to eternal repair while it suffered its due fate of rough handling, dirt, and rot.

Then he was made to stand and walk.

As the wind picked up and the snow grew frenzied he entered a small town. He walked barefoot and near-naked on the side of the road, his belly distended and his leg dragging along. No one can see me, no one would stop me, no one could help me anyway. They would just call the _____ but it would be too late. My only regret is _____. She'd have the coffee on. There was a time during my search for a cure when I tried everything to stop walking including giving up _____. The smell filled the _____. I loved to drink a _____ of _____ in the _____, to say _____ to _____ after we'd spent another _____ together. I'd tell her now it's going okay except for the poison. It's going okay except for how much I miss her and _____. _____?

_____?! I've never been a very good _____.

He came up a final hill alongside a street opposite a multi-level parking lot and a courtyard with a fountain and a few other professional buildings. He wondered where he would end up, in what outpost of trees or behind what building, inside what unused doorway or, if he was lucky, what unlocked bathroom or backseat, his final resting place. But then the other let go of its mineral grip and he saw the doors part before him.

He went down on his knees on the rubber mat. "You son of a bitch! You can't change the rules."

The nurse saw him and started from behind the station.

"He changed the rules!" he cried, as an emergency crew came forward.

You didn't really think I would let you kill us, did you?

He was lacking identification and admitted to the ICU under the name Richard Doe. He had renal failure, an enlarged spleen, sepsis-induced hypotension, cellular damage to the heart. He had trench foot and a case of dysentery. He required assisted breathing and intravenous antibiotics. He did not wake day or night.

The other made him say things. "Oof!" was one of them, "aaa, aaa" another. They entered into the type of interminable conversations that often break out in fevered dreams.

Q: What did you do for a living?

A: I was a _____.

Q: "Lawyer"?

A: Yes, that's it. Is this an interrogation?

Q: A simple word, "lawyer." Why can't you remember it?

A: Intelligence has its limits. Knowledge cannot determine in its entirety the measure of a man's _____.

Q: His what?

A: You know, his _____.

Q: "Soul"?

A: That's it, soul, yes.

Q: You believe in the soul now?

A: I do.

Q: I wasn't aware you gave any thought to such things.

A: I haven't, typically.

Q: Then what accounts for your sudden mystical impulse?

A: Without God, you win.

He didn't think the taunting was fair, but then the other had proven it didn't play fair. But how was it feasible? The other had co-opted his powers of recall and discourse. In his former life as a lawyer, the stress of an upcoming trial would cause him to dream of cross-examining expert witnesses on technical matters about which he knew nothing—handwriting analysis, abstruse accounting methods. The author of such dreams, he played both parts, interrogator and expert, but he knew only the interrogator's questions. When it came time for answers, he listened as the expert whom he had conjured conveniently mumbled, or spoke too softly, or omitted entire words.

It was like that now, only the other was the interrogator and he the muttering subject of its dream.

He was hooked to machines and monitors. He heard their pulse and suspiration, the steady mechanical beep of his heart. He realized that the other was content simply to lie there, to let the drips and antibiotics work their magic. He wasn't going to walk, the son of a bitch. The wily cunt wasn't going to walk. The wily cunt had been made to suffer and brought close to death and then he changed the rules. It wasn't fair. Tim tried to tear himself free. In so doing he learned how many fingers and parts of fingers he had lost. He was too weak to pull out a single IV and fell unconscious again.

Q: Are you aware that you can be made to forget words, if certain neurons are suppressed from firing?

A: Certain what?

Q: And that by suppressing the firing of others, you can be made
to forget what words mean entirely? Like the word *Jane,* for
instance.

A: Which?

Q: And do you know that if I do *this* —

[inaudible]

A: Oof!

Q: —you will flatline? And if I do this—

[inaudible]

A: Aaa, aaa...

Q: —you will cease flatlining? Do you really want to confuse
that for God's work?

He woke again, unable to move. He saw a man peering in
at him from the doorway. Was the man smiling? Just before
losing consciousness, he watched in horror as the man came
forward—unmistakably the same man he had encountered on
the bridge. The man was approaching and there was nothing
he could do, no defense possible, he was utterly paralyzed and
his eyes were closing. He was trapped inside. The paralysis was
worse than movement. He wanted to call out, but his throat was
plugged. The man stepped to the bed. Wake up! he cried to
himself. Tears leaked out from his closed eyes.

The next time he woke he found the strength to tear the lines
out of his veins and the tube from his throat. Alarms began to
sound. He slowly climbed out of bed, which kept pulling him
back in, as if he were in a gravel pit struggling to get a purchase
on the collapsing rock. A nurse caught him at the doorway as

he was leaving the room. He tried to scream but his vocal cords were out of commission and all he could produce was a long hoarse cry. "He's tormenting me! He's tormenting—"

He collapsed in the doorway, where he had another seizure. He shook on the floor with an animal gaze. His contorted mouth spat foam. The nurse came around quickly to cup the back of his head with her hands.

He was docile when the orderlies returned him to bed.

Q: If I can make you forget words, make you flatline, make you see things and seize up—

A: Oof! Oof! Oof! Oof!

Q: —is that not all the evidence you need that I control your fate, and that my fate is your only future? Why turn for comfort toward the fanciful conceit of corrupt men and frightened old ladies?

A: Aaa, aaa...

Q: It's just you and me, pal. Forget God. Act like a man. It's what we are.

He broke free every time he woke, so finally they strapped him down by the wrists and ankles, which made him thrash and weep and cry out without sound because hell was a bed, hell was a bed, while life, down the corridor and through the door, was out there—life and death both, it didn't matter which.

He raged when the tube was removed and his voice healed. He refused to tell them his name or the whereabouts of his family. He spoke of hallucinations and visions. He said he had the voice of the devil in his head. He disrupted the peace of other patients and hurled curses at the frightened staff. They transferred him to the psych ward, diagnosed him with paranoia and schizophrenia, and started him on a cocktail of antipsychotic medications.

They continued to ask him his name.

"Who are you?"

"Depends on what you mean by 'you,'" he said.

"Do you have family? Wouldn't they like to know where you are?"

"I never told her how sorry I was for the life I led her into. I had hoped to start over with the new apartment. Now I'm trying something different."

"Which is what?"

"I don't call home anymore."

"Where is home for you?"

"Home is where the heart is, right here." He pointed to his chest. "I go where he goes, and he doesn't give me much say in the matter."

The medication began taking effect and they no longer needed to restrain him. Still he snuck out of bed and wandered the hospital corridors asking patients if they had the poison. Some engaged him and others thought he was crazy. Some seemed to know exactly what he was talking about.

"I been getting help from the twelve-strand Orion healing technique. You tried that?"

"And they wanna call it a fascinoma."

"They keep threatening to cut me off."

"The whole family been eccentric with mental problems all along."

"Let me show you my scans."

"We need to discuss the voices you've been hearing."

"Voice," he said. "Not voices. Voice."

"Sorry, voice."

"And it isn't a voice. It's a point of view."

"A point of view?"

"A bleak and uninspired one, but convincing. Very evolved. He gains control of my powers—rhetorical, argumentative. Don't ask me how. There should be docket numbers to our conversations."

"Is the voice still there, louder, fainter?"

"Fainter. He makes it known when he's angry or wants something, but it's quieted down since you patched me up."

"That's good."

"Don't be fooled. He's just lying in wait."

"But if you keep taking the medication, there should be no problem."

"Pharmacology is only one tactical maneuver in a protracted war."

"What war is that?"

"The one we've been fighting for centuries. The one we've always lost, so far as anyone can tell."

"Sorry, I'm not sure I understand."

"Death. The will to live versus inevitable decay. What's not to understand?"

"Were you trying to kill yourself?"

"Depends on what you mean by 'yourself,'" he said.

He resumed eating voluntarily. He got up and voided himself of his own accord. He was quiet in the evenings. They gave him donated winter clothes and released him.

He walked out in a gray hunter's cap with fur brim and earflaps, a winter jacket. He stood just beyond the automatic doors where he had fallen to his knees almost two months earlier. He was trying to decide whether to go right or left, his breath visible in the cold. He had no impulse to undress and wander off into the winter. Ascension through annihilation wasn't his immediate concern. The other was happy. The other liked the warmth, felt a little hungry. He knew his first task was to get his personal details in order—to call a private banker he knew in New York, who'd help him restore his identification and credit cards. He had these clerical impulses. The good hospital staff had restored him to the land of the pragmatic. In his pocket sat several prescriptions, some of which he even thought worth filling. Pharmacology was a legitimate tactical advantage. Eventually, he decided to turn right.

She let go the second she heard his voice and for the first minute of the call she cried with an abandon that he, on the other end, did not entirely comprehend. "Oh," she said. He listened to her let out a heavy sigh in sobbing degrees. "Oh, Tim."

"I'm not dead," he said. "But I do have to take medicine."

"Oh," she said again. "I've been so…" She tried to collect herself. "Tell me where you are and I'll pick you up."

"But there's one I just don't take because it's probably better to be dead than to go around feeling like that, all zombie you know, just totally whacked out and exhausted and who gives a fuck you can't even think—I have two like that, actually—"

"Where are you, Tim? Please tell me."

"—but the second is for the seizures and I probably shouldn't, I don't know—"

"Seizures?"

"Probably shouldn't give that one up, I guess, even though I haven't had one since I was in the hospital so maybe they're gone now. I wouldn't put it past him to make something just—poof!—you know, disappear. He makes his own rules and what the fuck am I supposed to do if they keep shifting? It's like I told the doctors. Medicine can secure a base here and there but there will always be a battle going on somewhere else."

"Tim, please tell me, please tell me where you are," she said.

"I try not to pay attention and I do a pretty good job, too, when you consider how demanding he is, like I'm torturing *him*, you know, like I've taken *him* captive. For a while there we were trading retaliations in a zero-sum game. The chain of command was in constant flux. I thought I was winning but he changed the rules on me and that's when he got the upper hand, when I went down, and that lasted for, I don't know. I was under maybe three weeks?"

"Under?"

"Three weeks of torment. I was defenseless. He just had the run of me. He doesn't think much about God. I've come around on that matter. I believe in God now. Isn't that something?"

"Tim, please listen to me. I want to say something to you."

"Do you remember that doctor one time, he told us about the blood-brain barrier? Now, that's a distinction. On the one hand you've got the blood, just dumb as a train full of rocks, important rocks but dumb dumb dumb, and on the other hand the brain, which is where, you know, the me and the you, where the me and the you come from, and with this barrier in place, you keep the bastard *out,* you see. Integrity is maintained. There's a beautiful sanctity, when you think about it, a really holy and reverent sanctity that keeps the pure godlike parts from mixing with the rank and baser stuff, the rot, the decay, the blood, the rocks. That's where the real armies of God are, right there on that blood-brain barrier, doing God's work. I mean, that is the real frontline in the battle between the two—"

"What two?"

"The body and the soul. The blood-brain barrier and the synapses are the two main fronts. You've got both sides fighting for control of the dendrites and the axons and what all else I don't know."

"I don't understand, Tim, I don't understand."

"But he still finds ways to break through, even when I'm taking the medication. He commandeers my mind. That's my theory, anyway. Have you started drinking again?"

She was silent. "If I said yes," she said, "would you come home?"

He didn't reply.

"Tim, listen to me. Are you listening?"

He continued to say nothing.

"Scrub Island," she said.

He was quiet.

"You know what that is," she said. "Scrub Island. You remember Scrub Island?"

"Don't drink," he said. "Okay?"

"The little girl in the wedding dress," she said. "The ostriches and the man herding them with the bullwhip. I know you remember Scrub Island."

He stayed silent, holding the phone with one hand and the

cord in the other, staring down at his high-tops gone brandless with grime.

"Tell me where you are," she said, "and I'll pick you up."

"I have to go now," he said. "Don't drink."

He hung up and walked from the pay phone to the dining hall, situated in the church basement. The tables were laid with yellow plastic tablecloths. A faint odor of steamed food, bland and heavy, drifted across the room. Those eating wore their winter coats while the volunteers manning the deep basins of food behind the main table wore white aprons. He got himself a set of plastic silverware bundled in a napkin and a Styrofoam plate of food and sat down and ate his dinner as best he could.

5

I respected you more when you were indifferent to God. You were beset by matters of urgency in your life that took precedence over the lofty speculation of divinity students and men in pews on Sundays. You didn't have the time. You didn't make it a priority. You formed your notions on the fly, in flashes of grim insight, in brief feelings of certainty that consumed you entirely and then quickly faded into the background. When you die, you thought, you die. Why linger on that unpalatable truth? And the alternative, the alternative was a sham. You hated the institutions and the corruptions and the hypocrisies and the evils. You thought it was all a racket designed by the mighty to fleece the weak and keep them in check. The existence of the numinous, the mystical, the godhead itself—who knows? Maybe. But what evidence was there? You had been chiseled by reason to a diamond point. You were deferential to logic and evidence, skeptical of specious oratory, an enemy of hearsay. At best, you put the possibility in abeyance, knowing that even when one of your cases went to trial, when every detail was presented and picked over, every side aired and attacked and defended, there was slippage, lacunae, things no one would ever know. God was like that. God was a trial. But if pressed you sided with the disbelievers and sometimes you even showed contempt for those who spoke with the conviction of the weak and the credulous. You had that luxury. You stood outside of the wind and the rain. Your insights and arguments came to you in prosperity. Death was far off. You could afford to be leisurely. A drink was better than a thought. A meal was better than a conviction. Your family and your work were more meaningful to you than the ministrations of a hundred gods. That is, until you caved.

He approached the pharmacist at the drop-off window and handed her a number of prescriptions. She inspected them.

"These are all from out of state," she said, handing them back.

"What does that mean?"

"They have to come from an in-state doctor."

He looked over the writing on the prescriptions. Apparently he wasn't in Missouri anymore.

"I really need these," he said. "It's getting bad."

"I'm sorry," she said, "it's state law. You have to get them from a doctor here."

He took the prescriptions and walked back through the drugstore and out into the cold.

The rooftops and the rooms disappeared, and you caved. O weak thing called the spirit! O untested man! Nature proved itself to be indifferent on the mildest days, dependably vicious and antagonistic on all others. That this came as a surprise to you reveals the narrowness of your imagination and the naiveté that characterized every matter—

"You shut up."

—of so-called life and death. You made your steadfast convictions cradled in a swivel chair. Now you've shown yourself vulnerable to sentimentality. Your "belief" is no moral law or cohesive thought or even a beautiful speculation. It's a desperate search for comfort and has nothing to do with goodness, truth or beauty. You've simply weakened to the primordial fears that shook your superstitious forebears to the bones and convinced them to incant in extinct languages and drain their daughters of blood. For all your higher plane and beloved evolution, you now quiver in the same gradations of faith and testament, and your appeal is no less shrill. You want the old comforts and narratives—

"Shut up!"

—the folk mass and evensong—

"SHUT UP! SHUT UP!!"

—the great words repeated in the dark and over the heads of newborns and the bodies of the dead. Indulgent, happy to compromise, eager to see it all in a different light, in a finer and more noble and prettier light, the best light of man, the beacon and the hope. But that's just food—

"Food!" he cried aloud.

—just food. The verdict arrives in doses, century after century, and looks increasingly grim. The world is too old. The soul is the mind is the brain is the body. I am you and you are it and it will always win.

6

He laid out before him his morning's work. He uncapped his pen and folded back the legal pad to a clean sheet and began to write. Outside, the sun was baking the world. He didn't like his new office or the view that came with it and assumed they gave it to him to keep him out of sight from clients who might notice the bottles of prescription medication on his desk, or his missing fingers. One hand, with thumb and pinkie still intact, was fixed in a permanent expression of *hang loose, dude;* the other, with only the middle and ring fingers, looked like a roadside cactus. As for the medication, he had no choice in the matter: they refused to give him a desk with drawers. These systematic downgrades, which he suffered after every leave of absence, were humiliating. He usually forgot about them once he was lost in the writing. To be lost in the writing was to be absorbed, and to be absorbed was to lose awareness of everything—the shitty view and the third-class furniture, but also, and here was the paradox, even the contentment. To be lost in the writing was to be happy, but it required giving up any awareness of that happiness, of any awareness whatsoever, and so he was blissfully unaware—until the secretary came by and in calling him to awareness made him unhappy again.

"I don't need anything right now, thank you," he said. He made a kind of karate chop over the desk with his hang-loose hand. He couldn't look her in the eye, he was so annoyed. "I'll let you know if I do. Thank you."

She departed. He was given ten minutes of peace and quiet and then, sure enough, she reappeared. He had once argued during a partner caucus that secretaries were relics of an earlier era. You wanted something done right, you asked a paralegal to do it. Secretaries should be phased out. But too many partners treasured and coddled their secretaries, so he had to continue to suffer their anxious interruptions, their quivering attempts to justify their salaries. He realized he was going to have to give her something to do.

"May I have some coffee?" he asked. "Can you just bring me a cup of coffee?"

She had anticipated him. Her name was Ella, and she was coarse with premature age. He did not think, with those knees, she should be wearing a skirt. She began to pour the coffee into a cup on his desk. The coffee steamed upward and, almost against his will, he was momentarily grateful. It was a nice thing to have, a fresh cup of coffee, even in the summer. Never something to take for granted. As she poured, he pulled out his wallet with his cactus hand and using the middle and ring fingers removed a hundred-dollar bill, which he pressed into her free hand. She looked at the crumpled bill.

"What's this for?"

"An hour," he said. "An hour to work in peace, no interruptions, no inquiries. Surf the Internet, take a long lunch, talk to your kid on the phone. Whatever—for one hour."

She pocketed the hundred. "Sure," she said. "I'll surf the Internet." She shambled away.

Glare penetrated the window as cars went by. Semis with heavy loads rattled the plate glass. He kept his head down and slowly worked himself, word by word, back into communion with the other hours, days, years—there was in fact no name for this particular unit of time—that together formed a continuum of unawareness that was as close to transcendence as he would come. He was working himself, as if with a spade in a tunnel that finally yields to light, out of the physical world. Rested, at ease, contented by the coffee, the other had no complaints. He would get hungry soon, but with cunning, careful focus, Tim might have another hour to himself.

But before that hour was out, someone knocked gently on one corner of the desk. It was a visitor, and he had not had a visitor in a long time.

"Hi, Tim."

Fritz's tie was loosely knotted and his sleeves rolled up. He had dragged in with him a measure of the heat. "May I sit down?" he asked.

"Fritz?" He began to collect the work laid out before him into tidy piles. "Did we have an appointment? What the hell time was our appointment?"

Fritz climbed in across from him. "We didn't have an appointment," he said.

"Well, that's okay, hell. I'm just writing a brief. When I'm not being interrupted."

"Am I interrupting?"

"No, no, it's not you."

"Do you know what you want?"

"Not now," he told the secretary.

"Just some coffee," said Fritz.

Tim's hands returned to fussing with the loose-leaf paper. His eyes refused to meet Fritz's. Fritz noticed his missing fingers.

"Now's as good a time as ever," he said. "So where are we?"

Fritz looked up from his friend's hands. He hadn't known what to expect, but it wasn't this. "Where are we?" he asked.

"With the man. What progress?"

Fritz looked at him. "Nobody's seen you for months, Tim," he said. "We've been worried about you."

"Busy, you know."

"It took me a long time to find you."

He stopped fussing with his papers and sat up straight. "Now, look. We've been after this guy and after this guy, and while you guys are supposed to be the best, you still haven't found him. And every day we don't find him is another day an innocent man wastes away in that jail cell of his."

"R. H. Hobbs is dead, Tim."

The woman reappeared. Fritz turned his coffee mug over and set it right side up on the lacy paper doily. "Thank you," he said, and the woman departed.

"Do you know how long I've been petitioning to have secretaries phased out of this firm?" he said to Fritz. "What do they do? They fetch coffee. That's it. You want something done, you ask a paralegal. The only thing a secretary can do is fetch coffee, because fetching coffee is beneath a paralegal."

"Tim," said Fritz, "did you hear me? R. H. Hobbs is dead."

"No, he's not."

"He hanged himself in December."

"When did he get out?"

"Out?"

"Of prison. When did he get out of prison?"

"He was serving a life sentence —"

"I know what his goddamn sentence was, goddamn it," he said. "I know what he was serving."

His raised voice caught the attention of the two truckers

sitting at the counter. Ella stood across from them, smoking and staring. One of the truckers turned and said something.

"I'm asking a simple question," said Tim. "When did he get out?"

"I'm afraid he didn't get out," said Fritz.

Tim remembered sitting on the sofa watching TV with Becka when R.H.'s trial began. He was unable to leave the house for some reason. Why was that? He couldn't recall. Uninterrupted doses of *Buffy,* like an IV drip, kept the guilt at bay. After he went into remission, he went to see R.H. in prison. He sat across from him and noticed the gray hair on his arms. He had never really seen him until that day, an aging man in a prison jumpsuit.

"What about the man?"

"What man?"

"The man. The man, Fritz, who I saw on the bridge. And at the baths. At the baths, too, when he attacked me. Where are you with him?"

"We're nowhere."

"Nowhere?"

"It hasn't been an active case for a long time."

"Why did I establish a trust, then?" he cried. "I made a specific provision in the trust for your firm to be paid so that the case would continue."

"It's not a matter of money, Tim. We got the money."

"So what's the problem?"

"I refunded the payments."

Tim leaned back in the booth and looked at Fritz confidently for the first time. "What the hell for?"

"We can't find him," said Fritz, leaning forward over his untouched coffee. "We've looked, Tim. We've looked everywhere. We can't find him."

"So you just quit?"

"It's a cold case, man. I'm sorry. It's been cold for years."

"You can't find one guy, big firm like yours and one guy eludes you, when R.H. is wasting away in his cell."

"R.H. is dead, Tim. R.H. killed himself."

"How hard can it be to find one guy?" he asked. "You found me, didn't you?"

Tim sank down in the booth. His view now included the ill-swept tiled floor and the windowsill scattered with dead flies. Fritz looked at him intently, his elbows on the table, but said nothing.

"So if there's no news for me," said Tim, "why did you stop by?"

Fritz turned briefly to look out at the uneven slope of the parking lot, its potholes and crumbling blacktop. He turned back. Tim's obdurate eyes remained under the table.

"She was worried," he said. "She asked me to find you. She wanted to make sure you were okay."

"She? Who's she?"

Fritz pointed out the window.

"What?" said Tim. "What am I looking at?" He turned back to Fritz with an expression of outrage. "Oh, no, that's unacceptable," he said. "That's totally unacceptable."

"She's your wife," said Fritz.

"I'm working right now, goddamn it. I have work to do."

"She just wants to know you're okay," he said.

She talked briefly to Fritz before going in. Tim kept his eyes focused outside the window as she entered the restaurant and approached him.

She came up close to him and reached out and touched his cheek. He didn't want her to, but he did not move. He tried not to think of how he must look to her. He looked quickly into her eyes but then turned away. He did not want to read the emotion on her face. He did not want to see the particulars of her face again or how they came together to make her beauty. He did not want to know how she had or had not aged or what she wore, if it was something old or something he would not recognize. He did not want to be so close to her that he could smell her perfume. It was that faint but unmistakable scent and her pale eyes and her freckles that announced her inimitable self and called him back to everything he loved about the world.

"You haven't been taking care of yourself," she said. She glanced at the table for a plate that wasn't there. "When did you last eat something?" she asked. "You're too thin." She smoothed down the hair on the back of his head. "Please talk to me," she said. She stayed standing over him as if they had merely just finished eating and while he was collecting the change she was casually showing him affection in the instant before he stood, in the moment before they got back in the car together and returned home. "You need a wash," she said. With patience she picked a nettle from his oily hair, a nettle from a tree he must have brushed past. "Where you've been," she said, shaking her head. Her eyes filled with tears. She finally let her hand fall. "I'm going to sit down," she said. She slid into the booth, opposite him. She wore a light pink blouse of crepe de chine with three-quarter sleeves. The color highlighted the fairness of her skin, that reddish tint that maintained without effort the youthfulness of her face. Her laugh lines and the crow's-feet raying out at the corners of her eyes were an incongruity on that girlish face, like some unfair miscalculation. Her entire presence there was an incongruity. It brightened the dismal fluorescent brutality that such chain places wore like trademarks — unmistakable lighting from the highway, the national color of insomnia and transience. The hard booths were an insufferable yellow.

"Are you not going to talk to me?" she asked.

She reached out for him with both hands. He did not want her to touch his disfigured hands nor did he want to feel her touch, but again he didn't move. He managed only to keep his eyes averted. His apparent indifference might have seemed to come from someone hardened past the point of having his heart moved. With her arms outstretched and her hands covering one of his, her silence grew out into the kind of delicate pause that is called for when the other person is in deep mourning and minor gestures are meant to offer some portion of an unattainable solace.

She looked at his hand in hers. "Your poor fingers," she said.

He heard the quiver in her voice. He pulled away. He placed his hands together under the table, away. Soon he felt the phantom sensation of her hands. The advantages the other had over him, advantages that made hunger gnawing and pain vigilant and a touch from a woman bound up in memories of love more unbearable than all the other ills put together, were insurmountable. The senses were unvanquishable. He despised her for reminding him. There could be no stronger reminder. Hungry? Fuck you, two days without food. Hurting? Too bad, it's your funeral. But Jane. Jane was different. He resided behind armed checkpoints and coils of razor wire and slabs of blast-proof concrete, but her touch was a convoy.

"Becka misses you."

"Please don't talk about her," he said.

She was silent. "I miss you," she said. "Your apartment misses you. Tell me you don't miss it. Tell me you don't miss the muffins I make you. You try to find a muffin like that in here. Try to find one fifty miles in any direction. I don't know how we'll do it, Tim, but we'll do it. And you'll be there when the apartment fills up with the smell of muffins. Haven't we done it in the past? We'll do it better this time. We've learned some things. Tell me you don't miss it."

The ghost smell, triggered by his memory of her sweet baking, made his mouth water and brought on such a strong physical yearning that his body reasserted itself over his mind completely and he had to admit finally that he was not in the city and not at the office. He was in the front booth of a Waffle House on the unnamed borderland between two stagnating townships.

"Tell me you don't miss sitting in front of me in the bath getting your hair washed," she said. "Tell me that isn't a better consolation for your sickness than this."

"I have work to do," he said.

"Tell me it's not a better consolation," she said. "Tell me you don't miss my fingers in your hair. Let me show you."

"No."

"Let me remind you."

"No."

"Tell me," she said, standing and moving with a fluid grace from her side of the booth to his, and lowering her voice so that it entered only his ear, "tell me you don't miss your tongue in my pussy. Tell me you can make any sense of this world without that, without your lips on my pussy, making me come."

Her words shocked him. They started an erection he didn't want. He moved closer to the window to put distance between them.

"Tell me one of us should suffer without the other's help. Tell me you'd let me wander off on my own, forget to eat, forget to bathe, forget the promises we made. I know you think you're doing this for me. I know you think it's saving me by freeing me up to live my life. But that's not living. My life is you."

So much of who he was was involuntary. The watering mouth, the stirring erection, the unbidden burning in his eyes. The only control over the coursing world that he retained in his littleness was his selfless refusal to turn.

"Tell me you don't miss me," she said. "Tell me honestly that this is working out for you, that you've found the best way to live with it, that of all possible solutions, this is the only one, and it doesn't include me—you tell me that, Tim, and I'll go away."

He sat very still, like a sullen boy whose stunted brain lacked the resources to admit error and forsake the lost days for a better way.

With her arms around him, she pulled herself toward him, raising herself up a little on the hard bench so that her chin rested on his shoulder, and she fought her tears to speak as firmly as she had since entering, though he refused to turn to her even an inch.

"I've come a long way to find you," she said, "and it took so much longer than I thought it would, too long, and the wait killed me, but I was patient, because I promised your daughter that I would find you and bring you home, and I promised myself that, too, no matter how you objected or what you said. And if I leave here without you, my heart will break. But if you tell me you don't want me, if you tell me you still have to go it alone, then I will leave you alone."

He sat silent and unmoving. Her chin was against his shoulder. He felt her hot tears.

She felt his reply in the vibrations of his body.

"I don't want you," he said.

She sat next to him for a while, unable to rise right away. Eventually she released him but remained in the booth beside him. Ella and the truckers glanced over at them. Angled away from each other as they were, he and Jane might have seemed enmeshed in some petty domestic squabble. Jane slipped a napkin out from under the silverware and wiped her face. Then she leaned back into Tim, put her arms around him and hugged him, kissed him on the cheek, on the temple, and stood up and left the restaurant.

Her embrace stayed with him. He remained sitting in the same position, unable to move. There was nothing he could do now to reclaim unawareness. He had lost to the other. The rest of the day was shot. He was just dithering now, waiting for the walk to take him, and, following hard after the walk ended, the struggle to find shelter. He was lost in this grim forecast when someone knocked at the window. At first he didn't recognize her. She wore a simple red sundress and a pair of leather flats. The sundress was patternless and fell over her new figure. Her hair was long and layered and the natural chestnut brown it had been when she was a little girl. She was almost a different person, but he knew her. She stood close enough to touch. She waved at him. He looked at her, at his daughter waving through the glass, and without thinking of how ugly it might look to her, he raised his hand and waved back.

THEN THE LETTING GO

His condition never went into remission again, the walking never ceased. The nature of how he walked and his relationship to it as that thing which hijacked his body and led him into the wilderness (for everywhere was a wilderness to him who had known only the interiors of homes and offices and school buildings and restaurants and courthouses and hotels) changed over time, over a long adjustment and many misfortunes. The path itself was one of peaks and valleys, hot and cold in equal measure, rock, sedge and rush, the coil of barbed wire around a fence post, the wind boom of passing semis, the scantness and the drift.

He removed his medication from the labeled plastic baggies that had proven good for storage and transport. He placed the pills in a small pile on the floor of the tent. He poured water into the tin cup from the thermos and drank them down. Then he returned the baggies to the pack and rose to a squat. He released the air from the pallet and rolled it up and rolled up the bedroll and latched them tightly to the pack. Then he took down the tent. Finally it bulged fatly in its blue vinyl bag. He strapped it on top of the pack, so that as he walked, it hovered just behind his head. He loaded up the few essentials left by the campfire and doused what remained of the fire with creekwater. Then he set off under a full moon at the start of frost. He would look for some way to dispel his considerable energies in the downtime before a new walk began.

He came up from the arroyo and walked a mile down to an ATM. He withdrew enough cash to make it awhile. Then he walked across the street and ordered eggs and coffee. He stood up and took the newspaper from a nearby table, but none of it kept his interest. A strong breeze pressed against the plate glass and seeped diminished through the cheap glazing. Outside a woman was nearly halted by the wind and he heard a man's laughter as he reached back for her arm. His food came. He ate a late breakfast as the cloudburst moved in. Then he was on the other side of the glass in his transparent poncho heading toward the coastal springs, into the wind.

In the past he could sleep anywhere, in the snares of frostbite and the hothouses of heatstroke, exposed to ticks, spiders, snakes, the insult of birds, the menace of authorities and of the evil intentions of men.

The decision one night to sleep on the side of the road had forced him into the back of a squad car and his God talk and end-of-days ranting combined with some old-fashioned disrespect ended him up in the psych ward under physical restraint. He was given a more effective cocktail of antipsychotics and forced to take it, daily, until his release, upon which time the importance of finding seclusion and providing protection for himself became intuitive again. That's when he bought the tent, the bedroll and the new pack.

He established a rule never to linger too long at a campsite. He was not free to enjoy the ebb and flow of an hour, the leaves quivering in the wind, or the distant patch of drifting sky. Meditation and mindless wonder led to disaster.

He had once walked away from a campsite out of a valley and across a pine ridge, down an embankment to the foothills, where he awoke behind an Airstream in a designated vehicle area. Night rain on his skyward face woke him. He played back the image of the valley as it broadened and the tent receded. He had been forced to walk away from the few and only things he still possessed and they had taken on a value greater than any other man would have given them. The separation felt like heartbreak. He did not have the first hint how to return.

He searched for two days, and on the third day he started to withdraw from the medication, which was with his other things at the campsite. He became lightheaded and short of breath. He followed the arterial road into town and wandered around a Men's Wearhouse where he sorted unhappily through the tie racks. He paid for a double-breasted suit and arranged for its tailoring in anticipation of an important meeting. He burrowed further into mental daze after returning to the park. He started talking to himself again. He scolded the other and prayed to God that the foot soldiers of His army would vanquish the chariots and trespassers of the enemy on the frontlines of battle threatening him with chaos and death. His steadiness defected on the rain-slicked switchbacks, and he was laid out on a picnic bench, soaked through and bleeding, when the ranger came upon him.

"We've been looking for you," said the ranger.

"You have?"

"I'm with the angel mercenaries of God's army and the bugle blowers leading the charge," he said. "Here, let me help you."

The ranger reached down and helped him to the station and presented him with every item of his illegal campsite, the tent and bedroll and backpack. He took his medication and slept on a cot in the back of the station and when he woke up the ranger spoke much more harshly to him, fined him for failing to obtain a backcountry permit and for camping outside the designated area, and never said another word to him about the army of God.

Thereafter he pitched the tent immediately after coming to the end of a walk, slept, and, upon waking, packed everything up again. To own something was to keep it on his back or risk losing it forever.

A sonic flock of stealth fighters zipped by overhead, the briefest of black apparitions. He walked past fields of mesquite and tract housing and came to a Verizon store where he bought the cheapest phone and a package of prepaid minutes.

He called her at least once a month, sometimes twice, to let her know where he was and that everything was okay, he was safe, and she called him, but his cell phone wasn't always charged.

"We got twenty miles away from the Waffle House before I realized what a terrible mistake we'd made," she said to him. "I told Fritz to stop the car and turn around, but you were already gone. Did we really think you knew better than we did what was right for you, that you even knew how to take care of yourself? We should have dragged you out of there. Anybody could see you needed help. I don't know what we thought we were doing letting you stay there. I think we thought we were dealing with the old Tim. So I let twenty miles go by before I realized the old Tim was gone and that we had just abandoned a child. I stuck around after Fritz flew home and I drove around in the rental looking for you."

He said nothing.

"I have looked for you from the window of a moving car for so long now, I still do it out of habit. Even now, even knowing you're getting by, knowing you're taking your medication, I still look for you when I get in the car. I think I always will. I do it hoping to find you and convince you to come home. I'm used to it now, not having you with me, but I still look out the window hoping to find you so I can follow you and we can start over. Is there some way of starting over, do you think, some way we haven't thought of?"

He didn't answer.

"I'm just glad you're calling," she said. "I'm glad you're okay. You would like it here. It's smaller than what we had, but for me it's perfect. I could probably go smaller. Two hundred square feet maybe. I'm probably the only person in the city who wants a smaller apartment. Even Becka's is bigger. People ask me where I live and I feel the need to lie. If they knew the truth I don't think they'd trust my judgment as a broker. Sometimes I find myself describing the old house for them. I say I live in a house in the suburbs with my husband and they nod and don't think anything of it. They look at me like of course you do, where else would you live?"

The free health clinic in a college town was in a squalid corner of hell. He was there for a simple refill. His neighbors in the basement waiting room looked drained and ghoulish in the fluorescent light. His name was called. He waited inside the exam room until the official walked in. The official had credentials that made him the nearest approximation to a physician in the building. He handed the official his medical file. The official asked him if he still believed that God was waging an insurgency on the frontlines of his mind to capture that territory for the soul. He was quoting from the file.

"I'm not so sure about God anymore," he replied.

"It's an interesting theory, though."

"It wasn't always a theory."

The steady gaze that followed was unnerving. Silence filled the cubby in that warren of underfunded cubbies.

"God needs all the advocates He can get," said the official.

The statement sounded like a challenge. There seemed a right reply and a wrong one. The official stared at him without blinking. He didn't know if he was being tested for signs of continued madness or recruited to a cause.

"Of course He does," he said finally.

"You can't medicate the calling out of your life."

"I never would," he said.

He received his refills and took them to a pharmacy.

He passed up diners and hotels and the idle hour of rest in bars and bowling alleys because indulgence in the creature comforts during his downtime made him sluggish and contrarian when it came time to walk. He continued to think, "I'm winning," or "Today, he won," depending on how well his mind, his will, his soul (he did not know the best name for it) fought against the lesser instincts of his body. "He" or "It" or whatever you wanted to call it—but certainly not "I," he thought—still bellyached for food, needed water, complained of soreness in the joints and muscles. He tended to its needs while trying not to spoil it. He made every effort to remember a time when he was not just the sum of his urges.

"I guess I don't understand why it hasn't gone into remission. It went into remission before. You'd expect it would go into remission again. And then you could come home and we could pick up where we left off."

"That would kill me."

"Why?"

"Because if it went into remission, it would come back, and I don't want to have to do it all over again."

"Do what?"

"Resign myself to it."

"You wouldn't have to. We'd make it work."

"Go on with your life," he said.

"And do what?"

"Sell houses," he said. "Be happy. Remarry."

There was a pause on her end. "I can't believe you'd say that."

"I'm out here now," he said. "I'm doing what I have to do. You should do the same."

He stood outside a big multiplex reading the listings and showtimes. He was not current with the popular reviews but he could distinguish from the titles the political thriller from the romantic comedy from the animated feature. He badly wanted to be inside. There was a comfy seat in there for him and plenty of warmth. The distraction of mindless entertainment promised to shuffle off a pair of hours that might have otherwise been spent dwelling dully on a bench.

Against his better judgment he bought a ticket. He lost interest within fifteen minutes and dozed. He woke up to the credits and walked across the hall to a different screen and sat down before a story of intrigue whose plot was more sophisticated for his having missed the first half. When that show was over, he exited the building and bought a second ticket. He saw another show and half of a fourth before he was forced out of the warm plush oblivion into a torrid pace more odious for the dumb comfort that had preceded it.

He resolved never to indulge himself again. Then he woke and decamped and felt the blank expression of eternity boring through him again, downtime's merciless black-hole eyes, and in a small misfortune of time, he drank himself into a state watching a game on a bar TV.

After letting the dead battery languish a long time, he bought more minutes from an authorized retailer located beside a mattress store. He was unable to reach her on her cell so he tried her at the office, and there they informed him that she had left months earlier for another firm.

He dialed the number the old firm gave him and a casual voice answered. He was informed that Jane was on vacation and wouldn't be returning for another week. Did he care to speak to a different broker?

"How nice," he said. "Where on vacation?"

"I want to say Paris, but don't quote me," said the voice. "The south of France, maybe?"

He stood in the snow-patched prairie with the ice-blue brook running toward the rafting centers and trailer parks, far from the south of France, far from Paris, and a wave of death washed over him. Not biological death, which brought relief, but the death that harrows the living by giving them a glimpse of the life they've been denied. Its sorrow was a thousandfold any typical dying.

He pocketed the phone and walked slowly toward the russet uplands rising in the distance. Ravines in the granite of a north-facing slope sprouted green fronds in feathered clusters. He leaned back against the rock face and felt like crying. She was only resuming life. In the many months that passed between phone calls, she had done just as he had told her. He had no one to blame for it but himself.

He walked about the prairie until he got a decent signal. Becka was on a tour bus when his call came in. "Hello?" she said.

"Is your mother on vacation?"

"Dad?"

"Where's your mom?"

"Where are you?"

"Who cares where I am?"

"I do. Can't you imagine I might be curious?"

"I'm in a field," he said. "What more is there to say?"

She was silent. "Mom's in France."

"On vacation?"

"Yes."

"What's she doing there?"

"She's on vacation," she said.

"What's the name of the hotel she's staying at?"

She paused again. "Why do you want to know that?"

"I want to call her."

"What for?"

"Did she go there alone," he asked, "or with someone?"

Again she paused.

"Becka?"

"With someone," she said.

He bought a used car from a local dealership wreathed in flag bunting. He was dragged away from his new purchase by a long walk, and afterward looped back without sleeping. His body cried out for rest but he was determined to trump its dumb singular want by keeping constant attention on the pain of the living death he would suffer until he found his way back to her.

But he was too tired to drive straight to New York and did not make it a hundred miles before falling asleep. The road curved around while he kept straight. He went through a wire fence into a field where he struck a cow. The car undercut its hind legs and lifted the animal off the ground. It hit the hood and the windshield shattered into a cobweb. He slammed on the brakes and the beast caromed off. He stepped out, bleeding and dazed, and approached the animal, which lay flat, legs broken, and stared back at him with an unblinking eye that began to drip blood. He bent down and put both hands on it as if trying to keep the life inside, but the movement of its moist nostrils died out, and with it any final hope that he might make it back home.

He grabbed the pack and abandoned the car with the door hanging open as the rest of the scattered herd lowed at him, agitated and alive. He grew smaller in the shimmering distance and soon disappeared around the bend.

She called and called again. He let the phone ring into voice mail. He let the battery die. His right eye closed up from conjunctivitis and the pharmacist recommended that he see an ophthalmologist, but he settled for nonprescription drops that took effect slowly. Passing a downtown bank with an electronic clock, he noticed the date. He counted backward. Sixteen days earlier, it had been his birthday.

He recharged the battery using the men's-room outlet in a visitor center. He discovered fourteen messages waiting for him. One was from Becka wishing him a happy birthday. The others were from Jane. He had meant to be self-preserving, not cruel, in not calling her back, but he understood now that he could not have it both ways.

Still, he waited. The sun infused the green skin of the tent. He was staring up at it, preparing himself to rise and pack, when the phone rang. He answered in a voice he hadn't heard in days, maybe weeks. She spoke faster than he was accustomed to.

"Do you think I wanted this to happen? I wanted *you*. How many times have I called you since I came back from France? Twenty? I'm not trying to be heartless. This thing with Michael, it just happened. These things happen. Do you know how long you've been gone? Do you know it gets lonely? It gets so lonely. I didn't intend this. I kept telling you to come home. You told me to remarry. Go on with your life, you said. Well, that's what I did, I went on with my life. I went to France with a man I like. Can you blame me for that? You can't because you told me to. I'm not in the wrong here. All you had to do was come home, Tim. I kept telling you that. Come home. I'm telling you now. None of this matters. France, it doesn't matter. It was nice being taken care of for a while, that's all. I would be lying if I said it wasn't nice. But it's not what I want. I want you. Say you'll come home, and I'm yours. I'll come get you. I've always been willing to come get you. Are you there?"

He didn't reply.

"Say something. You won't call me back and when you finally pick up the phone you won't even talk. Say something, please. Say what you're thinking."

"I'm happy for you, banana."

She began to cry into the phone. "I'm sorry," she said. "I'm so sorry."

"I never imagined one of us taking a vacation without the other."

Her sob came from deep down in her chest. He told her she had nothing to be sorry for. She was exactly right. He had told her to do it.

"Can't you come home?"

"I can't."

"Can't, or won't?"

"I honestly can't," he said.

The call ended. He had told her to go on with her life only because her love and constancy had been so true for so long, he never dreamed they would actually be taken away.

She called a few months later to see if he would agree to make their separation official. Michael had asked her to marry him.

He was quiet. Finally he said that a few days prior, he had passed a Mail Boxes Etc., where he thought he could open up a mailbox. She could have the paperwork sent there.

"Are you sure you don't mind?"

"I don't mind," he said.

"Maybe the lawyer can just fax it."

"Either way," he said.

He spent a few days walking back to the Mail Boxes Etc. during his downtime and then called her with the fax number.

"I'm not asking for anything," she told him.

He didn't understand. Then it dawned on him that she meant money.

"You should take what you need," he said. "I'll sign whatever you send me."

"I don't need anything," she said.

He walked, and after he woke he returned to the Mail Boxes Etc. and found the fax waiting for him. The woman at the counter was also a notary public and together they signed the paperwork. Then he paid to have it faxed back to the lawyer.

He stopped in the alleyway and removed the phone from his pocket. The battery was dead and he hadn't bothered to recharge it for some time, maybe two months. He stood considering it awhile before tossing it inside a hollow dumpster where it hit with a cheap and lonely echo. He moved off, past the kids playing catch. He turned right and his presence was replaced by that window of space, no longer than a car's length, in which cars passed one another all day long, shooting off little sunbursts of glare.

He watched her from the back of the crowd. He wore his beard and snow cap and backpack, as if his age were not sufficient to set him apart. He was drowsy.

He had stayed put, approximately, near this ground zero, going on ten days. When he found himself twelve or fifteen miles out, he fought the urge to crash, turned around and walked back. Deprived of sleep, his body was pliable. It was his again. It was also sleep-deprived, and he struggled to retrace the dozen miles. He was not only tired on the return but weak and hungry, too.

She wore army-surplus pants and a denim jacket and a faded T-shirt that said Heavenly Lake Tahoe. She was moody and focused and she punished the mike stand. She moved around with iconic revolt as if the world that contained her was that murky bluish stage and she was thrashing and screaming for release. She removed her denim jacket and her T-shirt was soaked at the pits. She had gained back her weight and more.

He drifted over to where the crowd was thinner and rested his head against the wall and dozed standing despite the enormous sound.

To his surprise, she clung to him desperately outside the venue. She broke down in his arms while he worried that his clothes might smell.

"I'm sorry that it's been so long."

"You're so thin," she said, releasing him, but gripping his arms as if she feared that he might slip away.

They sat in a booth along the far wall of a Greek diner. Periodic voltage drops grayed the gold fixtures and darkened the cake display. Everyone at some point looked ceilingward.

She asked him if it was gone, and he said it wasn't.

"Then how did you make the show?"

"I've been circling the city since you posted the tour dates. I turn around and walk back."

"Without sleeping?"

"Part of the challenge, not sleeping."

"When do you sleep?"

"When I get close enough."

"And what do you do with your downtime?"

"Get closer."

"And then you walk away again?"

He nodded.

"Isn't that exhausting?"

He shrugged. "Gives the day its purpose," he said.

It was an act of willful defiance, looping, circling back, keeping within a certain perimeter. It imposed a pattern on the random arrivals and departures, even if that pattern was just to see a show, or to pick up a few pieces of mail from a p.o. box. He was collecting p.o. boxes, he told her, all across the country.

"Speaking of which," he said.

He unzipped the pack and brought out a freezer bag. He removed the two CDs he had ordered over the Internet. He showed her that he had uploaded them to his iPod as well. "I also have a concert tee and a poster of the show you did in San Francisco."

She was surprised and touched. "You're a good dad," she said.

He demurred. "Just a fan."

"I thought you only liked David Bowie."

"That was in the room," he said, remembering the months he spent in the hospital bed and the music she had introduced him to. "Out here I listen to everything."

He put the CDs back in the freezer bag and returned them to the pack. The power dropped out again and didn't return. There was a stir as people murmured and faded to shadows and shifted unsurely in the murk, as if from this point forward they would require absolute guidance as to how to proceed.

The waitress came over. "Your order didn't go through, hon."

"That's okay," said Becka. "Are you okay?" she asked him.

"I'm okay."

"Can we just have some more coffee?"

He wondered, in the dim light, if his eyes had played tricks on him. The sundress was gone. There was nothing skinny about her.

"The last time we saw each other," he said. "When was that?"

"I don't remember," she said.

"You were with your mom and Fritz."

She shook her head slowly in the darkness. "I wasn't with them."

"You look wonderful," he said.

"There's more of me, anyway."

He didn't reply immediately. Then he said, "Does it still bother you?"

She puffed out her cheeks like someone about to burst, eyes popping wide. Then she settled into a grin shaded with resignation. "It's my one go-around," she said. "What do you do—hate yourself till the bitter end?"

"I've always thought you were the most beautiful girl in the world."

"You've always been biased."

"I'm glad you don't hate yourself."

"Acceptance," she said. She shrugged. "It's a bitch."

Out in the parking lot she offered to give him a ride but he needed to be no place. Occasionally he stayed the night in a motel or at the YMCA and she tried to encourage him to do so that night but he said it was easy to fall back into the custom of television and a real bed, which later made his nights in the tent harder to reckon with. He was happier avoiding those places. And he no longer did cars.

"What does that mean, you don't do cars?"

"They're not an option," he said. "If I need to be somewhere, I walk."

"Not an option?" She rattled her enormous collection of keys in an unspoken admission that what he said was deeply strange to her. "Well, will you at least sit in the front seat with me a minute?" she asked. "There's something I need to tell you."

Her mother was sick. She had debated a long time over whether it made sense telling him. She knew his limitations and she didn't want him to feel guilty about what was out of his hands.

"Is it serious?"

"It's cancer."

"I don't know what that means," he said.

"You don't know what cancer means?"

"No, of course I know. I've just lost track."

"Lost track of what?"

He paused. "What does the man say?"

"What man?"

"The man she married."

"Michael?" she said. "She never married Michael."

"She didn't?" He was taken aback. "Why not?"

"I don't know the details, Dad. She broke things off."

How long had it been? He had lost track.

He looked out the window and down at the parking lot, a frivolous patch of blacktop into which one sprung toward a better destination or from which one departed in an onward spirit. But he would do neither. He would soon get out of the car and remain. Becka would drive away, and an empty evening ache would press down. And there was nothing he could do for either of them, for any of them.

He turned to look at his daughter. "There's nothing I can do," he said.

"I'm not asking you to do anything. I just thought you'd want to know."

He shook his head. "I don't," he said.

He entered a town of cattle murals and savings banks where he bought a mocha frappuccino. He walked with the coffee drink between a double row of single-story houses, many of which were for sale. The gate to one hung open. The realty sign was strangled under an unmown thicket and a stained mattress lay on the front porch.

He stretched out on the mattress and finished the mocha while watching a black squirrel with a frayed tail fitfully stalk the trees. A man with a cane came out of the house opposite. He sat on the porch and turned to his left, then to his right, then to his left again, with the cane between his legs and his hands on top of the brass handle. Then he stood, and with the deliberation of a man whose life had narrowed to a single task, he broomed pooled water from the porch. He sat down again to inspect the neighborhood. Eventually he went back inside.

Tim rose from the mattress and left the yard. He went back into town, passing the murals on the sides of the buildings, mostly of cattle and horses but one of Native Americans. He stopped in a camping supply store and bought another pair of boots, adhesive reflector strips, a new tent, rain gear, energy bars, an additional base layer and pullover, and a compass. He replaced the old goods with his new purchases inside the pack.

To be more than the sum of his urges. Part of the challenge, not sleeping. Something guaranteed to expend his considerable energies and lend purpose to the day. He loved her. He had always loved her. To return to her before she died—that would be the last thing ever required of him.

He started off at the end of his next walk. He turned sluggishly until the compass pointed him east. He crossed the road at its instruction and angled across a field of forage grass to a creek and walked along the bank against the downstream current. The water rippled white. He wanted to sleep. His exhaustion was that of a field soldier who debated whether or not living was worthwhile under such circumstances. But it was only his first day. He couldn't quit on his first day. He skirted a reservoir slower than shadow moves across a room. The black range in the distance stood against the sky like a spiked dinosaur.

He made it to the scenic drive. He fell to his knees in the rock beside the road. He told himself to get up. Don't fall asleep, he said. Tourists were gathered at the fence to behold the wonder. The green valley cut a snaking halfpipe through the brown monoliths of the canyon. He could curl up in one of their backseats, or in the aspen grove that sprouted above the ravine past the row of parked cars, or inside the room of the La Quinta Inn just down the road. But he stood up and continued on his way along the shoulder of the highway.

The tree was a terrible luxury. He leaned up against it and fell asleep. It was meant to be a quick respite, but as soon as he woke he fell asleep again. It was a lone willow in a field. He woke and slept, woke and slept, and every time he woke, he considered lying down between two of the willow's sinewy roots. But he slept upright for hours because to lie down would be indistinguishable from quitting.

He was taken far afield without water. Above him, daubs and strokes of rainless clouds. He came across a ranch house on a sloping dirt road nestled between sagebrush hills and knocked at the door. With a mouthful of dust, slow to conjure the name of the thing he needed, he said to the woman, who circled wide around him because he was a stranger and he sat on her porch with his back to her, "Water." The woman went back inside and returned. She watched him clutch the glass with his primitive assortment of fingers and gulp the water down before spitting it out and vomiting the rest. "You have to take it slow," she said.

It was a two-lane highway of blind curves and bent guard-rails. The darkness was so absolute that headlights leapt over the paved summits to the effect of a poor man's aurora. He sleepwalked from the shoulder into the lane. The car behind him flicked its brights on to find him drifting over. The driver swerved just as a pickup cleared the blind in the opposite lane, twenty yards away, and the two vehicles headed directly into each other. The truck lurched to a full stop close to the guard-rail, only a foot from the drop-off. The car's raging horn woke him. He stumbled back to the shoulder. The driver went around slowly, leaned into the passenger-side window and flipped him the bird to convey how offended he was by this show of dumb negligence. Then the truck pulled out and he was alone again on the highway.

A caravan of cyclists whirred past him in the slanting rain, leaving him in the wake of their fine, fast community. Their passing talk pierced him with longing. Geese with the white underbellies of bowling pins squawked overhead.

He sat in the back of a bar in a recess of tables with a half-finished beer in front of him, vaguely aware of a foosball game going on a few feet away. He fell asleep on the table. The bartender woke him at closing time. He went outside and resumed walking.

"Please don't tell her I'm coming," he wrote to Becka the next day, from a computer at a public library. "I don't think I can make it."

He broke a rule and spent a night in a rented room. He reentered a white world where scant traffic was treading delicately in the icy fall. It was a sanatorium of snow. Flurries mocked visibility and found cracks in his best gear. He did not make it east two miles when his will was pulled out from under him and he was forced to walk in a different direction. He woke later inside the tent and felt the pressing urge to make up for lost time. When he decamped, the sun was out and the snow had melted into a pristine damp that mellowed the earth like a trickling stream. He walked half the day only to come upon the same motel where he'd spent the night twenty-four hours earlier. His heart sank.

The glow in the distance appeared to intensify in pulse and color, it beat blood and energy like a diseased heart. The sun, reversing course, might have been setting in the east just over the edge of the lower range. He didn't know what it was. Night had fallen, and the snow was thriving after hours of indifferent drift. The glow was situated directly in his path. Two men on horseback came at him at a trot, followed by a tether of additional horses.

"What are you doing here?" asked one.

"What are you doing?"

"Taking these horses to safety."

Tim stumbled a little where he stood, having fallen asleep.

"You drunk?"

He got down on his haunches. "Just tired," he said.

"If you're gonna pass out," said the man, "better you do it away from here. Highway's closed."

"Is there another route that takes me east?"

The man looked behind him in the direction of the glow. "See that fork? No, it's too dark," he said. "You're going to hit a fork up there, leads you on if you take a left. Take a right instead. That'll take you to the Wal-Mart and such."

"Is that east?"

"If east is south."

He got to his feet. The weight of the pack made him wobble. One of the horses stirred. He smiled faintly in the torpid light and continued on.

He tried to make it through a wind-driven brush fire. The air was thick with ash and pine smoke. He retreated. Two days later he walked the same route when all that remained were black stakes of trees stabbed into the pale hillside.

"Okay," wrote Becka, "whatever, you won't fly, you can't fly. Whatever. At least let me come out there and get you. I drive to where you are, we tie you up and throw you in the trunk or something, and drive you back here. Why wouldn't that work?"

He reread the email. It was a perfectly reasonable proposition. He tried to think of what he might say to make her understand why it would not work for him.

The truth made him a monster. It put his struggle, the one he was waging against his weak and determined body, before Becka, before Jane, before everyone.

He decided to tell a partial truth. During every hour, there was a moment of despair, he wrote in reply to her email, and during every day, an hour. In that hour, he resigned himself to never seeing them again. But he had made some progress since his last email, and, despite quitting every day, he had not yet quit. He was on his way, he wrote, he was on his way, he promised. And then he dispatched her elegant solution with a single line that she could not possibly understand, obscuring his monstrosity, but clarifying for him nothing short of the reason he continued to live and breathe.

"I can't have you pick me up because I'm still at war," he wrote, "and I'm determined to win."

At first his body was subject only to little local breakdowns, to infections and inflammations, to aches, cricks, tweaks, cramps, contusions, retentions, swellings, fevers, tinglings, hackings, spasms, limps, displacements, dizziness, stiffness, chafing, agitations, confusions, staggerings, spells of low blood sugar, and the normal wear and tear of age. Yet it persisted to function more or less with an all-hands-on-deck discipline. He was certain that it had a mind of its own, an unassailable cellular will. If it were not that it needed sleep, and a bit of food, it would not need him. It would walk without him, after his mind had dimmed and died. It would walk until it collapsed into a pile of whitened and terrigenous bones.

He crossed the creek at a ford and continued east to lower elevations. He took the arterial roads that linked the logging towns
with the tourist centers. Ten days later he left the rain shadow of
the Rockies and walked out of Colorado.

Farewell Orion and the winter stars. He walked past a low-
lying billboard that had weathered into a long canvas of abstract
expression, above which stood a regal plastic pony in midstride.
The pony had a brown coat and a pitch-black mane. The black
mane matched the pony's hooves and forelegs. The billboard
pony was a Great Plains totem presiding over the safety of passing automobiles. He thought he could discern, in the far corner
of the billboard, a figure of piety wrapped in a nun's wimple,
which some attentive kook could legitimately claim was a silhouette of the Holy Mother. Little birds roosted at the pony's
feet.

He walked through the ten-mile-apart towns, past the water
towers and grain silos, and after several days arrived in grim
Grand Island. He slept in the skeletal start of a new house with
crossbeams and a cinderblock base. In the night he used the
on-site johnny. Plastic sheeting lay in the yard, weathered and
pale like a disintegrating shroud. Above him burned a pavilion
of stars in a final unfettered night. In the morning he walked
through Grand Island into rain.

Upon the plains the sulphur stink of the corporate ranch reached
many miles before and after him. In the middle stood ten thousand cows, an undulating field of Black Angus. He walked along
the fenced land to a strip of clean wire and bowed under it and
waded among the steer. Their crudely sculptured mass steamed

in the chill. They thickened the farther he went in until the crowd inhibited his movement and the sad things jostled him to the soundtrack of their discontent. The overcrowding had wearied them out of instinct. He squatted down in the atom heart of their huddling and drew heat from their bodies and drowsed on his haunches, bumped off balance from time to time by a shifting rump, dreaming of shit-strewn coasts and squall lines of black rain.

The clay-gray water lapped at the porches of the houses on both sides of the street. He was down in the water with the cars. Their rooftops were visible above the flood and a quarter, sometimes half their windshields, depending on the make and model. Everything was gray, the electricity poles, the saturated trees. He waded deep and slow through the water with help from the current. He climbed to the roof of a pickup to consider his options. Visibility was low but it looked as if the street he was on rose up in the distance. If he just kept wading straight, he would reach a clearing.

He climbed down from the truck and made his way forward. The shift in the current took him by surprise. He was lifted off his feet as if in the middle of a rapid and made to float downhill. He had not anticipated the crosscurrent at the intersection. There his own little street of rain was draining into a steeply graded side street like a gulch into a river. He paddled like mad but the pack filled with rainwater and pulled him down. He choked on the water. He grasped at nothing, at the air, at the rain, while houses floated by. A brief blur of red caught his eye and he reached out for a stop sign. He grabbed one slice of the octagon and struggled to get a better purchase. It was thin and slick and awkward. He hooked the top edge of the sign with a forearm. The rest of his body was floating downstream. He pulled himself toward the sign, against the force of the current. He pivoted around and pinned himself between the sign and the rushing water. He hugged the faceplate and struggled not to fishtail. The pack was latched to his back like an anchor pulling him down. He watched as trees, shopping carts, a section of fence coursed by.

"Do you miss me?" she asked.

He didn't reply. His medication was holding but the walk was having unintended consequences.

She asked him again. "Do you miss me, Tim?"

He stood with a finger in his ear trying to block out the video-game noise. Bad placement of those things, right beside the pay phone. The place was touted as the World's Largest Pit Stop, as if to draw tourists. He had paid for a shower and bought new clothes.

"Tim," she said, "why did you call if you aren't going to talk?"

"I hear you're sick."

"Who told you that?"

"What did you ask me?"

"Who told you I was sick? Did Becka tell you?"

"No, before that."

"I asked her not to."

"Before that, Jane. Before that."

"I asked if you missed me," she said.

He started to laugh. "Ha ha ha ha ha," he said. "HA HA HA HA HA HA!"

"What's so funny?"

All around him, the fluorescent illumination of tobacco ads, power-drink displays, heat-lamp chicken, postcard racks, shrink-wrapped magazines, scuffed aisles of candies and chips, and the purgatorial shuffling transients that fed off it all. His laughter gave way to strained tears. He turned into the pay phone so no one would see.

"Yes," he said. "I miss you."

It was summer in suburbia. The world smelled of well-mown lawns. The sprinklers churred round their rotaries. American flags wore gravity's folds on garage-mounted poles in all God's neighborhoods.

He had wandered off the path of greatest efficiency and succumbed to sleep in a park tightly bordered by town houses and cul-de-sacs. He was woken by a rooting noise. Something sizable was trying to burrow under the tent. Its odd shadow reared up across the slanted vinyl wall. He stepped out of the tent into the early-morning sun and humidity and came face-to-face with a tusked and rangy animal. The hairs along its scruff were gray and bristly. It looked up at him as he stood frozen with fear. He casually took one and then a second step backward and slowly retreated to the other side of the tent. He was relieved when the mad rooting resumed.

In the distance he saw the herd. They were up the small hilly incline near the glinting jungle gym. A few outliers were rutting under the wooden fence that separated the park from the houses. His own outlier was snorting and shaking the tent and very likely shredding the fabric.

He heard the slamming of a door and turned to see two men

stepping out of a truck. One man stretched and yawned. They wore identical dark blue slacks and short-sleeve work shirts and the door of the truck had some kind of decal he couldn't discern from such a distance. They each pulled from the bed of the truck a rifle with a scope, walked halfway up the incline, and began to shoot the boarlike animals. He threw up his arms and fled. He stood by the stone water fountain watching every member of the herd fall during the noiseless spree. He walked back to the tent. The boar that woke him lay on its side with a dart in its neck. One of the shooters approached smoking a cigarette. His shirt said Downers Grove Park District.

"Is it dead?"

The man shook his head. "We don't kill them here," he said.

"What is it?"

"Feral pig."

He took a drag from his cigarette in the punishing heat, sucking his cheeks in and squinting off into the distance. There his colleague was lifting the first of the pigs by a hoist into the bed of the truck. The man with the cigarette turned back and silently regarded the tent. Languid billows of smoke escaped his mouth as he spoke. "You can't camp here, you know."

He dreamed of a resurgent tribe of vanquished Indians. They materialized body and soul from the bloodred horizon of the central plains and walked out of the shores of the Great Lakes. Their mournful spirits had trailed him since the tepee rings in Wyoming. Their business outside the tent was bloody and serious. A collective chanting accompanied their war preparations. He was not welcome on their reclaimed land. He knew as much but he lay paralyzed with fever. Some ravishing pioneer bug, or perhaps heatstroke. The brute inarticulate chanting grew louder as the tribal chief entered the tent and demanded to know the name of the tribe, forgotten by the enemy and the descendants of the enemy who now inhabited the land and by the land itself. He tried vainly in sleep to remember the name. His recall would determine whether he lived or died, but it escaped him. The chief smelled of a popular aftershave. He filliped Tim's boot with his middle finger and Tim opened his eyes. A middle-aged man with a vigorous tan and a whistle lanyard dangling from his neck squatted in the mesh doorway. He wore a white polo and baseball cap. "I said what are you doing here, huh?"

"Where am I?"

"Christ, I thought you must be some kid," said the man. "You're on my field."

With chills and a fever he decamped from the North Side High School practice field as the sun beat down on the varsity team chanting their songs and running their drills at the vast eastern edge of the corn belt.

He woke on the hard curved pew inside a Methodist church, a small white monument to the simplicity and beauty of the Allegheny Jesus. He raised his head off the hymnal and sat up. He felt the fluid overload slowly drain down his limbs.

From the altar the preacher delivered a trial run of his sermon to the empty pews. Tim would have left were it not that he was lethargic and slow on the uptake. Beams of sunlight radiated through the stained-glass windows. He listened to the final ten minutes of the sermon, which concluded, "The wise man's eyes are in his head; but the fool walketh in darkness: and I myself perceived also that one event happeneth to them all." He thought he might be hallucinating again, but the preacher came down the aisle and reassured him: the leg cramps that had driven him inside the night before, common among extreme sportsmen, were the result of excessive muscular exertion, which led to inflammation, and to a buildup of a particular enzyme that his body was having difficulty breaking down.

"When that happens," the preacher continued, "you start to show signs of confusion, have visions, that sort of thing."

The preacher was seated in the pew in front of him, turned at an angle so they could converse. Were his words intended to put him at ease, or to make matters less certain?

"How do you know all this?" asked Tim.

"I run marathons."

He was a diminutive, bearded man with a serious face that did not smile falsely. He said he didn't think Tim was a regular member of the parish, and Tim explained that he was trying to reach New York to reunite with his wife, who was sick. Tim began to speak openly. On other occasions he had wanted to share with men like this the agonies of his circumstances, but it was difficult to overcome the fear that their reactions would be defined by incomprehension and a lack of sympathy, and that he would look weak before them.

"I'm glad to see you returning," the preacher said when he was through. "It is not good that the man should be alone."

"No," he said.

"But I'm curious. Why take such long walks?"

"I don't *take* them," he said. "I've told you. They're forced upon me."

"But, Tim, this sort of thing doesn't just happen."

He had never told the preacher his name.

"You only know my name because I'm hallucinating."

"I've assured you that you're not hallucinating," he said. "Now, why do you think you take such long walks?"

"You tell me. They have checked and double-checked the medical textbooks. They've searched for others like me, living or dead. I've been looking my entire life for just one other similar case."

"But is there anything whereof it may be said, see, this is new?" The preacher shook his small, round head. "No," he said. "There is no new thing under the sun."

"Okay, but I'm telling you: I'm not doing it."

"So all your life you've searched and searched for a rational explanation," he replied, "while presuming there is one. But if there isn't?"

"There must be."

"What is the rational explanation for the bees, Tim? The blackbirds? The fires? The floods? Do those things happen by accident, too?"

Tim stared at him blankly. The preacher finally smiled, in a small but comforting way. He reached over the back of his pew and kindly patted Tim's knee. Then he came around and helped him to his feet.

He carried on through rain-sodden leaves running in color from copper to yellow. They quivered in the wind with a high-pitched rustle and fell in sloping tumbles to the earth. In the Great Valley, north of the Piedmont region, he passed a lone farmhouse thrashed by a storm. Its roof was gone, its four sides reduced to timbers. A minivan looked as if someone had driven it halfway up the side of the aboveground pool. Lighter household possessions were strewn about as if the farmhouse had been a bag of garbage attacked in the night by a scavenging animal. And standing in the doorway, a child naked but for its diaper cried loudly into the void. A woman was running across the field toward the child. The clouds had dispersed by then. Contrails gone to drift in the upper winds littered the broad blue sky.

His conjunctivitis had come upon him outside Pocatello. It finally healed by Ogallala on the north side of the Platte River and returned on a desolate stretch of Highway 83 between Thedford and Valentine, during a despised detour inside the Nebraska sandhills. Leg cramps had plagued him by basin and range and became unbearable as early as the Laramie Plains. Around the lake region of Ravenna in central Nebraska he began to suffer from myositis, or muscle inflammation, which would lead through an inevitability of biological cause and effect to kidney failure by the time he was hospitalized in Elizabeth, New Jersey, ten miles as the crow flies from his final destination.

His infrequent showering brought on skin complications beyond the painful erosions of chafing and blisters, and in Mount Etna on the northern tip of Lake Icaria in western Iowa, he broke out in shingles that made carrying the pack an exercise in medieval torture. He would finally ditch the pack altogether when his back pain reached a pitch at the foothills of the Appalachian Mountains.

He was bothered by bug bites, ticks, fleas and lice, and after the heat burned off all memory of his participation in the flood that drowned an Iowa town, he let himself fry from Mount Pleasant to the western border of the Mississippi before the sun blisters appeared and he realized it was too late. He fought not very successfully against heatstroke and dehydration across Illinois and most of Indiana until he voided deep orange and finally not much of anything at all. Rhabdomyolysis was on him, medicalspeak for the dangerous elevations of a muscle enzyme released when the body undergoes severe trauma, so that by the time he was bivouacking in the windbreaks of barley, corn and soybean fields, in stands of bushy trees meant to protect crop yields from the unpredictable weather that punished the midwestern plains, his blood was berserk with excess potassium and he was at risk for a ventricular tachycardia that would have taken him faster than a bolt of lightning. Something with the delicacy of chisel and hammer set to splintering the bones down both his legs, a *tap, tap, tap* with every step, step, step.

The chain gas station with the logo of a dinosaur sold him a map, which he studied out by the propane tank. Everywhere he stopped he filled a cup with ice to soothe his burning tongue. His heels ballooned and forced him to unlace his boots and to walk on his toes which led to higher orders of osteal complications in the charnel house of his body. Beauty, surprisingly, was everywhere, in the wildflowers, the wheat fields, the collapsed barns, the passing trains, the church spires, the stilled ponds, the rising suns.

During another great diversion, from Tylersburg to Punxsutawney—which required him to cross I-80, his inconstant companion from the Continental Divide to his collapse in New Jersey—he walked past a field discharging one hot air balloon after another into an endless appetite of sky, on the same pink morning he was hit with a head cold. The cold developed into pneumonia with the leathery rales of pleurisy by the time he reached the twin towns of Peapack and Gladstone.

The first tasks of the specialists at the hospital in Elizabeth were to place him on mechanical respiration to fight the acute respiratory distress syndrome, tap and drain the excess fluid from his peritoneal cavity, and put him on dialysis for his liver and heart. His body played a game of touch-and-go with a team of doctors whose tender antagonisms were touching in the extreme. Uncompromising matter did not care for the abuses and insults of heroic stunts. It had the upper hand on practitioners of a medical science who believed they might speak to it fluently and convincingly when in fact they were deaf hostages to a great mocking laughter. They flooded his bloodstream with intravenous meds, fresh plasma and vitamin K, but how could they know if the brain swelling would subside or if he would ever regain consciousness?

A man came occasionally to visit him. He entered the hospital room pulling behind him a portable oxygen tank. On days he found Tim asleep, the man departed. On days Tim was awake but mute and unalert, he was no good to the man. Much later he was breathing on his own again, which was more than the man could say for himself. Many tubes had been affixed to Tim with flesh-colored tape. The man stood over him.

"Do you remember me?" he asked.

The world was blurry. He couldn't harden his focus on the man any further. He slowly shook his head.

"It's been a long time," said the man. He looked Tim over. "And you've been through one hell of a something." The man pulled a chair up to the bed and sat down next to him.

"What about him?" he asked. The man produced a photograph and held it above him, as steadily as his hand would allow, to give him a good look. "Recognize him?"

He stared at the photograph, trying to make sense of it. The shapes and colors bled into one another and into the room and his focus began to wobble and fade and before he could answer he was asleep again.

The man sat back in the chair and sighed. He returned

the picture to his suit coat and removed from the same pocket a business card. He turned the card over and jotted down his cell phone number. Then he realized there was no good place to set the card. The room was bare but for a small table affixed to the wall beside the bed. He decided to leave one there and to put another in Tim's sleeping hand. Then he walked out of the room, pulling his oxygen behind him.

He sat unhurried, not easily distracted, as if he had no plans or set arrangements and life was only a profligacy of time. It was a little past midday in Tompkins Square Park and other such men were on similar benches strung along the footpaths, unafraid to fritter away the day's frugal hours with the mildest curiosities.

Becka had brought her baby to meet his grandfather for the first time. It was an unplanned pregnancy but one that had given her mother a great deal of joy in a short amount of time, and Becka was grateful for that. She was curious about how he would react. She had gotten used to the idea that he would never return, would never meet her son, because he had not sent an email in months. He had given up, she thought, or he had died trying to reach her mother before she did, and in neither of those instances did she know how to find him, or how to be angry, or how to mourn. She went days and weeks without thinking of him at all, and on those occasions she did think of him, it was with an abstract sadness that transmuted disappointment, concern, and compromised love into a final resignation that as far as fathers were concerned, this—silence, mystery—was all life would have to offer her.

She stopped when she saw him. She moved off beside a tree under which a terrible pink fruit lay trampled, fouling the air. Jack was in the carrier, facing forward, and suddenly he moved his arms and legs in synchronicity while letting out a little squeal. She smoothed his pale hair as she stared into the distance.

It was sad to see her father so docile and inexpressive, and so thin. Much thinner than he had been when she saw him in Portland. He had explained in a totally unexpected email that he had been in the hospital a long time and now he was out, but he gave no specifics, made no inquiries, and requested nothing. She had had to arrange this meeting, though he chose Tompkins Square Park, where now, under a linden tree swiftly shedding leaves in the wind, he sat, as unremarkable a feature of the city as the park bench. She found herself lingering. She needed a moment to take him in so that she could greet him with a familiarity that would not betray any trace of the pity that had pierced and then repulsed her when he first came into view.

Jack was still doing a noisy dance of the limbs when she approached and yet her father didn't turn at the sound of her footsteps or their sudden halt nearby. "Daddy?" she said. He turned to her then, and in the long seconds that passed before he said it, she believed he had forgotten her name.

He had lost his way somewhere. He had forgotten why he had pushed and pushed to come so far. It seemed to him just another battle in the war.

Becka was carrying a baby in a harness. His grandson. It didn't touch him. She sat down on the bench next to him and introduced them. He repeated the boy's name and reached out and with one of his fingers gently lifted the child's soft pink foot. A small smile animated the weathered gray lines on his face, but that was all. Then they set off. Becka's apprehensions and warnings on the way there didn't touch him. Much more important was the matter of rising off the bench and starting off again and getting to where they were headed in one piece, with the pain under control, stopping for water or food if necessary, and making an end that got him out of the weather. He hoped not to be taken away by a walk, but otherwise nothing much else. And if he was taken away, there were other days to do this. It had waited a long time already.

She walked him down old city streets of old memories. When they arrived, even as he walked the hallway, he was still intent only on making the distance.

But he was not so far gone, for when he saw her in the hospital bed, swimming in that awful blue gown, he knew at once what it had all been for, why he had started off and why he had struggled, and it wasn't to win, it wasn't for God, and it wasn't stubbornness or pride or courage. He went to her and she looked at him standing over her. All time and distance between them collapsed, and without any mental searching for the word, he said to her, "Hello, banana," and then reached out to take her hand.

She was ready, she had been all packed up and ready to go. She'd made her amends and given herself final rites in a church of her own devising, godless, none of that superstition that cancer patients, some former incorrigible atheists, suddenly invent out of desperation. She had actually heard from another woman in the ward that God had created cancer, with its lag time between diagnosis and death, to give the disbeliever time to reform. Chemo and radiation weren't cures. They were modest foretastes of the hell the unrepentant could expect if they persevered in their godlessness.

When it came to God, she thought, ordinary people were at their most inventive.

God, if He was anything, was the answer to the mystery of why you got sick. She knew about the tree and the serpent and the temptation and the fall, but call that the broader cause. She wanted the revelation of the biological confoundedness. If He's in the details, He should be able to explain them. Upon dying you get paperwork that takes you step by step—the reason for the first errant cell, the exact moment of its arrival on the scene, and then, and then—and when you finish reading, the coffin light goes out, and you roll over for your eternal rest. That was the extent to which she permitted herself to believe in the existence of God.

Before he suddenly walked into the room, she hadn't heard from Tim. If he was dead, she wanted to believe that when his suffering ended, he was finally given an explanation, that his paperwork listed the cause or causes and unlocked the mechanics and offered a justification. That would be the least God could do for him.

Which was wishful thinking, no less than that of the conversion-through-cancer nutcase down the hall. Death was God's secrets extended into eternity.

Her modest size could not afford the weight she had lost. The tendons in her neck showed when she strained to sit up. To touch her back was to feel along an exotic scale of ribs and spine. She kept her hair in barrettes as a way of doing something with her hair at least. So few people had sent flowers. Dr. Bagdasarian had stopped by with tulips, and Becka's boyfriend had sent a mixed bouquet, and Michael, of course, who still loved her. She could not have made it any plainer to Michael and yet he would probably stand at her graveside as she was being lowered into the ground and profess his devotion once again. She didn't want it. Yet she did want more flowers.

They were counting on something new, a clinical trial. She was in it for everything she had.

She hoped he'd died indoors. She didn't think it was likely but the alternative was unthinkable, dying in a frozen field, or in some doorway in a distant city, alone until some inquisitive soul bent down, and the gapers started to cluster, and the cops found nothing, no wallet, no phone, nothing, and so had no next of kin to call. That was how they came to mourn him, she and Becka, without really mourning him, a totally unsatisfying way to mourn. Then he walked into the room, ravaged by the acts of time, thinner than she had ever known him to be, who knew every inch of him by touch, sundered from every appearance of happiness, suffering every ailment except immobility, and it took everything in her power to attribute his reappearance to the determination of a man who loved her, and not to a merciful act of God.

After Becka left with Jack, he drew a chair over to her bed and explained where he had been and how he had come to be there.

"I thought the worst," she said.

"That I would be alive and look like this?"

The film of tears that glazed over her dark and hollowed eyes quivered as she smiled. She squeezed his few fingers, no less bony and fragile than her own. "I think you look devastating," she said.

"Devastated?"

"As handsome as you ever were."

"Now there is a tender lie," he said.

They got reacquainted after so long a time apart. He said little at first because there was so little to say, confusing his experiences on the road for the ordinary banality of endurance. They came to know him at the hospital, where she referred to him as her husband again, and they adjusted to the sight of a man they would ordinarily expect to be tending to in a room of his own walking in and out of hers. He did not smile at them, at the nurses at their station. He hardly even cast them a glance. He said nothing unless it was to ask for something on her behalf, and he came and went like a tinker or beggar, in the same hitchhiker's outfit, if not the very same clothes, and with a heavy backpack swaddling his skinny frame.

Though returned to her at last, his body continued its demands and he was forced to leave her at a moment's notice. This was a new twist in an old cruelty, as time now meant so much more to him than those odious deposits of downtime and distant walks that had come to define these latter years. They could not say how much time she had left, and to leave under such circumstances was prodigal, ridiculing any sentiment of homecoming.

He discharged the walks with dutiful resignation, the way a busy hangman leaves for the day without scruple or gripe, and then he turned around and walked back.

"Where do you go when you leave?"

"I go lots of places."

"When you left yesterday, where did you go?"

"Yesterday I went to the beach," he said.

He removed from his pocket a smooth seashell with a swirl of brown leading into its dark hollow. The top of the shell spiraled to a sharp point. He put the shell in her hand and then sat down in the chair in the corner.

It was the perfect shell, exotic and intact. This was no Rockaway shell or Coney Island shell, not even a Jersey Shore shell. To get a shell like this, you had to walk to the Caribbean.

"Where did you get this? You can't find a shell like this around here."

"I told you. I went to the beach."

"What beach? What was it like?"

"At the beach? It was cold."

"What did you see there?"

"Well," he said. "I saw nothing, really."

"You walked and walked," she said. "You must have seen something."

"On the way I remember seeing an old woman. She was in her nightgown but with a heavy overcoat. She wore a pair of pink boots and she was raking leaves in front of a brownstone."

"What else?"

"People leaving a building for the evening."

"What else?"

"I ran my hand along a chain-link fence."

"What else?"

"That's it. That's all I remember."

"In all that time?"

"That's it," he said.

For the first time he began to pay attention to the things he saw on his walks, so that when he returned to her, he had observations of the outside world to share. They were fleeting, they were middles without beginnings or ends, but they were diverting—for him to witness, for her to hear. She soaked them up. They seemed just as much nourishment as whatever the doctors were providing.

He realized he might have been doing it wrong for years. He might have seen interesting things had he been able to let go of the frustration and despair. He wondered what kind of life he might have had if he had paid attention from the beginning. But that would have been hard. That would have been for himself. It was easier now, doing it for someone else.

"I saw a woman in a leather apron outside a beauty salon, smoking a cigarette. I saw two cops standing around the remains of an accident, broken reflector bits on the pavement. I heard kids running behind me and then they overtook me like a herd of cattle and they all wore the same school uniform but each one still looked so different. I smelled chocolate for almost a mile. I saw some men playing soccer and I thought I could even see the steam coming off their bodies. It's getting colder."

She interrupted. "When I get better, do you think it might be possible for us to go on vacation together?"

"Of course," he said. "Of course that's possible."

They discussed different places. She offered a new country, and then he suggested another, and they grew more and more excited. There was nowhere the two of them would not have enjoyed. They agreed on the African safari they had planned many years before but had never taken.

He stood in the window holding the baby in his arms, rocking back and forth to keep Jack dozing happily against his body. The weight was a glorious burden. The little lumpy fellow and he each shared their body heat. Jane was asleep in the hospital bed. Becka sat against the far wall of the room, reading a magazine. They had worked out the procedure for what to do if he suddenly had to go, but for the moment, in that unlikely place, a wonderful peace was holding. He had even taken off his boots. The window was radiant with cold sunlight. The only noise was the imaginary one that came from dust motes slowly tumbling in the light.

He came into the room and pulled the chair close and sat down next to her.

"I saw a dog in a purse. I saw bread being delivered, loaves of bread in paper sacks, dropped off in front of an Italian restaurant. Later in the morning I saw a bodybuilder in nothing but a T-shirt and sweatpants, such an enormous pair of arms, leave a health club and trip over himself. He went down with his gym bag, and a woman with a baby stroller stopped to ask him if he was all right. I saw a quiet street where I thought you and I could live very happily, a street of brownstones with good little yards. I saw a man chipping the ice off his windshield with a butter knife. And it was working! I saw the Metropolitan Museum of Art. Even at this time of year, people are sitting on the steps out front like it's the Fourth of July. I saw the last of the last of the light. Should I go on?"

She had her eyes closed. "Close the door," she said.

He stood up and closed the door. She took down her pajama bottoms. He saw what she was doing and reached out for a chair and placed it in front of the door. He turned off the light and walked back to her as shadows began to assert themselves in the room. He climbed on from the foot of the bed and pulled her to him until her head left the pillow. A small spray of hair still clung there. She began to unzip him. He wasn't sure what to expect. He couldn't rule out one final treachery of the body, which if it had its way, he thought, would crown its triumph of cruelty by depriving him — them — of this too. But he overestimated its power, or underestimated his own. Or did they both want the same thing? Now was not the time to wonder. Now was the time to forget his body and to look at her. He needed nothing but the look she returned. Then she shut her eyes, and he shut his, and they began to concentrate. He found more strength in her than he expected. She moved under him with an old authority. He listened as she began to come, as she was coming, as the coming wound down to a long final sigh that accompanied a burst of static from the nurse's intercom above the bed. He used the pillow to muffle himself. It was a two-minute triumph for both of them, and afterward they calmly restored respectability to the room.

He was sitting in a booth in a gas station convenience store. In the booth ahead of him sat an old man drinking coffee and reading a newspaper.

He tapped one edge of the business card against the table until his middle and ring fingers reached the bottom edge. Then he flipped the card over and tapped it down again.

He stood up and walked outside. He crossed the lot to the pay phone and dialed the number on back of the card.

"Hello?"

"Hello," he said. "I believe you came to see me in the hospital."

They met at a diner on the Upper West Side. He sat at a booth with a view and while waiting watched a man on the corner,

closer to the diner than the street, take a final puff from a cigarette and snuff it out under his shoe. It would have been unremarkable if not for the thin clear tube that ran from the man's
nose down to a portable oxygen tank. It caused him to look
closer, and by the time the man entered he realized it was the
same man he'd been waiting for, which should not have surprised him. He had been told to look out for the tank.

He stood up and waved. He didn't think he'd be recognized
otherwise.

"Hello."

"Hello," said Tim. They shook hands and the man sat down
across from him.

"You've recovered."

"More or less."

"You were in a bad way there for a while. Taking care of
yourself?"

"Trying to. Every day I feel about a year older."

"Oh, I hear that. Try doing it all with emphysema," he said,
grabbing the clear tube that ran up to his nose. "That's fun. Let
me tell you. A-plus fun-o."

"I can't imagine."

"Fucking cigarettes," he said, tapping the pack in his front
pocket. "Fuck them to hell."

They talked awhile longer. Then Tim said, "You said you
had something to show me."

From the inner pocket of his suit coat, Detective Roy
removed the sketch from long ago that presented a likeness of
the man who had accosted Tim on the bridge. It was quartered
by heavy creases and he took care in unfolding it. Then he took
out the photograph he had tried showing Tim in the hospital
room. Tim patted his pockets in search of the eyeglasses he was

still unaccustomed to having at his disposal. He removed the glasses from the case and gazed down at the sketch and the picture sitting side by side on the table. "What am I looking at?"

"This is your sketch. The sketch of the man you thought might have had something to do with the, uh—" He stopped and peered at Tim. "Sorry, do you remember...do you remember a man named R. H. Hobbs?"

Tim looked up from the table. He nodded.

"Sorry," said the detective. "Stupid of me ..."

"Why are you showing me this?"

The detective tapped the picture. "Is that the same man as in the sketch?"

Tim picked up the picture and studied it. "This is an old man," he said.

"Taking that into account, do you see a resemblance?"

He stared hard at the photograph. It was taken at an office party. The man stood some distance from the camera in a huddle with six or seven others, among cubicle divisions and fluorescent lighting, holding a red plastic cup. The longer and more willfully Tim looked, the more distant his memory of what the man had once looked like grew. He looked frequently to the sketch for help. "Maybe," he said. "The nose is the same, I think, with that knob in the middle. But it's not a very good angle."

The detective coughed violently. "Look harder," he said, collecting himself. "Concentrate."

"You don't have any other pictures?"

"This one's it."

He looked back down at it. "I don't know," he said. "It's been a long time."

The detective resumed coughing. Soon his eyes were red and teary. His words issued out in the brief staccato pauses. "We

want him for another murder…last year…victim like Evelyn Hobbs."

"How?"

"Same pattern, same stab wounds…and there are others."

"How many others?"

The woman in the booth behind them turned to see if the detective was going to be all right.

"Do you want some water?" asked Tim.

He dismissed him with an abrupt shake of his head. "And he harassed the lawyer."

"Harassed?"

"Provoked…as he did you …"

"How?"

"On the street…knew the details. It's how we got on to him." Now the detective was having trouble breathing. When he wasn't coughing, he was wheezing to take in air.

"Do you have him in custody? I could take a look at him, maybe then—"

"Can't locate him…he might have fled…" The detective stopped talking and abandoned himself entirely to coughing. He was barely able to say he needed some air before standing and walking out of the diner, trailed by his oxygen tank.

Tim waited for the waitress to bring around the check. He paid up front and then joined the detective outside. He found him smoking a cigarette. His coughing was all cleared up. Tim handed back the photograph and the sketch.

"I can't tell you one way or the other," he said. "I'm sorry."

The detective looked down the avenue and exhaled before returning a baleful gaze. "Right now he's just a person of interest in a single murder. But if we can tie him to Evelyn Hobbs, we can maybe tie him to the others. There are six, maybe as many as eight. And people, family members, who need to know what happened."

"You were adamant," he said. "Remember? Only one suspect."

"I know."

"He hanged himself in prison."

"I know," said the detective. "I know."

The detective thought he knew something but he knew nothing. What did it matter, these other people? R.H. would never know the details. He would never know the name of the man who might be responsible. That was the travesty. This death-sealed ignorance, and the indifference to that ignorance by any power higher than man.

The detective snuffed his cigarette out under his shoe. "You're the only one we've got," he said. "The one guy in the world if we're going to get anywhere on this."

"Don't pin that on me," he said. "You're the one who didn't believe my client."

"And I feel awful about that."

"Awful enough to kill yourself?"

The detective was taken aback. "To kill myself?" He had fired up a new cigarette and now blew out a dismissive stream. "No," he said. "Not to kill myself."

"Then you should feel indifferent," said Tim.

His departures from the room were peremptory. A sudden movement, a glimpse of him passing through the doorway, and he was gone. "Going now," he might say. He might be in the middle of recounting for her things he'd seen. "Back soon."

If they were lucky, he had time to turn his head so that she saw he was addressing her and not some ghost standing before him.

Some days he left, and as he walked, he brooded that his final words to her one day might be, "Going now."

He did not want his final good-bye to be a hasty good-bye.

He returned one morning smelling of fresh snow and brick mortar, car exhaust and woodsmoke. Was that all in her head? She wanted him to resume telling her what he'd seen. He brought the world inside for her. He stood over the bed.

"I want to say good-bye" he said.

"But you just got here."

"I mean as if it were for the last time."

"Why do you want to do that?"

He explained. They had the opportunity, before it was too late, to preempt the regret that nothing or too little had been said between them. She agreed that that might be important. He assumed a serious expression. He did not have anything prepared. He took her hand, kissed it, and said good-bye. She thought there would be more to it, but nothing more came. She started to laugh.

"Is that it?"

"I guess so."

"Well," she said. "Good-bye, then!"

They spent the next several hours in each other's company, long after they'd said good-bye. Then, against everyone's sunniest assessments, in defiance of the grimmest percentages, and to her own astonishment, she began to recover.

It was wonderfully swift. He watched as her weight started to hold. Every time he returned to her room, she seemed to have gained back some measure of strength. She was up. She was getting off the bed to go to the bathroom. She was walking the hallways on her own. The final phase of the clinical trial came to an end and she was released.

She went home to that apartment where they had lived happily during the time between his second recurrence and his third, final, permanent one. She hadn't sold it, as he had assumed, but had kept it, hoping someday that he would return to her and that they would resume their life together there. It was the same old place with the same furnishings, the lived-in chairs and pretty Persian rugs, the books lined up on the built-in shelves, the fireplace. He stood in the doorway a nostalgic stranger.

He had been living in parks and rented rooms, his home base the cancer center on the Upper East Side. Now it shifted to the parlor-floor apartment in the West Village. He left and returned frequently, but discovered this difference. Upon his arrival, he no longer found her hanging over an uncharted abyss, but rinsing a glass or making herself a grilled-cheese sandwich, or doing something downright vigorous, like scrubbing the bathtub. It occurred naturally then, as the days passed and he came to the ends of walks and faced the myriad challenges of reversing course—the tedious backtracking, the physical exhaustion—that the urgency to return, the motivation to get back to her, began to wane.

A livery wrangler orchestrated the waiting lawyers through the drizzle into towncars on Eighth Avenue, holding an umbrella over their heads, opening and closing the back doors. The sky was wrecked and darkening.

He stood outside the old bastion under the arcade, staring at the revolving doors. Once upon a time, he could have taught a master class in entering with authority. Now he was building up to something, summoning courage. There was some dismay.

There was also indifference. He struggled to recall all the significance, investment, meaning, now petrified.

He entered, walked across the lobby, and stepped on the escalator. Midway up he glided toward a man he recognized. It was Peter, his old associate. He stared at Peter, unafraid to size up or be sized up. Peter's hair had thinned and he had grown enormously fat. He was cultivating a massive heart attack under an expensive wool coat. The flamboyant signature of a red bow tie sat framed between the coat's lapels. Just as they passed, Peter finally graced him with a glance. He might have quickly turned away again if Tim hadn't been staring as hard as he was. He flipped Peter the bird. Peter continued to descend, now following the hostile stranger with offended eyes.

Frank Novovian had also gone fat. His head no longer shaved to the skin, his dirty gray hair was clumped and patchy, like the quills of a feather permanently skewed by a rough hand. His retiring slouch behind the security post said there was no going back. "Can I help you?" he asked.

"My name is Tim Farnsworth," he said. "I wonder if you remember me."

Frank held him suspended in a surprised and penetrating gaze. He lifted an inch off the chair, righting his jellied form, which immediately settled back into place. All at once his expression broke into clarity.

"I sure do," he said. "Like it was yesterday."

He waited around for Frank's shift to end and then they walked to a bar on Ninth Avenue. Frank continued to express surprise at his reappearance after so many years. He might have thought Tim was dead. Most likely he hadn't thought of him at all. Tim didn't ask.

They sat at the bar and talked about the people they once had in common. Frank asked him if he'd heard about Mike Kronish. It was policy at Troyer, Barr to make partners "of counsel" when they turned sixty-five—an emeritus-type designation that furnished them with an office and an income for perpetuity, but stripped them of responsibility and power. When they tried to make Kronish of counsel he declared a fight. He made it clear that he had no desire to be the defanged old man coolly sought out on occasion for some niblet of sage advice. He campaigned hard to have the bylaws changed. When the vote was rejected at the partner caucus, he threatened to sue for age discrimination, but he knew as well as anyone that the bylaws were the bylaws. Troyer, Barr was bigger than any one man. He resigned and started his own firm downtown. He was, Tim guessed, siphoning off clients and billing like a bull fresh out of law school.

Frank told Tim the details of Sam Wodica's death. Unlike Kronish, Troyer, Barr's former managing partner had been happy to retire. He moved to Malibu and devoted himself to surfing and flying. His antique biplane drifted off course and ran into trouble during a sudden ice storm over the desert. He radioed for help and then went silent. The wreckage was spotted a few weeks later between broken canyons, and his remains were confirmed by dental records.

"An ice storm over the desert?"

"That's what I heard, Mr. Farnsworth."

Mr. Farnsworth. He had not heard those words spoken in years. It was someone's name, his name, but it was no one he knew. It had belonged, if it belonged to anyone, to a fiction, the name of someone who might never have walked the earth.

"There's something I've always meant to ask you, Frank," he said. "Do you have kids?"

Frank was tipping back his beer. He nodded with his brows. "Two boys," he replied, resettling his bottle on the coaster.

"Do you have pictures?"

"Pictures?"

"With you. In your wallet."

"They're grown men now. Twenty-eight and thirty."

"No families of their own?"

"One's married. The other . . . I can't say one way or the other about that one. To be honest, he's always sort of confused me. Maybe he's gay. I don't know."

He turned away and drank his beer. Tim did the same, and for a moment they looked like perfect strangers forced together by the confines of the bar. After a moment Tim removed his leather wallet, water-stained and contoured by age. He opened it to a portrait of Jack at just a few months, sitting on Becka's lap. Next to them sat Becka's boyfriend what's-his-name, the producer. Jane stood behind them.

"That's my family there," he said.

Frank took the wallet offered him and admired the picture. Then he handed it back with a kind word. "Looks like a happy bunch," he said. When they were through with their second beer they left the bar.

He walked with Frank to the subway terminal. They walked leisurely, avoiding the puddles. He spoke freely to Frank. He told him about his wife's sickness and recovery, his daughter's music career, and his walking. He admitted that a breakdown some years back now required him to take a cocktail of antipsychotic medication. He wasn't confiding, for there was nothing to keep secret anymore, and no one to keep a secret from. Surprised by the candor, or simply attentive, Frank said very little.

When they reached the entrance he held out his hand,

something he never liked to do because of his missing fingers. "Mr. Novovian," he said.

Frank showed no reservations in taking his hand. The two men said good-bye, promising that if the chance arose in the future, they'd do this over again. Then Tim watched him as he disappeared into the terminal, heading toward the train that for all these years, night after night, had taken him from the city into New Jersey, toward home.

Months before his reappearance, Becka had mentioned that he was trying to return. She wanted to give her mother reason to live. But Jane didn't want him to come and she didn't want to live. She had made peace with dying. She had watched him struggle for too long to pretend that struggling was profitable. If it was her turn to go, she would go. She would go peacefully.

Then he returned and she wanted to live.

If he could suffer like that, if he could endure such an ordeal. If he could be so valiant.

The equipoise she had struck was ruptured the minute he walked into the room. Going peacefully, that was history. She began to rage as he had raged.

Did he think it was the clinical trial? The clinical trial wasn't what saved her.

He didn't believe that. With him it was just working or failing to work. Cells lived or they died. The heart beat or stopped beating. Then the entire thing returned to ashes and dust. He'd come a long way from the man who once believed that God was in the trenches surrounding every atom, fighting the devil for the soul.

"There's no soul," he said. "No God and no soul."

"What about your mind, all the miracles of your mind?"

"It's captive."

"Captive to what?"

"The body. The body's decay."

"You don't believe that," she said. "I don't believe you believe that."

He did. The medicine had set him right at last.

She stood up and went over to the window. She looked out for a while before turning and sitting on the ledge. "When you recover from an illness," she said, "as I have, no matter what you thought you believed, you start to think maybe there's something."

"I wouldn't know about that," he said. "I've never recovered."

"Don't be self-pitying."

"I'm not self-pitying," he said. "Just stating the facts."

He had walked and walked to get back to her, and now that she was home, there was nothing more to do. Returning to her, returning to her, returning to her again and again, was not a possible life. It was twice the challenge as the going because he was working on low energy and no sleep. He could do it when it was a matter of life and death. But now, now he needed to let himself rest when it came time to rest, and to move on when it came time to move on, and to do so in the direction of the moving on.

"What about the vacation?" she said. "We planned a safari."

He didn't reply. The safari had always been pure delusion.

If he left now, she told him, he would be leaving her worse off than when he found her. She would not want to live, but she would not want to go peacefully, either. She would rage, and her raging would be pointless.

She became deeply afraid and began to cry. He made no move to comfort her. He had kept his backpack on, which made it hard to read his intentions. Did he mean to leave now, that night?

Not wanting to wake the baby, he thought twice about ringing the buzzer so early in the morning. He settled himself on the stoop. Becka's boyfriend rescued him an hour later, coming home from a late-night recording session, and brought him up to their third-floor walk-up where the coffee was brewing and Bob Dylan was playing low on the radio. Becka's boyfriend said, "Look who I found." Becka turned and showed surprise. She poured him a cup of coffee, which he drank on a vintage barstool with a sparkling red vinyl seat. Her boyfriend finished his beer and excused himself to get some shut-eye. He kissed Becka on the forehead and left the room. There was a certain unorthodox domestic tranquillity here that made her father happy to have witnessed.

She placed Jack in his arms while she went to the bedroom to change out of her pajamas. When she returned she was wearing a pair of denim coveralls and a faded 7UP T-shirt. She asked him if he wanted breakfast.

"No," he said, "no breakfast this morning."

"Let me make you some breakfast, Dad."

"My iPod is a wasteland," he said. "I wondered if you could give me some new music."

She took his iPod and walked over to the computer with it. For the tenth time he requested her new CD but she wasn't completely satisfied with the production and didn't want to give it to him until it was perfect. He said she was acting unconscionably toward her biggest fan. He threatened to get down on his knees. He had every intention of getting that album before leaving. She gave in finally and uploaded it. He took off the backpack—to store the iPod, she thought. But then he put the iPod in his pocket. He put his arms around her. He went over to the crib where Jack was now lying contentedly on his back. He picked the baby up and held him above his head and brought his exposed belly down to his face, breathed in his baby's scent, and kissed his smooth skin.

The phone was ringing when he shut the door behind him.

He crossed the George Washington Bridge and an hour later turned off the primary road and walked the sidewalk past the day-care center and the library that were nestled inside the residential neighborhood. The road dipped and came to a second primary road where he turned left and the traffic picked up again. Past the gas stations he walked to the overpass and followed the shoulder down the on-ramp to the divided highway where the cars washed past with an old familiarity that quickly settled back in his ears.

He regained an eye for those locations that best served his needs for rest and renewal. He landed on a final redoubt of trees, he slept behind deserted buildings. There were occasional run-ins with unsympathetic authorities who pressed on him their provincial dogmas of safety and propriety. People did not like him on their private lawns or inside their public parks. He made no appeal to their sympathy. He simply packed up and moved on. He had proven long ago that there was no circumstance under which he could not walk if he put his mind to it.

He never returned to New York. Months passed before he could even bring himself to call home again.

Three years after leaving, he drifted into a community library in what remained of central Louisiana to use the free computers alongside the homeless and the refugees. Becka had sent him an email that had languished in his inbox for over a month. She told him of test results that confirmed with near certainty that her mother was no longer in remission. What Becka did not mention was that those tests had come in months ago and that Jane had asked Becka to wait until the end to tell him, so that he wouldn't be tempted to return to her bedside.

He called that afternoon. He stood on the exposed side of a gas station as a heat wave issued from an incinerating and merciless sun.

"Why do you put any stock in those test results?" he asked Jane. "What are your symptoms?"

"My symptoms?" she said.

"You've already proven it was bogus, Jane. The whole thing was bogus."

"It's different this time."

"What are you saying? That you're dying? Who's telling you that you're dying?"

"Nobody needs to tell me," she replied. "I'm dying. They tell me I'm dying because I'm dying."

He had to inform her that she wasn't dying. She simply wasn't trying hard enough to overcome the nihilism of the body. The soul was inside her doing the work of angels to repulse the atheistic forces of biology and strict materialism and she needed to do her part to show God which side she was on. He suggested going for a jog or cooking a large meal.

His medication required tweaking from time to time, and then the clarity would come flooding back to him. He spoke a mile a minute. She could hardly get a word in. She asked him if he was taking his medication and he became furious. The obnoxious certainties of some people! The rigid orthodoxies of cause and effect! Whenever anyone was presented with the one true eschatology and the work of the divine, they wanted to drag those verities through the rivulets of shit dug and tended to by Western medicine. *They* were the drugged zombies, not him. He wasn't crazy. He just saw things others could not see.

A week later he sat weeping in the waiting room of a psychiatrist he had seen on two other occasions. The doctor had been closing in on setting the cocktail straight again when Tim failed to return, clear-eyed once again to the bullshit and the lies. He wept because in the midst of such lucidity, he could only be confounded by what mysterious force had compelled him to return now, by the layers and layers of complexity in a war he would never comprehend.

He called home again within the month. The phantasmagoria of heaven and hell that had whipped him into a frenzy the last time he spoke to her had been replaced by the cool and measured assessment of someone observing the objective differences in a before-and-after picture. Gone was his manic pace. The soul was once again unlikely. It was despairing news. It meant that he would not see her again, not here, not in any afterlife.

He would tell her anything, of course. Yes of course he would tell her that he loved her and that the soul was vibrant and real and death only an interlude. His banana, how she had taken care of him. She had come to him in far-flung places no matter the time of day or night. Of course he would give her every reassurance, he would say anything.

But Becka answered and told him that she was already gone.

He maintained a sound mind until the end. He was vigilant about periodic checkups and disciplined with his medication. He took care of himself as best he could, eating well however possible, sleeping when his body required it, and keeping at bay to the extent his mind allowed it a grim referendum on life, and he persevered in this manner of living until his death, which took place in the far north on a day of record snowfall, during a morning blizzard.

By then he was something a passing car couldn't resist. Gaunt and weathered, limping sturdily, he walked the shoulder of the highway like a wasted beggar moving between two ancient persecuting cities. The driver turned to look at him as he blurred past, then picked the sight back up in the rearview mirror. There he receded slowly into a terrible smallness, into nothing, not even memory.

By then he was paying attention, as Jane had taught him, and had learned to distinguish between a hundred variations of unnamed winds. He couldn't name the twitchy burrower with the black-tipped tail that scanned an upland prairie for danger, but he knew it as well as the raspy grass with the flowering spike that left soft yellow pollen on his pant legs, and he knew it as well as the bright constellation that suddenly resolved itself out of a confusion of stars. He knew *fee-bee fee-boo, fee-bee fee-boo* came from a small bird with brushed gray wings and a tail as firm as a tongue depressor, and he knew the sharp clear whistle of *set-suey, sedu-swee-swee* of a scythe-beaked bird he saw often in winter, and he knew the French-inflected call of a small stately black and white bird who sang *teehee tieur, teehee tieur* — though he knew none of them by name.

By then he had stood on the riverbank and watched men shoot into the running water. He was startled by the echo. He watched them pull their mauled catch from the water to the parched rocks. Half the meat was missing. He had to wonder the point, if it was a matter of sport, or a supply of bullets greater than hooks and nets.

By then he had remembered the morning he returned to her hospital room to tell her he worried about the insufficiency of the final words they would say to each other. They had an awkward ceremony that made her laugh. "Good-bye, then!" she had said to him. He could not forgive himself that he had urged her to cook a meal as she was dying, so he clung to the memory of that morning.

By then he had given up everything but his need for shelter and nourishment, but there had been afternoons he spent in community libraries, reading books he would not finish and sending and receiving email. That was how he learned one day that Becka had married. She sent pictures of a small outdoor ceremony. He had never seen her look so healthy or beautiful, or so old. He was sorry that neither of her parents were in attendance. He wrote back to congratulate her. "How big Jack has gotten!" he said in response to seeing the little man in his tuxedo. He left the library with an uncertain heart, grateful that he had been spared the disappointment of anticipating an event he could not attend, but hopeful that she had done so out of mercy and not forgetfulness.

By then they wondered if he had the money for the things he brought up to the counter. He was a certain type, mute and suspect. Some contrariness kept such old men moving, as if to stop and settle would be to fall back into the human business of bickering and violence. Better for all if he was on his way. They watched him leave the store with his small bundle and stand on the other side of the road packing as if for some journey by foot, and they wondered if he knew which passes to avoid, what roads

closed at the start of November, and if his permits were in order.
They predicted some quarrelsome run-in or tragic end. He had
a whippy sort of strength and an old rapport with his pack,
which he shouldered on with a burdened grace. They watched
him walk along the side of the highway, asking nothing of the
passing cars and leaving town without having uttered a word.

He wanted a drink of water. It was deliciously painful, his thirst,
a thought to relish quenching.

He had yet to open his eyes. He was lucid and alert as he usually was in the first few minutes after waking. He heard the wind
outside, sonically layered and multidirectional, and he heard the
crackle of descending snow and the slight sizzle of one flake as it
caught hold of the combed bluffs accumulating against the side
of the tent, shaped by the wind. His thirst persisted beautifully.
What gratification would come when he finally rose and poured
a cool cup into the lid of the thermos.

He made no effort to move, though, so content in the bedroll, so warm and easeful, while the wind howled madness outside and drove the snow to frenzy.

A similar feeling had overtaken him the night before. He had
pitched the tent at the end of his walk and climbed exhausted
inside the bag, expecting to fall quickly into a long and satisfying sleep. Despite the severity of the weather, he liked it up here
almost better than any other place in the world. The bustle and
tempo of people proceeding with their eventful lives could not
cripple him with longing here, and it was unlikely that he would
be awakened by a meddlesome authority or a group of noisy
jerks. He relaxed into the warmth of the bag and felt his body,
still humming with the jangle of his recent walk, wind down into

a stillness that eventually made its way into his deepest interiors. The wind was just then starting to pick up, but beneath its bellowing he became aware of his heart whispering *listen... listen... listen....* He heard the blood pump out of his chest and flow down his arteries to pulse faintly at his wrist and in the hollow beside his anklebone, and his breathing lifted him up and down, up and down, and he heard the calmness, like the coals of a settled fire, of his rested bones. He luxuriated in his exhaustion. The weariness was inseparable from pleasure. He half struggled to stay awake just to stretch the moment out for as long as possible.

Now it was morning. It was wrong to dawdle like this. Wake up, pack up — that was the protocol. This sort of indulgence could be dangerous.

But was there anything comparable to a languorous morning in bed, under the warm confines of a blanket, while you kept the vicious cold at bay another minute, and then stretched that one minute out to five? It was only a bedroll set on top of an inflatable pallet inside a makeshift shelter, but he didn't open his eyes. He listened to the wind. He heard other sounds, too: a clock ticking in a warm kitchen, the coffeemaker sucking and percolating on the counter, Jane treading lightly across the floor, gathering the cups, opening the refrigerator for the milk. "Tell me where you are and I'll pick you up," she said from somewhere in the distance.

Five minutes gave way to ten, and ten to twenty. There was no question now that he was starting to press his luck. He had to rise and dress. He had to break down the tent. He still had to find food for the day. There were many things that awaited his command, not least the pleasurable taste of the water he promised himself as a reward for disturbing such a delicate peace.

He languished another twenty minutes. Then he absolutely insisted that he rise that instant and take care of business or else he might find himself wandering out there in the blistering snow, fighting the wind with his bare hands. But just then he realized that, at some point during his sumptuous idling, he had stopped hearing the wind. He didn't suppose that it could have died completely and so quickly, recalling the terrible fury it was kicking up. He expected the vinyl to whip taut again in its stitching any second now, or at least to hear a few high-pitched, snow-borne whistles of the storm departing, but time marched on and there was nothing. He thought he might open his eyes to see if the silhouette of the falling snow continued to dapple the skin of the tent, but he decided not to exert himself unnecessarily. Instead he chose to do as he had done the night before: settle deep inside himself and listen to the strange, subtle operations going on inside his body. He listened for his heart to whisper its soft word. He listened for the breathing that lifted him up and down inside the bag. But *listen… listen… listen* was gone. His quiescent nerves gave no signals and received none. He detected nothing but an enormous, gentle stillness from the things he could name and those he couldn't inside him, the organs and muscles, the cells and tissues. He never had to rise again, the silence informed him. Never had to walk, never had to seek out food, never had to carry around the heavy and the weary weight, and in a measure of time that may have been the smallest natural unit known to man, or that may have been and may still remain all of eternity, he realized that he was still thinking, his mind was still afire, that he had just scored if not won the whole damn thing, and that the exquisite thought of his eternal rest was how delicious that cup of water was going to taste the instant it touched his lips.